Belldeep

Where chimera jousts with reality

Verity Short

ISBN 978-0-9929542-7-7

For Olive, Christine and Cynthia
who came through for me

Table of Contents

Part 1: Denouement or Prelude? 1

1. Bored Meetings 3
2. Exeter Beginnings..19
3. Trysts 34
4. Eiderdown Fluff 51

Part 2: The Jousting Jester, Hera and the Peacock ...69

5. Getting Away 71
6. The Stolen Child..89
7. Ancient Monuments.......................................106
8. Moulin Rouge 123
9. Kingfishers 138
10. The Goblin Market 153
11. Milner's Inferno 176

Part 3: The Accounting.................................197

12. *Le Bouffon et le Chat* 199
13. The Howler...203
14. Begging a Stone to Talk................................220
15. The Lion's Den 239
16. Lady Sibylline...255
17. *Tragedie*...279
18. Madame Wanhope...299
19. A Long Night's Journey into Day 313
20. The Cat Whisperer......................................333

By the same Author..347

Laws and principles are not for times when there is no temptation: [.....]

If at my individual convenience I might break them, what would be their worth?

—Charlotte Bronte, *Jane Eyre*

PART 1

Denouement or Prelude?

CHAPTER 1

Bored Meetings

THE PHONE VIBRATED. *At last,* thought Milner. *Control yourself. Keep calm and keep jugglin'. Don't, whatever you do, drop the ball now. Concentrate. Steer this meeting to the outcome you spent ages engineering. That'll mean two victories to gloat over. Keep your grip meanwhile. Indulge yourself later.*

He wanted to punch the air and shout, but restrained himself. He mustn't allow the slightest upturn of his lips. If he did, the executives in front of him would get the wrong idea. Not the moment to give his game away. Control was key. He had 'em in the palm of his hand. He'd taken a risk leaving the phone on, but having waited an eternity for this text, reckoned it was worth the gamble. But a nagging doubt intervened. He needed to be sure it was 'THE' message. *If my long-anticipated hopes and plans have come to fruition, I'll take it as a good omen. It'll be confirmation I'm meant to secure this victory.*

"Gentlemen, let's break. Need to point Percy at the porcelain."

The tension of the moment dissipated as seats were

pushed back and torpid limbs pressed into action. As Milner rose, he sought to hide a heavy inward sigh behind a smile and nod of approval. *Trust my grin convinced 'em – pity some of 'em are as good at false smiles as me, makes it difficult, but they've never bested me in this boardroom. Hope my text shows my other project has succeeded. Disappointment has been my lot too often in that connection.* He reached the toilet, phone in hand, and focussed on the small screen so hard he didn't realise he had company until a gentle cough forced him to look round. He hoped whoever it was failed to see him slip the phone into his pocket where he became conscious of it burning a hole.

"Strategic withdrawal, old chap – give 'em time to stew eh?" suggested Jack.

"What?"

"Seen you in action over the years. Wouldn't be the first occasion you employed this tactic. Didn't earn the nickname 'Prophet and Loss' for now't."

"What? Oh yeah. You know me too well, obviously."

"See you in there for the kill," said Jack, as he dried his hands and winked at Milner. Alone again, Milner fished out his phone.

Relief. It was the text. *Two arrived at flat.* How lucky was he, its arrival coincided with a strategic break moment! A positive portent. His incantations last night worked – that and careful planning. He'd been ages getting the fruit to ripen so he could pick it. He'd given up hope the dolts he practised his magic on would ever succumb. *Can't remember a plan with so many setbacks and delays. Finally, my patience is rewarded. I'll finish screwing that lot to the floor in the board room, then go and perform my long-imagined victory scene at the flat.*

Concentrate, Milner. Focus. Don't let impatience to get to the flat ruin this outcome. This project has been in the boiler-room forever. Keep Calm and Keep Screwing. Now there's a thought. I'll adopt it as a motto seeing it's appropriate to both situations. Come to think of it, what a great Tee-shirt slogan for the DIY business where I'm a non-exec. Must make a note and suggest it to the marketing department next week at their board. Someone may have proposed the idea already, but won't hurt to check.

With a tight schedule to get across London and spring his surprise, Milner hurried back to the meeting and called it to attention.

"Now, gentlemen. Agenda item eight. We debated to death the risk assessment in your papers on the downside of this share floatation. Been through pricing tactics and marketing strategy in minute detail. Any objections before I press go? Are we in agreement?"

"One more issue," piped up James Hester.

Milner groaned inwardly. *What a pedantic, pontificating prat. Assumed I whipped him into line on the phone last night. Obviously not. Idiot always manages to upend me with something.* He glared hard at James, who made the mistake of meeting him glare for glare.

"Come on then, what is it?"

"Just wanted to praise your brilliant action plan."

"Good. If that's it, gentlemen…"

Milner rose, gathered his papers and nodded at the minute taker.

"Minutes ready for checking by the weekend?"

"Sure."

Milner left without lingering for the usual chit-chat. Needed to procure a taxi – must hurry to Bankside. He texted the concierge. *Assume two still there? Yes,* came the response. He hailed a cab and checked his phone for other messages. His annoyance and impatience grew on each occasion the driver hit his brakes and jerked Milner into awareness of the volume of London traffic. *Time is supposed to fly when you're having fun, but this is tedious. Why can't the congestion clear, and I get where I'm going?* After what seemed forever, they arrived. Milner paid the fare. As he gained the street, he noticed the theatre opposite boasted a performance of Shakespeare's *As you Like It*, with the strapline 'All the world's a Stage, And all the men and women merely players'. Milner hurried into the building, nodded to Akim as he crossed the lobby to the lifts, then proceeded to the second floor. He stood for a moment outside his door, inhaled deeply, inserted his key and entered.

 C3 C3 C3

As Milner's key turned, Julian froze. *Surely not? Blast the man; come to rob me of postcoital satisfaction.* Julian's anxiety and stress took over and stopped him marinating in his own testosterone. He fingered his waist to find trouser belt loops to hitch up his pants up and calm himself, but blushed. He wasn't wearing any. *Gronya said Milner had a board meeting all afternoon and wouldn't be using the flat today. What the hell is he doing here?* Thank goodness they'd finished and the bedroom door was shut. *I'll ponder it later.* At that moment a phone rang. Julian heard Milner curse, then turn to traverse the passage to the kitchen where he addressed his caller.

"James, what can I do you for?" grunted Milner as he rapped the counter with a pen. "But we discussed that. Voted and passed it. What's your problem?"

"Shhh!" whispered Gronya, who put a finger to her lips as she rose from the bed. "I'll sort him."

She donned pants and a top and padded through the door, pulling it closed. After what seemed ages, Julian heard Milner's conversation end.

"Hello, Milner," said Gronya, "didn't expect to see you. Said you'd go straight home after the board. I've a slight headache after shopping so decided to rest before I set off. Shall I get you some tea? Then I'll freshen up and we can go together?"

"Good idea. Rooibos, please. Need to make notes. Won't take long."

Julian listened as the kettle boiled and Gronya riffled in cupboards for cups and teabags. Then the living room door banged shut. *Must've carried the tea in and put wood in't hole. They're speaking softly. Can't hear. No doubt Milner's gloating or moaning. If he's wise, it won't be about boardroom victories or hassles or whatever he's been up to.*

Gronya made it plain over the years she found Milner's business affairs boring, uninteresting and irritating. Didn't mean she didn't enjoy exploiting its proceeds. She loved to revel in driving Milner's Bentley or using the latest tablet computer or gadget he never failed to produce for her. He was generous that way. They were probably discussing children or cats. They had two of one and four of the other. All of them kept Gronya forever busy with neurotic behaviour. She spoiled them at great cost to herself as she never stopped telling him, and Milner. Julian's view was they were demanding, unreasonably so sometimes, but with a few handling techniques, were manageable. *Still, now she's spoiling me*, he gloated, as a self-satisfied grin spread over his face.

Julian imagined the City where Milner worked as some disembodied entity, more so after he met Gronya and listened to her complain about it. His only evidence of it was once a month Milner paid money into Julian's account to settle his bills. Even that transaction seemed surreal as it happened online. Julian never handled cash; left it to his wife, Adelle, who'd been his office manager before they retired. Adelle issued the monthly invoices to Milner. He was aware Milner described his relationship with money as a Gordian Knot that demanded 'thinking outside the box', but if you understood how to disentangle it with patience, you would end up with the whole thing intact and in your possession. Like Gronya, Julian hated business-speak and turned off whenever Milner indulged.

C03 C03 C03

GRONYA CARRIED THE TEA into the living room, placed Milner's cup on the table, and closed the door. Milner stood in front of the oil painting that dominated an entire wall – a retirement gift from the board members of the large financial institution where he'd been chairman; commissioned from a painter of Milner's choice. Didn't take him long to decide on the artist although the subject matter was left to his colleagues. When the work was ready, Milner went to view it. He became mesmerised the minute he spied the canvas in the artist's studio, but until now, hadn't understood why. He remembered waiving an opportunity to discuss it with the artist. *Didn't need insights. My creativity is sufficient to amplify and bring understanding of what I'm looking at. It's what makes me good at recognising art with high commercial value.* The scene was a hilly landscape, set in a blue horizon, with a single, stick-like figure, descending a hill towards the viewer. *Perhaps I had a vision of the future I wanted away from Gronya when I saw it. Now I think about it, must have subconsciously believed I was alone.* Milner turned to look at Gronya.

"Your grins suggest you're happy," said Milner.

"Perfect. Better than I hoped. Wish it hadn't taken so long to get him here."

"Told you often his ethics would be easy to break. It was the strong moral code that would be harder to smash."

"Don't understand the difference between ethics and

morals."

"Good job I do and stuck with it."

"Still insist you should've got him here before now. Made me wait too long."

"Tested my patience for sure, but finally closed the deal," said Milner, turning away to peruse the papers he pulled from his briefcase.

"Even better than I fantasised," said Gronya.

"What? Oh. Right. Pleased for you. Don't go on. Don't want the nitty-gritty. Are you interested to learn if the board meeting proved successful since the proceeds will finance your new life with Julian?"

"Couldn't care less. Got what I want, and as long as you give me a house big enough to enjoy setting up with Julian, don't need details."

"Right. Don't consider anybody except yourself, dear. No point changing the habits of a lifetime. Better finish this charade."

Milner rose, opened the door and headed along the passage towards the bedroom. He turned to Gronya and mouthed at her.

"Come on then, protest."

Gronya shook herself and started her prepared speech.

"Milner, darling, finish your tea. We must get home to feed the cats." Gronya injected the right amount of panic into her voice to sound convincing – just as rehearsed.

"Need something from the dressing room before we

leave," he insisted.

"I'll get it. Don't go in there. There's a mess to clean up."

"I'm used to your clutter. It's not a problem. Unless you're hiding something? Are you?"

Milner opened the bedroom door to find Julian by the window pulling up his trousers. Milner turned to Gronya behind him in the doorway.

"How could you? And with Julian. Guessed there was something going on. How long have the pair of you lied to me? Didn't we have an understanding, Julian? Thought after your retirement you were my friend. Didn't for one moment consider agreeing to continue a friendship with you and Adelle was so you might pursue Gronya. How will Adelle take this?"

"Milner, please understand," blurted Gronya.

"Understand what? It's clear what a pair of liars you are. Nothing to say for yourself, Julian? No? Clearly not. I'm off home. You better stay here and tidy up, Gronya. See you later. I'll feed the cats, by the way. Don't rush back for me, or the kids for that matter. Finish your dirty little tryst. I'll make all judgments and decisions on progress from here. Don't trouble yourselves on that score."

CB CB CB

"WHAT DO YOU suppose he'll do?" said Julian.

"Nothing hasty, never does. Plans responses. You know that."

"At least we can now explore making a new life to-gether."

"Let's not be previous. Needn't rush our dreams. Telling my girls will be difficult," said Gronya.

"My family won't find it easy, but they'll be OK. Laid a lot of groundwork with Sabina. She's sympathetic, though has no idea how far it's gone."

"How d'you manage that?"

"Never respected her mother. Been simple to under-mine what little affection existed. Sabina will go where she calculates she can get the best for herself. Thinks that's with me. Daniel will find it more difficult, but should be amenable. Likes to pretend he's fair and non-judgmental. We'll see, though."

"They'll come round in the end. Once they realise our love and affection is the only thing that matters, and how our relationship was made in heaven. Pity we took so long to find each other."

"You're right. Everyone will bask in the glow of our happiness. Our contentment will spill out and convince the world it's right. It'll be OK."

"Better get home or my girls will wonder what's happening because I've done something out of the ordinary for myself for once."

CR CR CR

MILNER JOURNEYED HOME content. He heaved a sigh of relief as he settled down for the short train journey. *At last.* He was rid of her. He'd put up with forty years of moans and complaints about his inadequacies. There were loose ends, and the next few months would be difficult. But he was in control. He was steering this ship and if all he had to listen to was some emotional ranting for a bit, he'd cope. He was adept at closing his ears and tuning out when he didn't want to hear. It was a useful skill at home and in the boardroom. He'd honed to a fine art an ability to make optimum use of imagined metaphorical headphones to block out unpleasantness.

He walked up the hill from the station anticipating a glass of excellent Bordeaux and some of the foie gras he collected from the flat. Madame Jouffre had dropped it off when she stayed a week ago. It was her own stuff, made fresh each year. He anticipated savouring the loving ritual of tradition in every mouthful. He'd bought French bread from a London bakery to accompany it. His taste buds salivated. *Just reward for a plan well executed, even if overlong in its realisation.* As he fumbled with his key, the door was wrenched open by Ollah and Hattie plus four felines. The girls were angry, while the cats mewed and cried, curled and uncurled their paws in distress.

"Where's Mum?" the girls demanded in unison.

"Coming later. Got business to finish in town."

"But she never does that. Where is she? She hasn't fed the cats. What does she think she's doing?"

"Can't you find cat food and sort it? Two of them are yours anyway."

"Mum does it. She should be here."

They followed him into the kitchen.

"What's for dinner then?" demanded Ollah.

"Wasn't expecting you, you'll need to forage in the fridge. You know – the big white thing with the double doors. Blasts cold air into the room when you investigate its entrails."

"Sarchasm, Dad, doesn't become you."

"Sarchasm?"

"You know. The abyss between your sarcasm and my uncomprehending but simple requirement to be fed and watered."

"Ha, ha, Ollah, very clever. Is that original?"

"May be. Might have read it somewhere, who knows."

"Your banter will get you into trouble."

"Will? Already does, without fail. Do I care? Not one jot."

Milner put the bag containing the foie gras on the counter. *Guess I'll have to leave this pleasure to some other time.* Hattie grabbed it and groped inside.

"What's in here? Eeugh! It's that disgusting stuff you insist on eating. Smells foul. How can you stomach this muck?"

"Is nothing private?" he demanded, extracting the parcel and putting it in a cupboard. "Anyway, since I supply the food here, I'll eat what I want. You get fed to pander to your pickiness so you've no cause to complain."

"My eating habits are just fine. My psychotherapist

says so."

"Mum lets us open her parcels," shouted Ollah, her nose in the fridge searching for a beer.

"I'm not Mum. Things will need to change around here."

"What's that supposed to mean?" they demanded in echoing bellows.

"Nothing – for now," said Milner to the air, as he realised they were exiting the kitchen, his rhetoric wasted – as usual.

"Hold on – before you wander off. What about the cats? Must I feed them? Neither of you seem bothered, despite the caterwauling." *Suppose I shouldn't criticise, they're both chiselled from the same piece of driftwood.* "Your empty stares show you don't care so I'll do it. Then I'll shower. If you want to eat sooner, you must stir your carcasses, otherwise you'll need to wait till I get round to it."

"I'll wait," said Ollah.

"After seeing that vile stuff you brought home, my appetite has gone," said Hattie.

♋ ♋ ♋

AFTER A MEAL alone with Ollah – Hattie stuck to her guns – Milner climbed the stairs with Hera at his heels. She was his favourite cat. They shared a special bond; she understood his angst at having to be the one in the household who provided everything – not just financial security, but the steady, practical guidance that anchored everyone's foothold in reality, all that kept them grounded. The girls exhausted him emotionally. He closed his study door and slumped into his comfy chair aided by a large single malt. Hera curled up on his lap and purred with contentment. Gronya hadn't come home, and while he was unconcerned, the girls were angry with her. He listened to their invective for her not being here, for neglect of the cats, for not having dinner ready. He reminded them they hadn't been expected, but that didn't stop them. They went on and on. Ollah was furious. She wanted to talk to her mother about her latest love interest. Hattie just wanted to moan at her. The competition between them to get their mother's attention always led to arguments. Despite a spacious house with a study to retreat to, their voices penetrated the thickest of walls. He loved them dearly, they were his pride and joy. *Just wish they weren't so much like their mother. Or is it my imagination because I'm tired but full of anticipation now the end is in sight? They are both so clever and have achieved heaps. Maybe what's coming will help them think a bit less about themselves and more about my happiness. You never know. Some good has to result from putting myself first for once.*

Milner reminisced about when he met Gronya. He sipped his whisky with closed eyes, pictured the scene. He'd been a law student in the West Country. He saw her first with a group of girls at a bar. A friend from university was acquainted with her crowd. They joined forces one evening, and he got introduced. It grew from there. It was difficult to remember why he fell so hard for her charms, but he had. That and the big blonde hair and bust. Perhaps it was her vulnerability. She let him know she valued his anticipation of her every need. As the youngest of seven, she'd always been noticed last. It gave him pleasure to look after her, satisfy her whims. It was what drove him in those early days. They were content at first. Gronya was glad to be the object of his attention in private. She complained about how her large family overlooked her. Hinted at how she wished to be the centre of her own happy household, be a hub, dispensing and receiving love and affection in copious amounts. She'd been pleased when his career took off and she could have babies. Her ambition was to be a stay-at-home mum. Said she wanted to be a homemaker. He was content he'd found a woman who didn't want to chase a career or compete with him, satisfied to concentrate on him and his children.

A knock on the door roused him from his reverie. It was Gronya. He sensed anger.

"What's the problem now? Thought you were sated when I saw you at the flat."

"I was. But you didn't manage the girls tonight. Had to listen to angry complaints about not being here. Meant I didn't get more duvet time with Julian."

"What's the worry? He won't want to carry on?"

"No. He's on the hook. Your tactics were brilliant."

"So I'm good for something then?"

"Pity your dick couldn't match your plans."

"Gracious as ever," said Milner. "Let me remind you of the deal. I secure Julian and the sexual prowess you crave. You take the flack from the girls."

"Had no idea they'd be so angry. If it's a measure of what's to come, it won't be easy."

"Too late now. You signed the contract with the devil."

03 03 03

CHAPTER 2

Exeter Beginnings

G RONYA LEFT, SLAMMING the door behind her. *Make your feelings plain, why don't you?* Milner glared after her, sighed then settled down to enjoy his single malt. He listened as she banged about her bedroom. When this noise abated he detected the low hum of muffled conversation. *Must be indulging in a long-winded love rant with Julian. They go on for hours. Pity neither thinks about who pays her bills. Still, it's a small price to pay.*

Milner's thoughts turned to the beginning of his own courtship of her. Tried to recollect if they shared lengthy phone calls. *What an old fashioned notion – courting. Doubt Ollah and Hattie understand what it means. Not sure I could explain it. Suppose the main criterion it represented was 'No Sex Before Marriage'. The girls would mock that idea as quaint.* The luxury of mobiles didn't exist then. Conversations were on the family phone in the hallway, listened to by all and sundry, or from a red telephone box on the street. *Darned inconvenient in miserable weather, them kiosks. How to freeze your whatsits off in the cause of love, presumably sanctified by the Queen, 'cause after her coronation in 1952 she had the Tudor crown that adorned the top of the kiosks changed to the one used at her ceremony, the King Edward Crown. Another useless bit of ephemera that swirls around my brain. Whatever, conflabs must have been haphazard as public phones tended to be non-functioning. Mind you, vandalism wasn't much of a problem in the West Country then, so maybe I did call her from red boxes lots. Ah... Don't get cynical, Milner; you have hope on the horizon.* He did recall in detail her demand for constant reassurance. That's what made her bewitching. Never hid her desire to be pandered to. Always ready to let him sort everything out. He found it disarming; played to his need to feel wanted and necessary. He could just remember his infatuation. Not all emotion had withered from her relentless compulsion to elaborate on his failings. Few other memories of his first year at law school remained. She overwhelmed any that did.

Hers was a large clan. Her father headed up a substantial family building firm. This gave rise to an enigma around Gronya he found difficult to unravel. She'd get behind the wheel of any vehicle – huge trucks, diggers, small cars – and handle it with panache. The conundrum was she insisted on a navigator for all journeys, long or short. She handled the Bentleys better than he did, but wouldn't drive anywhere alone. He wondered if this presaged a hidden meaning, a foreshadowing he failed to register. It was one reason for his ambivalence over wizardry. He couldn't see the future, despite a natural desire to want to. That was a skill he reckoned worth the effort to cultivate. But it was beyond him. So he developed skills that allowed him to manipulate people like chess pieces. On balance he calculated this to be a more satisfactory challenge given the unpredictable nature of human behaviour meant you'd to be ready to tweak planned strategies at a moment's notice. The trick was to stay several steps ahead; something he believed himself more than capable of.

"Well, Hera, time for bed, I guess. You'll curl up with me, won't you?"

CB CB CB

BREAKFAST NEXT MORNING was tense.

"We need a conversation before I leave." Milner tried to catch Gronya's eye, but she glanced away determined not to meet his gaze.

"What about?" demanded Ollah. "I must see Mum. She refused me when I phoned last night so I get priority."

"Not fair?" wailed Hattie. "I had stuff to spill to her yesterday. I phoned before you, Ollah. You wait till after me."

"My priorities take precedence," said Milner. "You'll both get a turn – after me."

"You can all wait. I've business of my own," said Gronya. She picked up her phone and headed off upstairs, three mouths agape behind her.

"What's up?" chorused the girls. "Got a cheek walking off," said Ollah.

"For goodness' sake, you two. Look after yourselves for once," said Milner heading off to follow Gronya.

"Why should we?" demanded Hattie. "She's nothing else to do. Isn't that why she's here?"

"Have you and Mum rowed again?" demanded Ollah. "You'll get over it. You always do."

Milner turned and glared at Ollah. *Keep calm. Don't give the game away.*

"Sure we will, but I'll talk to her now. So back off. Sort yourselves out for the next few hours."

Gronya had closed her bedroom door, so Milner knocked.

"Get lost!" she shouted. "I'll see you when I'm ready. Right at this moment I'm talking with someone more important."

Milner hung around in hopes the murmurings would cease. Didn't want her to escape before he spoke to her, so thought to hover until silence descended, then try again. He paced impatiently for ten minutes then took the initiative. He knocked, opened the door and entered, then hovered, determined to get her attention.

"*He's* come in. Better go," said Gronya, glaring at Milner. "Can't wait for more duvet time. I'll phone later to fix it up. Love you lots, darling."

"You must control yourself until we speak to the girls," said Milner.

"Don't tell me how to behave. You've no power over

me now," Gronya spat back as she lifted up her phone and began to enter a text message.

"If it makes you happy to believe that, go ahead. But whatever you think, there are repercussions from your little amour to deal with."

Ollah burst in.

"Who the hell were you on the phone to, Mum? We/I demand your attention. Speak to or text whoever later?"

Milner admitted defeat and left the floor to Ollah.

"We'll talk this evening, Gronya. Make sure you're around and have your daughters sorted, so you and I can have a proper discussion."

He retired to his study to prepare for his board meeting. A substantial pile of papers demanded attention, but his thoughts were dominated by three women who resembled Joan of Arc; one bore Gronya's face, another Ollah's and the last Hattie's – dressed in martyr's armour and waving a pennant. *Why do I see them that way? Because they find it deplorable that others' sacrifices take precedence over their own? Ollah and Hattie are scandalised if their mother does something for herself, while she finds it intolerable to do anything to ensure my happiness. All make a virtue out of insisting others sort their own problems; that everyone and everything is here to serve them. Anyone who puts themselves before Gronya, Ollah or Hattie is wrong and selfish, particularly if it prevents that person spending empty time on Gronya, Ollah or Hattie.*

CB CB CB

"MUM, MUM, MUMMMMMMMMMM," bellowed Ollah.

"What?" demanded Gronya, looking up from her mobile. *Will send this text – drat the girl. I will get it off. She'll wait till I'm finished.*

"Pay attention. Stop it and look at to me," insisted Ollah as Milner exited. "Who are you texting that can possibly be more important than me?"

Gronya determined to finish her message, so typed in the last few words and read it over. *'Sorry darling, can't talk. Milner demanded attention. Eughhhh! Ollah chased him off and insists I listen to her. Can't wait for more duvet time. Will phone later when alone with house to myself.'*

Gronya glanced up, phone in hand. "Can't anyone get privacy around here? Is it necessary to burst in threatening to rip the door from its hinges? What did the door do to you?"

"Mum, I demand you listen."

Gronya turned her back on Ollah, pressed send then spun round. "OK, shoot, what's so important I can't text in peace?"

Gronya listened. *Better seem to pay attention. The quicker she gets through, the sooner I get my phone call.* Gronya, who could recite Ollah's litany by heart, tuned out. Nods and appropriate umms sufficed. It'd be the usual thing. Complaints over Milner moaning about her cat peeing everywhere; specially up the new lounge curtains. Work issues followed, then boyfriends, weight and health problems – in that order. It was a constant background hum that never ceased. *Must be why I sympathise with people who suffer tinnitus.*

Gronya's mind drifted to Ollah's birth. Milner claimed to be a proud father. The image was clear; Milner leaning over the cot, cooing. He didn't pick it up though. That happened later. When he did, he handled Ollah gingerly. *Told myself he was nervous; that explained it. I was so on edge I didn't think.* It made perfect sense – then. When Hattie came and he behaved the same she began to wonder. *Was so in love with my little girls when they were born. When did they turn into monsters that leave me exhausted and drained? Ollah never got enough milk from me. Ended up bottle feeding her. So much extra work. Wretched girl couldn't be satisfied. Still the same. Wasn't my fault. Tried hard to do everything right – for both of them.* Milner got angry when she failed to cope. She was a mother. Why couldn't she perform like other mothers – naturally, without difficulty? He declined to help, left the nurture part to her. Said his role was to earn money to make them secure. He paid for her to see a psychiatrist to prescribe sleeping pills and antidepressants. Meant she slept while the nanny he hired a few days a week attended baby. *But there was always the next exhausting battle with Ollah. Like a roundabout we couldn't dismount. The child never let up. Vociferous, best describes Ollah now. Knows how to twist her father round her finger. Mind you, both girls are proficient on that score. Reckon Ollah has the advantage though. Maybe because we are physically alike – heavy-chested, thin-hipped with shortish legs, and blonde hair. Hattie's the looker. Well-*

proportioned figure, slim with long legs and dark blonde hair; never looks mousey or wispy like mine and Ollah's.

She puzzled over Milner's behaviour. Down the years, he subsumed household duties. Not the housework – a cleaner undertook those chores with Gronya required to supervise. *Expected me to keep an eye out for maintenance or repairs, but if I suggested how to solve problems, ignored me and hired workmen he approved of.* Milner took care of cooking and food buying. Gronya gave him lists, but he brought home what he considered necessary. *Said if he did the shopping, he'd buy what he liked/wanted.* They muddled along. No one went without and he improved at it as time passed. Milner shopped for gifts. Gronya's job was to enquire what people wanted then he'd source requested items. She hated shops. If forced to go, equipped herself with antiseptic wipes to clean trolley handles and wouldn't travel on public transport in case someone sneezed and spread germs over her.

Ollah jerked Gronya from her reverie with a tug on her arm.

"You ain't listening – what's the matter? You always listen. What's going on?"

"Nothing. I was paying attention. Heard you mention the doctor?"

"You weren't. Can tell. Not sure I should bother to repeat it."

"Sorry. Don't mean to seem distracted. Come on. What about the doctor?"

"You have to go with me, Mum."

"I always do. Every time. What's the problem now?"

"Need HIV tests."

"What?"

"Got drunk and slept with a gay guy again, unprotected."

"For goodness' sake. Why?"

"Don't know. Can't help meself. Will Dad cough up? Used up maximum claims on my private insurance cover."

"Ask him yourself."

"Why can't you? He bends over backwards for you just now."

"You reckon? Go. Make the appointment. I'll use my credit card and deal with it at the end of the month if he queries it."

Gronya retrieved her phone to see if she had a reply to her text. She hadn't been so cheerful since, well forever. It took ages, this getting to be in heaven. She'd found someone to concentrate on her and her alone. Said he'd do anything to make her happy, fulfil her every need, no matter what the cost. *There won't be too big a price to pay. Our happiness will shine. Everyone will agree we were meant to be together. I'll be a better mother because I'm content. Julian will help me cope with them, instead of Milner shuffling off issues by offering money. Thinks cash solves every problem. Why did it take so long?* Julian told her not to worry; it'd be OK.

Hattie burst in as Gronya's phone bleeped. Hattie

gasped in annoyance as an arm shot up in front of her.

"No need for the Hitler salute, Mum, I've every right to demand your attention."

"All in good time. Need to see who this is from."

"For goodness sake, Mum, everyone else got attention. Put that thing down. Concentrate on me? It was bad enough you didn't talk to me more than forty minutes last night. You owe me now."

"I'll read my message first. Stop me and it'll take longer to attend to whatever you want."

"Put the damn thing down and listen." Hattie tried to snatch the phone. Gronya held on tight, retreated to the ensuite and slammed the door. Blessed relief spread through every inch of her as she devoured the words – *Dying for duvet time too. Speak asap. Your slave.*

Gronya emerged to face Hattie's anger.

"For goodness' sake, Mum. This isn't right. It's your job to be here when I need you. You always are. What's the problem? You sorted Ollah. It's my turn. I should've been first."

"Calm down. You've got my attention."

Gronya tuned out of the detail of the loud, rehearsed monologue. Could list the moans word-for-word. Cat, studies, latest project, exam prep. There'd been a huge fuss last month when Hattie refused to take exams. It took heaps of patient persuasion to get her to sit them but, as usual, Hattie used food to manipulate and control everyone around her. Threatened to starve herself to death. It was Milner's fault. He gave way to them far too often, and they learnt how to wheedle everything they wanted from him. *I hate money – he uses it to solve problems – they play up – he hands over more of whatever they ask for – our lives would be better if we never had much. Mind you, won't suggest that to Milner. Need him to pay for me and Julian to get a home together so I can enjoy the happy life I've earned. Julian can't afford it.*

CB CB CB

CALM SETTLED OVER the house as everyone left to pursue the tasks that filled their working hours. Gronya listened as cars exited the driveway, her main hiatus achieved when the Bentley purred out of the gate. *Must make sure I get to use the Bentley when I move in with Julian. Milner will agree. Should be easy to persuade him to let me have it sometimes. Must ensure he pays for maintenance though. The sacrifices I'll have to endure. Still it'll be worth it to bask in one-to-one attention from Julian.*

Her phone rang. It was Julian.

"Darling. Just got rid of the tribe. Couldn't wait to hear your dulcet tones."

"What are you wearing?"

"Not what I'd like to be. I'll do a selfie in my undies to send you. Keep you interested."

"No picture necessary. Imagining you next to me naked is enough."

"Been looking at getting away. I'll book our cottage in the West Country for a week. Can you come?"

"Absolutely. Adelle won't be a problem. Knows

something is wrong, but trusts me. Won't say anything. We hardly talk anyway. Don't feel obliged to explain myself."

"When will you tell her?"

"End of the month. We're away for a family thing. I'll do it after."

"How do you reckon she'll take it?"

"She's still besotted. Will do anything for me. Believes those antiquated vows we made on our wedding day. I can handle her. It'll be OK, she'll fall in line, stay friends with you and we'll be happy. Just like an extended family."

"Milner assumes that'll happen. Reckons he can manage Adelle. Not too difficult – says she's always loyal to those she trusts – is sure she trusts him. Says it took him ages to get her confidence, but managed in the end."

"Adelle is gullible. Wants to believe the best of people. Believes folks until they give her reasons not to."

"Let's change the subject? Want to hear how you adore me."

"You're the only woman on earth who can satisfy me. Known it for ages. Nothing I wouldn't do you for. Shall I go on?"

Gronya was forced to hang up ninety minutes later. The front door bell shrilled with incessant urgency and her ear was red from pressing the mobile to it. She promised to phone after everyone went to bed that night. She opened the door to Ollah.

"Forgot my keys."

"I should put them on piece of elastic and thread them through your sleeves like I used to with your gloves when you were little. That way you might remember them."

"Never mind that. We've to get to the doctor."

"Right. I'll fetch my handbag."

℃℧ ℃℧ ℃℧

MILNER GOT HIS AUDIENCE with Gronya that evening. It took a while to steer the conversation to his objective. First, he'd to listen to moans about the girls.

"They took up my whole day one way or another."

"No. Surely not. Surely you exaggerate. You mean you didn't even get one moment for a longwinded mutual adoration session with Julian on your mobile?" asked Milner.

"Drop the sarcasm."

"Thing is, I know you spoke at least two hours with him. Don't doubt you'll get in another few after everyone has retired tonight."

"You're a selfish, jealous man."

"Really?"

"Always were. Never satisfied me, emotionally or physically."

"Don't wanna hear it," said Milner, presenting an outstretched flat, upraised palm to her. "Listened to enough of your rehashes. Blame me for everything. Like a dog returning to its vomit."

"How crude. But then you always were where I'm

concerned."

"Can't resist, can you? No more. I'll ignore it. Our shared life, such as it was, is over. I want to concentrate on getting you and Julian together and out of my hair. I've waited long enough. How quickly can we proceed?"

"Can't tell the girls before Julian tells Adelle."

"Suggest he gets on with it then."

"We talked it over. He'll do it after his family occasion. Says he can't do it before."

Milner left her alone. He knew she blamed him because she projected her own negative qualities on to him. First heard of the syndrome in therapy sessions. Then came across it in corporate training days on how to conduct negotiations. He registered long ago that individuals seek therapy because they want to be understood and supported. The successful therapist did this by validating a patient's condition – not by challenging self-indulgent wallow. *Never did that meself. Guarded against it as it's the surest way NOT to achieve goals. Remain objective is my mantra. What I do know – although she'd deny it – is she can be as aggressive as any man I've met in business when it comes to getting her emotional needs satisfied. Julian'll learn soon enough – ignorant fool. Prides himself on being an expert in understanding people. Fact is, he's a happy-go-lucky amateur compared with me, the seasoned professional. It's why I'm rich and he's relatively poor – money wise.* Milner calculated you wasted time seeking to explain projection to unsophisticated souls, hampered as they were by a congenital inability to grasp such concepts. You simply took advantage of the weakness it created in them. Milner approached bargaining with the image of a maze in his head. This helped him plan the achievement of his aims with precision. *Everyone gets to the centre, but the guy with the strategies to deal with dead ends reaches the middle first.*

છ છ છ

CHAPTER 3

Trysts

JULIAN STOOD, SIGHED heavily, hitched his thumbs through the belt loops on his jeans then wiggled his bum till he felt comfortable. He knew Adelle admired his small hips and waist and how he'd not developed a beer belly; a trophy many men over sixty lugged around in honour of a misspent youth. The family chatted, but he was uneasy, struggled to join in. He was here, but not here, didn't want to join in the proceedings. *Gotta escape the stifling overtone of connectedness and reminders of duty. It's too much when they're together – can cope with Adelle alone – ignore her – but as a group, shoving commitments in my face – don't want to deal with it. Wish I was with Gronya – must get out of here – find somewhere private – phone Gronya – strengthen my resolve.*

Imitating an automaton, he forced his legs to carry him from the room, staring briefly at each individual as he did so. Adelle, he reserved till last. Guilt and alienation overwhelmed him. *Don't meet her gaze – she knows something's wrong – her eyes reveal it – can't bear to see them haunted with sadness.* He must act to re-establish his autonomy; divorce himself from feelings for Adelle; satisfy his needs independent of her. Gronya understood. She helped him appreciate his personal happiness was paramount – identified how he sacrificed his very being to Adelle – how taking Gronya as his lover liberated him.

Forty-five years he'd known Adelle, forty-two of them married. He'd been besotted with her since she was sixteen and he eighteen. Spent hours composing poems and hanging around waiting to see her. Remembered how at work one day he found an adding machine roll, then scribbled thirty-nine inches of nonsense spilling out his adoration. When complete, he fashioned and fitted neat handles either end, rolled it up, stamped it with the office 'confidential' stamp; then covered it with lots of xxxxx's. *She's still got that inane token, kept in a special box together with my love letters. How stupid, hoarding immature rubbish? How idiotic was I to believe I'd need her forever? How naïve was she to be taken in by twaddle about 'till death us do part'.*

Dreams troubled him. In them, Adelle stood before him, smiling that lovely smile which lit up her eyes. She'd a beautiful face and perfect figure. He longed to possess that body. Needed her so much he risked his relationship with his mum, whom he adored, to make Adelle his. In the end his mum accepted Adelle and loved her as a daughter. They were happy until not long ago. *It's a good job Mum and Dad are gone. Couldn't have broken with Adelle with them around.* Gronya pointed out how Adelle abused him over the years, demanded loyalty and took him for granted.

Adelle grew up with a father who based his role in life on a personal need to undermine her self-confidence. Julian realised early on the key to unlock her devotion was to make her happy about herself. Gronya had pinpointed how Adelle manipulated this aspect of their lives and exploited his compassionate nature. Thanks to Gronya he'd singled out this weakness in himself. One of Adelle's tricks was to reiterate her unworthiness while praising his self-deprecating honesty and steadfastness; then seek reassurance that he needed her as much as she him. Gronya spelled out how this manoeuvre had become as troublesome as flies buzzing around cowpats. Continual adoration becomes tiresome, not that he didn't deserve it according to Gronya. He dialled Gronya's number, impatient for her to pick up.

"Hi, darling," she purred. "How d'you guess I longed to hear your voice?"

"What? Oh. Must be another sign of our deep under-standing of each other's needs. I need your dulcet tones to restore my equilibrium."

"And here's me believing it's because I need you, the answer to my longings."

"Please tell me I'm doing right," he said. "With the family around I can't shed my anxiety."

"You'll always do what's right. Everything you do is perfect, from phoning me to making me into a proper woman under the duvet."

"Not now, Precious. I need control and can't get at

you."

"Trying to keep you on your toes, or should I say…"

"Stop. It's enough you haunt my dreams." *Won't admit Adelle features in them, more than Gronya.*

"I've arranged the cottage hire for two weeks' time. Can you come?"

"Sure. I'll tell Adelle next weekend. Thank goodness you persuaded me to rent a flat near Sabina for a few months. It'd be more difficult if we lived in our house with constant reminders of our years together. Must go, someone's calling. Will ring later when everyone's in bed. Love you, need you."

Julian stuffed the phone into his pocket as one of the grandchildren burst in to demand attention. The family were gathered for a week of celebrations in a rented house big enough to accommodate everyone. The kids soon found their way around, exposing potential areas of escape to play hide and seek. He gave up ideas of privacy for the next couple of hours. *I'll indulge them until tea and bath time. Won't get such opportunities again. Better make the most of 'em.*

A while later, Julian sat down with a gin and tonic. Sabina was upstairs bathing the children before story and bed while Adelle prepared dinner. He poured everyone a drink, then was dismissed as unnecessary to proceedings until the food was ready. He excused himself to secure a quiet haven to aid his contemplations. He picked up an arts magazine to leaf through. He reminisced on how Adelle had been instrumental in developing his own appreciation of it; *proved fortuitous when we discovered Milner knew a great deal about art.* When Adelle questioned why Milner pursued a friendship with them, Gronya persuaded her it was because Milner loved to visit exhibitions, retrospectives and auctions. Said he valued the opportunity to discuss these with her; appreciated her input to his collection and potential purchases. Gronya admitted she didn't understand painting or sculpture, just accepted Milner's recommendations because they were sound investments.

He turned up an article on the significance of unicorns in iconography. His mind spun away as he pictured the unicorn tapestry hung in the main porch of their house. They'd visited Stratford to see a Shakespeare play. *Another interest Adelle encouraged. Not sure why I went along, other than to keep her quiet. More ways she exploited me. On the plus side, it did create something in common between Milner and Adelle that Gronya used to explain the dynamics of their friendship.* Although it was thirty-five years ago, he remembered it like yesterday.

"Look, look, Julian. See what I bought in that shop opposite The Globe."

"What?"

"A unicorn tapestry. Don't you just adore it? Bet the fence and the flowers around the animal are symbolic. Can't wait to explore the meanings. Need to visit a library and start research."

"Can we afford it?" he asked.

"Wasn't expensive. We don't have many pictures.

Was hoping you'd fall in love with it too. If you dislike it, I'll take it back, get a refund."

He hadn't liked it, but to keep her quiet, agreed it was agreeable. Later, when he saw the satisfaction it gave her to investigate the meanings of the plants and flowers, he realised the tapestry had more value than the image it portrayed, so found the money for a frame. It proved expensive, but kept her happy. Since then it always hung prominently in their home, admired by everyone who visited. Adelle explained the unicorn's significance as a mythical creature from medieval times that could only be captured by a virgin. Julian didn't consider the matter important until Milner, through Gronya, alerted him to the implications of the icon in terms of his relationship with Adelle. Milner told Gronya, who told Julian, that for Adelle, albeit unconsciously, it represented the way she tamed Julian, encircled and enclosed him and robbed him of his autonomy.

After dinner everyone gathered in the living room. Julian wished they'd go to bed. He didn't feel sociable, wanted to be alone with his phone. He sensed it in his pocket, his fingers itched to press the buttons that represented happiness, freedom, fulfilment and those other things he was sure he'd missed forever. Someone started flicking through TV channels.

"Stop," said one of the viewers. "It's the lottery draw. Find my ticket. Quick."

Julian stood, hitched up his trousers and walked toward the kitchen. *What losers to hope their numbers will come up? Don't they appreciate the odds? Ironic the one with the ticket ain't long for this world but still reckons money is the answer.*

"Excuse me, just going to get a drink," he said.

He crossed to the sink glass in hand, wrenched hard on the stiff tap which abruptly gave way and splashed water everywhere. *Why does that remind me of my misery?* Adelle was talking in the other room. She'd got up to stand near the kitchen door.

"Never needed to win a lottery. Won that when I found Julian. My lucky million pound draw in life."

He froze. He heard her say it often enough. Watched people nod in acknowledgement and accept the rock solid strength of their partnership without question. He put the glass down and riffled in his pocket for the phone. If he phoned Gronya, she'd reassure him that Adelle was manipulating him. The sooner he talked to Gronya the better. She'd help strengthen his resolve to tell Adelle next weekend that their 'marriage' – that sham institution Adelle worshipped – was over, that he was no longer going to ossify in a worn out, jaded faded relationship.

CS CS CS

GRONYA STARED AT her phone, willed it to ring.

"If you stare at that thing any harder, it'll disintegrate," said Milner.

"Shut up. I'm desperate for him to call. He's vulnerable this week with his family. Won't change his mind, but I won't be happy till Adelle knows it's over."

"To take your thoughts off him, let me remind you of the stuff you need to say to him."

"Can manage by myself."

"I want to make sure he doesn't wiggle off the hook," said Milner. "There's a lot riding on this for me. I'd rather we went over tactics you can employ to reassure him."

"If you must."

"Use clever-sounding expressions. He can be uptight and words that sound articulate impress him. Remind him how to 'reformulate' the past to cope with the current situation."

"What does that mean?"

"Doesn't matter. Write it down so you don't forget. He'll understand. Will be under the illusion you do too, and won't question."

"But what if he does?"

"Then get on to sex. Tell him how randy he makes you. Talk of the moment your eyes met over those champagne glasses when you knew he was yours. The day he realised the truth. Emphasise how you adore whorish romps – something you've told me he complains that Adelle no longer wants because she likes cuddles and comfort. Say you make each other young again – that he is still virile enough for dirty, filthy orgies. Do I have to amplify?"

"No thanks. I get the picture."

"Good – don't mess this up. I've waited too long and

worked too hard to put this one to bed – excuse the excellent pun. Another thing. Express it different ways. He'll fool himself what you repeat is new; not just the same old, same old. Will stay convinced you're better for him. That's Adelle's weakness. Like most people, she thinks repeating something makes it true. She forgets it works some occasions but not all."

"You've lost me now. Go away and leave me alone. I'm going to text Julian to phone me."

℃ ℃ ℃

JULIAN CLIMBED THE STAIRS to the flat. He was on his way to tell Adelle, unable to decide which emotion was uppermost – anxiety, fear or relief it'd soon be over. His stomach churned; he woke that morning in a sweat with painful cramps. He attributed this to his nightmare, parts of which haunted him. He couldn't dismiss the scene as he awoke; the one where he was seated on a river bank, head in hands as Adelle called to him. Around lay lifeless, gutted swans. It irritated that he couldn't remember if he found them dead, or whether he killed them before he sat down.

Adelle was ironing.

"We have to talk? I've something to tell you."

"You want to talk? To me? Avoided that for ages. Why now? Decided you've tortured me enough?"

"Sarcasm won't help. Just listen. I'm in love with Gronya. She's part of my life; I'm going off to spend two weeks with her in the West Country."

"What are you wittering on about?"

"You and me. We'll live together, but I'll go off and be with Gronya when I need to. That way I can watch after you and make sure you're cared for. You won't be alone."

"Is that all I'm getting?"

"You don't need any more."

"Why don't you stop this nonsense and help me fix our marriage?"

"That'll never happen."

"You mean just like that – forty-five years – over – no explanation – no attempt to sort anything out."

"Take it or leave it – don't ask why – you'll never get justification from me – don't owe you any."

"Are you serious?"

"Dead right – best way to deal with it is don't think on what we had or what you'll miss."

"Just like that – do you realise how cruel and callous you sound?"

"Don't care."

"What does Milner say?"

"He's happy."

"He's what?"

"Happy."

"You're joking, aren't you?"

"No."

"What about your colleagues?"

"Two years since I retired. They won't make any comments."

"You're sure? Shall we ask them?"

"Don't threaten me."

"I wasn't. Just want to know what they'll say. Or are you too afraid to ask because they'll disapprove?"

"None of their business."

"You're twisted if you believe that."

"No name calling or nastiness, totally unnecessary."

"Do you realise you sound more and more pathetic and stupid as this goes on? You cannot justify this behaviour on any grounds, and you know it."

"I can."

"Then do so."

"I've told you. You'll get no explanations from me. I owe you none."

"And that is the most twisted, distorted part of your delusion. You do owe me. The fact you choose not to discuss things properly means you know what you're doing is wrong on every count – absolutely, completely, utterly wrong."

"Think what you like. It won't change anything."

"Get out – get out – get out – get hold of your piece of filth. Let her arrange for you to stay at that stinking London flat. Don't ever come back here."

"I told you. We'll have no name calling, thank you."

"Why? Because it's the truth. That woman has pre-tended to be my friend for the past however many years, but it's clear she used me to stalk you. She's a liar and a manipulator. She whores herself around anywhere she thinks she can get what she wants irrespective of the cost to the people she preys on."

"How dare you? I said no name calling."

"Your performance doesn't give you the right to dictate my behaviour. Fact is, you don't want to listen to the truth. You and that piece of filth that called herself my friend have tried the case between you without a judge and jury because you know you'd be found guilty of disgusting selfish behaviour."

Julian had expected an outburst, but was determined not to lose his temper. The way to deal with it was remain calm. Ignore her. It'd blow over, Adelle would accept the situation and understand that his and Gronya's happiness was paramount.

"Nothing more to say," Adelle said as tears streamed down her face. "Then get out – just get out."

"As you wish. I'll make lunch first though. Would you like toasted cheese?"

C3 C3 C3

ADELLE WATCHED HIM prepare his food. The fog of pain enveloping her was unbearable. It crept into every part of her body and took up squatter's rights. Deep breaths couldn't disperse it. Sobs prevented her taking too many, and breathing became difficult as the physical discomfort in her heart forced it to miss beats. Her stomach churned as she swallowed what resembled nails that scratched and tore at her throat. The sensation was of them being hammered with precision into every inch of her insides. She wanted to be sick, but regurgitating imaginary nails would be more painful than swallowing. So she clutched at the idea that she mustn't vomit – not at any price.

Through the mist she observed Julian hitch up his trousers with his thumbs every few seconds, a sure sign he was uncomfortable. His pallor was ghost-like and he rattled and cluttered the tray as he attempted to push it in and out of the oven. He cut his finger as he sliced the cheese and went in search of a plaster. The silence added to her pain, and she sat stunned, unable to accept what he said. Julian finished preparing his food, and she watched him eat. She examined that adored face she knew each detail of. She saw him go through the motions; chew his food as if it tasted of poison. She was aware of his pretence that he was in dignified control. He learnt that from his mum. The thought of her sent Adelle into paroxysms of tears. Thank goodness his parents died long ago. If they hadn't, this would've killed them.

Julian finished eating, took a bag and left. From the window overlooking the street, Adelle watched him drive off. Bereft and torn apart with fear and misery, she paced the flat, encompassed in pain that she believed would never lift or disperse, no matter how many times Julian said she shouldn't think about it. *He might be able to turn off affection and trust like a cold tap, but I can't. How he could he do this – to me, to our children – to our grandchildren? Has he been lying all these years? Never loved me? How can he – how can he hurt me this way? I love him so much. He's the only thing I've lived for my whole life. How can I live without him? Why can't I lie down, fall sleep and never wake?*

෬ ෬ ෬

MILNER SAT IN the dining room while Gronya sorted stuff in the kitchen. The girls were due. He'd ordered them to come, told them he'd something critical to share. They grumbled. He expected that – wouldn't be normal if they didn't – but they did, in the end, grudgingly agree. He spent ages preparing. It was no different to a board meeting. Needed to get his ducks in a row, be ready to handle protests or arguments. There'd be the additional feature of excess emotion, but he'd plans to control that. *What I'll do is persuade them to focus on the notion that love of power is superior to the power of love. They must empower themselves to make the most of it and not let the idea that their mother loves Julian and not me take over. Must visualise the spider web I'm drawing them into. Once caught they'll be OK; they'll go along with everything, will have no choice.*

"So what's this about? What we done this time?" Ollah sounded drunk. Milner hoped she wasn't too far gone – he needed her calm.

"Mum and I have something to share with you. It's important not to overreact and discuss the matter calmly. We can do that, can't we?"

Hattie glanced from one parent to the other. "It's bad, isn't it? Can see from the way you look at each other. It's in Mum's eyes. She's like a rabbit in headlights."

"Rubbish," insisted Ollah. "What can be that awful? Dad'll tell us off, we'll say sorry. Then go back to normal."

"Ollah – their faces say this is serious. Don't think I want to hear. Can't you shut up and listen? Drink coffee or something, sober up."

"Enough!" Milner hoped his best boardroom voice would call everyone to order. "Your mother has taken a lover and will move out to live with him as soon as it can be arranged."

"A what? You're joking. Not April first is it? Why would Mum do that? She's here to take care of us. If she's got a bit of rough on the side, she's not doing her job. Stop messing around," Ollah burst out.

"Ollah, look at Mum's face," said Hattie. "She's gone bright red and is sweating like a pig. Dad's telling the truth."

Ollah and Hattie stood up and advanced on Gronya, who jumped up to stand behind her chair. Milner put himself between them.

"Sit down. We must exercise control and not get angry; there's no point. Everything's done and dusted. I'm OK with it. You should be too. Let's look forward to how it will work."

"You won't brush this under the carpet, Dad. I want answers. You owe us that much."

"In reality, we owe you nothing. We've brought you up and given you a good education. You're adults.

Behave like it and let's discuss how to move on."

"I want answers. Who's the disgusting idiot Mum 'made lurv to'? How dare he come and wreck our family?"

"Don't forget your mother and her lover have upset his family. We aren't alone in our betrayal. We must ensure we cope better than his lot. That will be our strength. You're capable of that."

"Just like that? How long have you known, Dad?"

"A while."

"So why tell us now? Why not let the nonsense go on till it fizzles out?"

"Because his wife said she won't tolerate a ménage à trois or quatre or whatever; has kicked him out. She may stand on principles, but is the one who'll lose out; we'll be friends and enjoy good times together; she'll be cut off."

"Maybe she's right."

"Don't think so," said Milner. "Given it a lot of consideration. Mine is the way to tackle this."

"Well – Mum – come on– who is this great lurver – don't stand there mute. Tell us."

"Julian."

"That snake!"

"Don't call him that. I love him. He's going to make me happy in ways none of you ever managed."

"Gronya. Don't be provocative." Milner glared at her. *Need to keep this lot focused on my target. Can't let that slip away.* "Let's get back to how we're gonna deal with this."

"Are you saying Dad and us, we don't make you happy?" wailed Ollah. "Why not? It's unthinkable. We're your kids. Your job is to put us first. What do you imagine you're doing? And what about Dad? He gave you everything you ever wanted. Just look around."

Gronya was not to be distracted. "You father never gave me the one thing I need most."

"And what on earth is that?"

"None of your business."

"Come on, girls," interrupted Milner. "Remember the love of power, not the power of love. Let's stay rational and not get incoherent – otherwise we'll be lost."

"I can't stop my irrational feelings," insisted Ollah. "Mum's betrayed us. If you accept this betrayal and condone it, you'll be betraying us as well. I'll never, never, never, never see that creep, talk to him, share any bit of fresh air with him or do anything that shows I accept his disgusting behaviour in taking Mum away from us."

"I'm with Ollah," said Hattie. "I'll never speak to him. Don't ever bring that snake anywhere near me or us."

"Girls – calm down – don't act in ways you'll regret. If we stay cool, we'll get what we want from this situation. Trust me. I've got everything worked out." *Must keep my voice low-key, don't let them get any hint I'm not in control. I'm the master manipulator here. Gronya won't beat me on this, won't let this lot get away.*

ભ ભ ભ

CHAPTER 4

Eiderdown Fluff

THE GIRLS RETIRED to their rooms. Anger resonated through the house, fuelling Gronya's insecurities and sense of guilt. *Why won't they understand? I need this. My life has been one long, slow sacrifice for them.* She needed to talk to Julian who'd put a stop to her bothersome conscience. *Want my guilty feelings soothed. Can't feel like this. I deserve to be happy.* The girls shed tears of frustration because she refused to give him up. Milner insisted they take time to consider positive ways to deal with the situation. Told them he wanted no reprisals or criticism, just solutions. He'd to go out to host a business dinner; trusted them to behave during his absence. Instructed them to come up with ideas for discussion at breakfast next morning which he stressed would be conducted by him in a calm and constructive manner.

Milner prepared his papers and left. Gronya waited for the purr of the Bentley engine accompanied by the crunch of wheels on gravel, then retired to her room. It was the only way to escape the worst of the echoes from Ollah and Hattie's intermittent sobbing. *You'd think with such a big house, it'd be easy to hide. Will never understand how the noise carries even with their rooms at opposite ends of it.* Gronya closed her door in the hope they wouldn't trouble her. Inevitably, they did. Soon after Milner departed, they burst in on her.

"Not talking to the snake are you? Hang up. Talk to us," Ollah bellowed.

"Shhh. He'll hear you," pleaded Gronya.

"Do we care? He needs to know we despise him, and you, for his disgusting behaviour. How dare he snatch your attention from us? You make sure he knows what we think. Is he listening? Good." Ollah snatched the mobile from Gronya's hand and shouted into it. "Don't ever come near us and if you know what's good for you, you'll give up this idiocy. That's everything I have to say. I'll never talk to you or see you – ever."

Gronya retrieved her phone. Glaring at Ollah, she spoke to Julian.

"Sorry, darling. I'll phone later."

"Darling... Darling... Darling," screamed Hattie. "How dare you utter that word in front of us?"

Gronya tried to dial Milner, but couldn't get through.

"Say what you have to, then leave me in peace."

"What's the point?" said Ollah. "You don't care anyway, do you?"

"Of course I do. I'll be here to support you whenever and whatever happens."

"Damn right! We'll both make sure you are. If that

snake thinks he'll grab your attention when we should have it – he better learn he won't. Dad and we need you and, angry as we are, you're our mother first. Incidentally, did you feed the cats before we arrived? Brought my dog too so you can find food for him as well," snapped Ollah.

Gronya listened to their rants, overcome with emotional exhaustion. Once their immediate anger was vented they returned to their rooms. Gronya made her way downstairs, fed Ollah's pets, then retreated to her haven. When the house went quiet, and she thought it safe, she phoned Julian.

"Sorry about earlier. Girls took it badly."

"Never mind. We didn't think it'd be easy. If they take precedence for a while, we'll cope. We've our trip to look forward to."

"Tell me again we're doing what's right."

"No question. We owe it to ourselves. My mum used to say everyone else would demand and get what they wanted attention wise. Sometimes you must concentrate on your own needs."

"But we've hurt so many people."

"Don't dwell on it. They need to accept it. If they insist on being sorry for themselves it's because they're the selfish ones. They'll see our happiness should be supreme. You're the most gorgeous, wonderful, beautiful lady in the world, and nothing will keep me from you."

"I've changed so much because of you. You bring out the best of me. Milner brought out the worst. Used me to take the heat from the girls all these years. It's why we're meant to be. You make me young. You're the first one to appreciate me, better than I do myself."

"Funny. That's how I am about you. With you I'm complete. Never felt so whole. Nobody ever did that for me."

"Not even your children?"

"Not even them. Although wouldn't say it to them. They'll understand because I love them, I'm doing this for their good."

"Mine need a great deal of reassurance – more than usual. I can manage because you make me strong."

Gronya ended the call ninety minutes later. It was past midnight. *Wish I could stop being on edge and agitated. Can't cope. Better take a pill. Julian is the only medicine I want, but he isn't here. Perhaps I should phone him again. He won't mind. No. Mustn't. He'll get fed up. Especially hearing how horrid the girls have been.* Without realising it, Gronya was imposing discipline on herself to make sure she kept the affection flowing. It was difficult. Someone once told her how love had to be created and earned through hard work. She was certain she'd accrued points with Julian by hanging onto the idea they'd be together, but hadn't had a chance to show how much he deserved her. Julian might escape; lose his autonomy to Adelle again if she dropped her vigilance. It was a nightmare when he spent time with Adelle. At least he'd moved out of Adelle's bed and wasn't sharing that with her. Said he slept on a blow-up mattress when he went there.

I'm sweating so much I need another shower. Gronya got up; as she rubbed her face and the back of her neck with a towel she kept in readiness beside her, she knocked over a bedside table and broke a lamp. *Damn.* She paced the bedroom and bathroom. She ran taps, then turned them off. *Must talk to him.* She compromised with a text. *Please darling, tell me you're OK. Say you still love me.* Julian's phone bleeped. He replied. *I'm OK. In bed, on my mattress on the floor, longing for you. Will love you for eternity. Go to sleep. Rest. Will chat tomorrow.*

Gronya tried to recall something she was sure Milner told her. How if she got Julian to bring his objectives into sharper focus it would energise and keep him concentrated on being with her. *Business/boardroom speak; what did it mean? Can't do without him. Simple as. Must get him to myself soon as.* The shower called. Gronya stepped into it and let the cool water wash away her perspiration. After drying herself, she climbed into bed. Several hours later, her towel soaked with sweat from her face, neck and armpits, she lay awake. Blessed unconsciousness hadn't been granted. *How will I manage till we go away together in a couple of weeks? It's no good. Can't follow the advice on those mugs and posters – 'Keep calm and carry on'.*

CƷ CƷ CƷ

JULIAN PUT THE PHONE down after texting Gronya. His

hands were sweaty, his heart beat fast. He desired her so much. He turned over and closed his eyes. Gronya behaved like a whore when they were together. She'd talk dirty – would go on about 'ff' – filthy fornication – about how virile he was, how big he was and how satisfying. He wondered where the 'ff' came from. Didn't question her, liked the notion and savoured it instead. He remembered learning about alliteration in school. Played around with it in his mind, fantasising about the next time he got hold of her for 'fff'; the middle 'f' standing for fantasy, fantastic or something else ending in 'ing.

Intimacy with Adelle long ago settled into peaceful considerate sessions; more about cuddles, comfort and cream to smooth things along. Adelle tolerated his snoring, under the illusion she would adore him till she died; it was the bargain, the good with the bad. Gronya adopted the opposite approach. She loathed it. Years ago she banished Milner from her bed, on the excuse of the abhorrent guttural wheezing he emitted while asleep. Saw no reason to change her stance now. So when they got together she'd arrive in Julian's bed for mad passionate sex; then go sleep elsewhere. He wanted more snuggles but Gronya wouldn't tolerate too many. Didn't like to cuddle up because of her tendency to sweat. Said she hated being uncomfortable when she got too hot. It was OK during the day, she'd consent to fondling if they were in the kitchen or downstairs, but spontaneous hugs were brief. Made it clear it was all right to sneak up and grab her bum or tits as long as he didn't do it too often. Would laugh and talk vulgar when he did, except her hot flushes confused him, left him unsure. Mixed messages became the order of things. On balance he reasoned that as he achieved almost everything he needed and more intercourse than he dreamed of, it didn't matter if he'd to snore alone.

ೞ ೞ ೞ

MILNER DECIDED HE must see Adelle. *Need to get her on side, make her believe I'm as unhappy as her, persuade her I'm a friend. Then I can keep her in my orbit with an eye on what she plans or gets up to. Can't allow her to wreck it.* The ideal opportunity presented when Adelle wrote seeking a reference for some voluntary organisation she wanted to work for. It gave him the chance to invite her to tea at a neutral venue. He'd to chair some board meetings near Langley Street Station and as there was a hotel nearby, invited her to join him one afternoon. On the day in question she texted saying she couldn't come and was sorry. Then texted again to say she'd changed her mind. *Nuisance, but I suppose she has the right to be up and down after what we've done to her.*

Milner watched her walk towards him. Her expression was downcast, she'd lost weight and looked sad. *Mustn't be concerned. She deserves it. If she couldn't hang onto him it's her own fault, not mine or Gronya's or anyone else's.*

"Hi. Didn't recognise you. Was looking for a dark-haired lady. You changed your hair colour."

"Let it go natural," Adelle responded, her voice flat and unanimated.

"Shall we take tea in the hotel outside the station?"

"Sure – lead on."

They settled down in a corner. Milner ordered afternoon tea. Adelle didn't fancy biscuits or cake. *Fine, makes it easy.* The first thing she handed him was a bag.

"Would you be kind enough to return these bits and pieces to Gronya?"

"What are they?"

"Every gift she gave me the last few years. Since they were bribes and none of them sincerely given, I cannot keep them."

"I'm sorry you feel that way. They were from me too."

"I wasn't aware. Was always under the impression she was the one who chose and bought them."

"No. Gronya enquired what you wanted on my behalf. I sourced and purchased them."

"Not sure it helps to know. In any event they carry painful memories and I can't look at them without breaking down."

"In that case I'll take them. I understand. I've also been devastated."

"Really?"

"Have loved Gronya more than forty years. Hasn't been easy, but I need to keep her in my life for my family's sake. We have a grandchild who needs her.

Don't want to see Julian, but plan to take care of Gronya. Told her there's no way back and I'll divorce her. I'll ensure she has a large home and a good income, but it will be painful."

"You do realise it was her plan the whole time, to steal Julian from me?"

"You reckon? I'm sure it only started last August."

"Don't want to sound rude, but as a man of the world, you must be aware how naïve that sounds. I've been a fool. She stalked him for years. In August Julian became remote, but I sensed something wrong ages before. August was when he stopped speaking to me and wouldn't tell me why. The first I realised it was Gronya was when he told me a couple of weeks ago. I trusted her and cannot understand how my so-called friend has betrayed me this way."

"Let's not talk about betrayal. Need to look forward. It'll be difficult but I can recommend some reading if you like."

"Self-help twaddle? My world is shattered, everything I believe in destroyed, and you surmise there's solace to be found in well-meaning, misguided rubbish about forgiveness and moving on?"

"You'll have to eventually – build a new life. I want to help as a friend."

"You're sure, are you? You seem calm and unworried. Is there more to this than I sense on the surface?"

"No. But there's no point fighting battles already won. I have to ensure my children and grandchildren benefit from Gronya's love. It's not easy, but I'll concentrate on what makes her and them happy. I'll find my own happiness again. Need the idea to sustain me. You should adopt it too."

"You sound like a used car salesman. I'm too sore to reason that way. Can barely get through each day."

"You will. Don't worry. You'll cope. You're strong."

They finished. Milner excused himself to go and chair his board. He walked away from Adelle pleased he could report success to Gronya.

"It's OK. Got her in control," he reported on his journey home on the train. "She's sore, but won't do anything stupid."

"As long as you're sure. I'll let Julian know you're happy with the outcome."

"Jubilant. I told her I plan to divorce you."

"Why?"

"Because she'll tell Julian. Then you can say you spoke to me and I denied it."

"The point being?"

"Must I spell everything out in minute detail?" said Milner in frustration. "You need to build on his belief that she exaggerates and lies to get attention. It's part of my strategy. Makes her look foolish because Julian believes you. You've been at it for years under my guidance. Isn't it obvious? Haven't you learned anything?"

"Right! I see. I resemble that remark," said Gronya as she burst out laughing. "Very clever."

"She's returned the gifts you gave her. It's not worth worrying about. One of her stupid standing-on-moral-principles ideas. Tends to revert to them if she feels threatened."

"It's a weakness she has," said Gronya struggling to get her words out as her laughter became almost uncontrollable.

"What so funny?" asked Milner.

"Nothing. You wouldn't understand," she spluttered.

I understand more than you give me credit for, girl. You suppose you won an easy victory. I'm not so sure. No point worrying you with it. It's annoying when you put on your obtuse questioning attitude as if you're naïve and lost. Think I don't know you do it instinctively. If not, you should by now. Been at it long enough. Milner hung up and fished in Adelle's parcel to see what she'd returned. He was disappointed to note it was everything he remembered he wrapped and gave her the last three years.

CB CB CB

GRONYA ARRIVED IN EXETER at the cottage. She travelled separately from Julian, who'd taken a temporary job in a nearby town. It was hard. Living in London offered no chance to see Julian in the week. She'd investigated a house for rent near the marital home with Milner, who agreed to sort out the legals for a two-year rental, but Julian didn't want to commit. Said he wanted to wait till he knew where he might get a permanent job.

She told him not to worry. She'd sufficient income to keep them until he found work, but he was being stubborn about his contribution to household expenses. *Stupid male pride. Doesn't matter he'll never have enough to pay rent. Still – must pander to his ego. It'll be worth it in the end, he'll be so completely mine he won't escape. This is the one time I can ignore the old saying 'be careful what you wish for'. This is everything I want, I won't regret it.* She complained to Milner Julian was taking too long to persuade over renting the house. Milner said to be wary. She could tread on his dignity as well as his dreams. If she trod too hard, he may struggle and break away. This trip was a means to secure Julian within her meticulously spun web by demonstrating how wonderful life could be for them together – alone. Milner had promised to deal with the girls' inevitable crises for the next two weeks so she could weave her mesh as tight as possible.

Gronya set about unpacking the Bentley Milner had loaned her. *No way I'm travelling around the countryside as a passenger in Julian's jalopy. I want to drive and be comfortable. Thank goodness Milner understands I can only go so far in lowering my standards.* As she carted supplies and bits and pieces into the cottage she hummed. She was excited. She spoke to Julian last night for the usual couple of hours, but also exchanged emails with him during the day. The girls complained loud and long while she packed up the car – moaning incessantly about how she talked on the phone to the jerk all day, and they couldn't get hold of her. *Who cares?* As long as neither of them had a crisis Milner couldn't cope with, she determined to enjoy herself.

Milner and her, Julian and Adelle had stayed in this cottage the year before during the town's literary festival. Gronya and Julian hadn't slept together then. It'd been eye contact, emails and texts. During that week Gronya carried around her secret; Julian was hers and not Adelle's. Adelle commented to Gronya how relaxed she seemed. She deflected Adelle's enquiry about the reason for her happiness and gloated in private how Adelle would never guess, she was too trusting of Julian. Milner noticed Gronya's smiles and warned her not to seem too dreamy and content. He also admonished her about the stolen glances. It'd been difficult not to indulge them too much, but she succeeded in controlling herself, because at the end of the week Adelle didn't suspect. It was a few weeks later Julian made love to her for the first time. *I shan't forget. Was so nervous here last September, but Milner kept telling me we had the whole thing done and dusted and not to worry. Now here I am. Julian's coming to me. It's so exciting when he tells me how beautiful I am and how he has longed for me his entire life. Be still my beating heart.*

Her email to Julian yesterday earned a rebuke for gloating over an email they'd received the previous week from the literary festival committee inviting ticket applications for this year's event. She told Julian she expected one had gone to Adelle who'd get upset when she opened it. Suggested Adelle's emotions might surface and make her volatile. Julian got annoyed, said he didn't want to consider it, and Adelle had to cope. He'd instructed her often enough not to ruminate on their failed marriage and relationship. If she couldn't take his advice it was no longer his or Gronya's business. Gronya wrote back and justified herself by saying she had sympathy for Adelle, which was why she'd mentioned it. *Didn't really experience guilt over it, but Milner told me to say it to pacify Julian.*

Julian's car pulled into the driveway. Gronya rushed out, fell into his arms and kissed him passionately.

"Come and see. It's like I emailed yesterday – Our First Home," purred Gronya.

"I take it you are saying that With Capital Letters the same as in your email yesterday. Makes it more real and important with capital letters, doesn't it?"

"What are you talking about?"

"No matter. I'm happy to be here. Where's the bed? Let's get to it, make good use of our duvet time."

"Now there's a phrase you've learnt from me," said Gronya leading him towards the stairs. "We'll finish unpacking later."

"There's only one item I want to unpack," laughed Julian. "I've brought clothes to stand up in and some pyjamas, and don't plan to wear the jim-jams."

The time sped too fast for Gronya. Several phone calls came from the girls, but Milner managed to keep those to a minimum. He worked out a strategy for him and Gronya to deal with them.

"You'll owe me big time," he said to her. "It's going to be hell."

"Don't care what the price is. I want two weeks of heaven. You have obligations to me for the miserable years I endured," she spat at him.

"Don't push your luck," he responded.

Gronya and Julian spent lazy days. They got up late after 'duvet time', ate something light, then walked along the shore, holding hands like teenagers. She'd go into raptures about how happy she was. Laugh at how it took so long to find each other. They determined this would be their special place where they made their First Home together. Wrapped in the sounds of the sea and lost in each other, they'd search for a café to take coffee – he always had full-leaded, she stuck to decaffeinated. They'd joke about how he could give up caffeine and share her decaf, he was virile and energetic enough not to need it any more.

Afternoons were whiled away in hunts for places to eat in the evening; menus outside local restaurants were examined in detail to see what appealed.

"I know what I fancy," Julian would say as they stared at the menu and squeezed her hand.

"Now, now. A girl must get nourishment and rest to keep her good looks in order."

Forced to return to Milner and the girls at the end of the two weeks, Gronya did so with reluctance, angry at missing romantic walks along the seafront with Julian. She pined for Julian, her physical ache unbearable.

Added to her misery were Julian's phone problems. Julian never bothered about phones or computers. He left that to Adelle, who in turn relied on Milner to keep her up to date with the latest gadgets. The difference was while Adelle used equipment as an aid to help smooth out life's challenges, Milner was always desperate to try out the most recent piece of kit. Gronya benefitted from this because once Milner tired of his current toy he gave it to her while he moved on to another. Gronya heard Milner describe himself as an 'early adopter' and Adelle as a 'get it when thrown off the ark as no more use to anyone' type of person. Said it was because Adelle was too mean to pay the upfront development costs and would buy when it came down in price because it was old news.

Communication between Gronya and Julian became intermittent. With no landline at his accommodation, she'd to feed her longings through a series of frustrating short phone calls.

"*Quel dommage,*" said Julian when he managed to get through one evening. Having hitched up his pants to be comfortable on his hips, he dialled her number more in hope than confidence. Caught unawares when she answered, he was so surprised he pressed the phone to his ear and adjusted his trousers, but with one thumb.

"Just a quickie. Sorry – quickies on the brain. Hope the phone doesn't die on us. It's a crisis. May have to resort to pigeons to get hold of you – if they can make time between bonking – I'm jealous you understand."

"Been watching the pigeons here – they're too speedy for what I have in mind – although I'm envious because they get going frequently. Practising until perfect – or beyond three seconds – something I intend to do to you – soon – get beyond three seconds you understand. Anywhichway, there were smiley beaks all round and a lot of feathers flying. Another thing I'm aiming for asap."

"It'd help communications if I could get my dongle going."

"Naughty boy."

"Keep talking. Need to hear your voice. I'm so love-sick. Want you with me under my duvet. Proves we belong together forever."

"I know. Keep working on your dongle."

The phone went dead. *Blast. I wish I'd paid more attention on how to get comms in order when Adelle tried to show me.*

ભ ભ ભ

PART 2

The Jousting Jester, Hera and the Peacock

CHAPTER 5

Getting Away

MILNER DID IT often, but this would be the first occasion alone. It was his job to organise supplies and pack the Bentley, but doing it on his own provoked strange reflections, which he struggled to understand. Why did he miss Gronya's nagging and complaining? He was aware it arose from her anxiety, but as a routine it was comfortable. They shared the driving to Dordogneshire, the affectionate name adopted by expats. Meant they didn't need frequent stops. This time he'd be forced to take more than the usual number of breaks otherwise he might nod off at the wheel. *Who'd have guessed it? It'll be a long journey, but needs must.*

Milner set off from London early next morning. The route was busy. *Perhaps I should've cancelled. I'd plenty of opportunity to give Madame Jouffre notice. Trouble is, she doesn't get a lot of business this season of the year.* After lengthy and anxious deliberations he decided it would be good to visit her and his friends in the village one last time. He also had to show his coping skills, so Gronya, in her own perverse way, couldn't criticise him for needing, or not needing, her depending on her mood at any given moment. He was relieved they agreed the cats wouldn't go to a cattery. Gronya would visit the house daily to feed and water them. Despite their marriage of over forty years, he organised most of that. Gronya left him to it. *So why do I feel desolate? Don't make sense. Been isolated inside the relationship for ages. Why does this loneliness seem more awful? It is, after all, what I planned.* He must behave in an appropriate manner, be seen to be gracious. He struggled to decide how to play the whole thing. If he overplayed the chivalry or, alternatively, pretended to display intense anger, the game would be up. Given his long experience of boardroom management, it made no point to doubt himself. On future holidays, he'd take a girlfriend, but that'd have to wait. For now, he'd to set the right tone.

The motorway was busy with its usual mixture of large lorries transporting the world around in containers. *Rolling advertising – effective – wonder if the guy who dreamed that one up got a fortune from it – whatever – lots of people made heaps from it.* He accelerated the Bentley past cars with roof racks piled high and trailers packed to the gunnels with badly-tied canvases flapping. *Why does Easter make it obligatory to fill roads with vehicles like that? Still, they bought their stuff somewhere. Means someone has done well from them. They'll be a nuisance all the way south. Will ignore them as much as possible.* His Eurotunnel crossing was nine-thirty am. He was on schedule. He arrived at the Folkestone terminal and decided not to call in at the shops, but go straight to the car parks by the barrier. After parking up he wandered over to the catering trailer to ask for a mug of hot water. He offered to pay the cost of a drink to get it. He wanted to use his Rooibos caffeine-free teabag. No *stimulants required; I'm stimulating enough.* As he stood by his vehicle, the wind picked up. *Wouldn't fancy the ferry today.* He examined his watch. Sufficient time to visit the gents before boarding. *Hate those cramped, smelly train toilets. Space is my must have – for everything – it's not luck I can buy comfort whenever and wherever I want.*

He returned to find the barrier about to be raised. He started his engine and followed the lead vehicle around to the ramp and down to the train. The conductors waved him on and he drove through the carriages. *Good – nearly first on, nearly first off. Means I get away quicker t'other end, leave behind some of those awful canvased trailers.* He studied the guard who worked to minimise the gaps between vehicles, then instructed each driver to apply their handbrake, put their gear stick in neutral and open a window. O*ne French guard today.* The man closed the safety doors for each compartment. *Smooth and efficient – a business after my own scruples.* Milner looked at the notices and adverts on the carriage sides that extolled wines and places to visit in France. *Pity I can't advertise here but wouldn't suit my operations. Targeted advertising keeps marketing costs down. Although sometimes it can pay to go off piste.* He peered through the rear window of the vehicle ahead and saw a family of four. The children watched cartoons on screens suspended from the seat in front of them. The parents had their own screen resting on the dashboard. They seemed absorbed in a car chase. *Mindless entertainment for mindless people. Dumb cartoons and movies for dumb people. Still, someone made a killing from them.*

He sat back as the train glided out of the station. He'd be in France in about an hour. *Better rest my eyes. Not tired, but they've been scratchy since I got up.* He fished around in the glove compartment and found a small bottle of eye drops. He adjusted his seat and laid his head against the headrest. The power of the train's diesel engines pulsed through the Bentley floor and Milner visualised them pulling the carriages along in the darkness. The engineering amazed him, given the gentle almost subliminal rocking ride it gave. *That's the way to do it. Manipulate people and make them grateful because they are too stupid to realise they've been had.*

Despite closed eyes, he remained conscious. He wished to sleep, but it wasn't possible sitting up. After a while, he glanced at his watch and, as he did so, became aware he couldn't feel or hear the soothing throb of the diesel engines. *Have we stopped? Wonder why?* Perhaps he'd fallen asleep. He was convinced he hadn't. He straightened his seat to sit upright, looked around and realised he was still in the tunnel as there was no light visible outside the train windows. *Did I miss an emergency stop? Why are we stationary?* He shook his head to force his senses back into alignment with the situation. A guard emerged through the doors and approached his vehicle. *Is that the same guy who loaded the carriage earlier? Not sure. Thought I'd paid more attention, but don't know now.* The guard leaned over and spoke with an English accent. *Must be different chap, t'other bloke was French.*

"Please vacate your vehicle and accompany me to the service tunnel where carriages wait to take you to the French side."

"What's the problem?"

"Engine failure. Evacuation necessary. A relief will pull these carriages out, but meantime you must leave the train. 'Elf and safety and all that."

"Very well. Should I bring my briefcase and passport?"

"Good idea, sir."

Others walked in single file in front of him. Milner sensed something brush against his leg. He looked down to see a cat he was sure he recognised walking beside him. It was a dappled tortoiseshell and white she-cat with a brown and black coat, white paws and dark amber eyes. He stopped, leaned over and picked her up.

"You look like Hera," he said aloud. "How did you get on the train? You must belong to another vehicle. I wonder which one. In the meantime I'll keep you safe. We'll need to find your owner. They'll have your pet passport."

"I am Hera and I won't require a passport where we're headed," said the cat.

Milner stopped. Had he imagined it? The guard called out for people to hurry so Milner resumed walking. He followed the line through the door into the service tunnel and boarded with the other passengers. He looked down at the cat.

"Must be going bonkers. Did you talk?"

Hera blinked at Milner as, unconcerned, she licked her paw.

"I did. I'm assigned to look after you on a journey we are to take together."

Milner gasped. "Journey? What journey? How did you get here?"

"Sit back and relax. All will be revealed."

They headed into the darkness. *Must be dreaming. Need to wake up. We'll arrive in Calais soon.* The train slowed and pulled into a siding. He looked around to establish bearings. Belldeep Acres was the name on the sign. *Never heard of it. Are we in France? It's not a French name. Where on earth am I? What am I doing here?*

"Chillax," said Hera. "Don't worry. I know where we're going. Follow me."

Milner disembarked and followed Hera along the platform.

"I realise you've doubts," said Hera as they approached the ticket office, beyond which Milner observed an archway to a cobbled street.

"Hope that's not for us," he said, horrified, pointing at a pony and trap.

"As I stated, before you so rudely interrupted, despite

your reservations, I'm here to help. It is our transport, by the way."

"Why?"

"Because you've never ridden in one before. Do I need any other justification?"

"Won't question further and will humour you for now, but I reckon it'll be bumpy over those cobblestones."

"True… But they are an improvement on the dirt road to the chateau. Lots of potholes, especially after heavy rain. You might end up walking if the trap falls in one and loses a wheel."

"Trust it's not a sign of what to expect. Where are the other passengers going?" asked Milner realising his transport was only big enough to carry one passenger beside the driver.

"They're chateau-bound. Hay carts will collect them."

"Why do I get special treatment?" asked Milner.

"You have the most to learn."

"What's that supposed to mean?"

"You'll see."

The pony and trap set off. Being used to his Bentley, Milner didn't appreciate the bouncy, bumpy motion of the wheels on the uneven surface. *Am I dreaming?* His body and the loud clack of horseshoes on cobbles indicated he wasn't. His wizardry knowledge told him portals to other worlds were something his ancestors had experience of, but he'd never been through one. He prided himself on being a modern wizard who didn't have to rely on crude spells, although the occasional incantation in private did no harm. His gift lay in a talent for exploiting skills through which he manipulated individuals to achieve desire outcomes. Getting others to bend to his will made him wealthy. He'd no need to resort to the sort of magic his predecessors relied on. It was why he smiled whenever someone congratulated him with the phrase '...that was wizard, old chap...' not realising their proximity to the truth. The thing he could count on was, however sophisticated people might be, gullibility was a trait they never discarded. Pride in his capacity to take advantage of that endearing/enduring aspect of human nature imparted quiet satisfaction. He harmed nobody, just secured more choices in life because of the flexibility afforded him by wealth.

The pony trotted along the gravelled dirt road. Milner, absorbed in his thoughts, ceased to be discomforted by the bumpy ride. When he did pay attention to his surroundings, he noted they were transiting a small wood. *Must be ancient. The trees are gnarled. Look at the huge oak ahead. Its girth indicates it's several hundred years old. Will ask someone when I get the chance. Maybe Hera knows.* In the distance he saw the spires of a chateau roof.

"Is that our destination?"

"It is. Although we'll make a short stop in the wood."

"What for?"

"To collect briefing papers."

"Briefing?"

"Yes. Otherwise you'll be unprepared to reap the full benefit of your trip to Belldeep. You always insist on value for money and a good ROI – Return on Investment – so you should be the first to recognise the usefulness of a precise rundown to help you extract maximum advantage from the experience you are about to enjoy."

"Will I get to rate enjoyment after by completing a customer satisfaction survey?"

"Don't get ahead of yourself," said Hera. "I'm in charge of witticisms, if you don't mind."

Milner smiled as the trap halted beneath the oak that he wondered the age of. It occurred to him it had more significance than he realised. He studied it intensely. Its gnarls and knots showed intricate patterns in which he traced facial outlines. He was sure he recognised people he knew, but then they transmogrified into other familiar individuals. A smartly dressed fellow stepped out from behind the tree and distracted him from his contemplation of the metamorphosing quality of the trunk's scarred bark. Milner was reminded of images he'd seen of Toulouse Lautrec or that painting of raining men by Magritte. This guy wore an expensive suit, handmade black brogues and a bowler hat. An umbrella was hooked over one arm. In the other he carried a clipboard and folder. Milner's attention was drawn to the small creature perched on his left shoulder. It was identical to clipboard man, right down to replica clothes.

"Good afternoon and welcome," said the man.

"Here's your agenda and briefing papers. Sign where indicated to acknowledge receipt."

While he spoke the creature offered its own greeting.

Hello there, prat. Come to see what you can see? You look like a right tosser who needs taking down a couple of pegs. We'll have sport with you, I reckon.

Taken aback, Milner reasoned his imagination must be working overtime. He signed, took the papers and handed back the clipboard. The man disappeared behind the tree. Hera nodded to the driver to start up the pony.

"Did I imagine it, or did that thing on his shoulder just insult me?"

"Don't take it personally," said Hera. "Where we're going everyone has a doppelgänger. It will reveal what the person thinks as opposed to what they say. A bit disconcerting, but you'll get used to it. The main point is not to betray to the individual addressing you that you know what their doppelgänger reveals. You pride yourself on your ability to read people, but hearing uncensored thoughts while you stand in front of them will shock. Why don't you read your briefing papers while we make our way towards the chateau?"

Milner opened his folder.

Belldeep – Mission Statement
To create lasting solutions to arrogance, pride and complacency

OMG – or in the words of a certain person of tennis fame – they cannot be serious, man.

"Why can't they?" asked Hera.

"How did you know my thoughts?"

"You have your own doppelgänger, although only I can see and hear it."

"What did I do to deserve this? I pride myself on work well done as long as it hasn't harmed anyone. Pride is not something negative as this briefing suggests."

"Really? You're absolutely convinced you never harmed anyone?"

"Why am I debating this with you?"

"What's wrong in a debate with a cat? You do it at home. Or is it only in order when I can't answer back?"

"I'll accept the question of pride might be discussed at some point. But as for the other issues, I'm not arrogant or complacent."

"Really? You do have a lot to learn."

"And if I don't want to? Can't see the necessity?"

"For once you've no choice. You can't resume your journey or holiday until this experience is complete. Might as well settle down – get on with it."

"So... to coin a phrase – there isn't a cat's chance in hell of getting out of this."

"My, oh my! A sarcastic paws for thought," said Hera as she placed her paw on his knee and batted her eyelids at him. "Whatever – you clearly retain a sense of humour. Better hang on to it. It'll come in handy, or should I say pawsy?"

The pony and trap left the wood to wend its way up a gentle incline. The chateau loomed ahead, surrounded by a high stone wall. Presently they stopped before a sturdy, heavy oak double door covered in iron hinges studded with nails. In the middle of the right hand panel a smaller door boasted a substantial knocker. It was fashioned in the shape of a clenched gloved fist. It looked eerie to Milner. Above the centre of the doors, carved into the stonework was the figure of a Hanged Man, upside down. Below this was a sign –

We aim to challenge complacency
You aim too, please

This lot have a real downer on complacency. Still, not a problem for me. Never been that.

"We'll see," said Hera.

Milner glared at her and alighted. The knocker disturbed him. *I seem to have landed in a commune with a surfeit of symbols. Suppose this curled fist carries meaning.*

"It does," said Hera. "All will become clear, but for now you are right to be uneasy about the doorknob and the image it represents. You must, however, use it to summon someone to gain entry."

"Aren't you afraid I won't be as open as I might be if you know my thinking?" Milner asked, poised to grasp the knocker.

"I reckon you'd boast you can cope. Are you suggesting you can't?"

"Got me there. Need to contemplate that one. Meantime, suppose I better get on with it."

"Good idea."

Milner took hold of the disembodied fist, aware of a surreal sense of unease as his fingers closed around it. It was heavier than he surmised, and he'd to grip hard to lift it to bang the sounding plate. The door was opened by a concierge, with his compulsory doppelgänger. Both looked as if they'd worked at a posh London hotel in the 1930s. *Nice touch. Obviously paid attention to period details.* In his turn, the concierge inspected Milner up and down.

"Welcome, sir. You must be our expected guest."

Oh boy, said the doppelgänger. *Clipboard man reported this one was a right arrogant idiot. Wonder how many falls he'll take till his pride is well and truly dented.*

Milner turned to Hera.

"Good job he can't hear my doppelgänger. He wouldn't like what I'm thinking."

"Told you it would be disconcerting. It's part of the training."

"Training? Explain why I need any?"

"You'll see," purred Hera. "For now I'll escort you to your accommodation so you can install yourself, read the rest of the agenda, and familiarise yourself with the facilities."

The concierge opened the double gates. Milner climbed into his seat and was carried along a path to the chateau drawbridge, which they crossed over into a cobbled courtyard.

"This way," said Hera who led Milner through an archway, and up some stairs to a covered loggia, off of which a series of doors offered access to rooms.

"This is your suite," said Hera. Carved on the door was the name La Sérénelle. A card representing a hermit adorned the right side doorjamb, beneath which Milner's name was inscribed.

"Another tarot card?"

"You recognised the one at the front gates then?"

"I did. Never studied them in detail, can you indicate their significance? Not sure I appreciate the image of the upside-down hanged man. Doesn't it suggest sacrifice? Isn't a hermit someone who retreats to be alone? Aren't I here to network and meet challenges?"

"Quite so. First lesson. Your assumptions are based on narrow interpretations as a result of ingrained ideas. You wouldn't tolerate such an approach in business. Why accept it here?"

"So what do the tarot figures represent?"

"They have many meanings. For you the Hanged Man exemplifies a challenge to contemplate old patterns of behaviour and bad habits that restrict you, and the Hermit a need to examine your past actions through honest introspection."

Milner smiled. *Goes both ways. I assume they are ready for my challenge to them.*

"Don't forget I know what you're thinking," said Hera.

Milner entered the room to be his private space for the next few days. *Comfortable refuge at least. Bed looks warm and clean.* He stopped dead. *How'd they get hold of that, for goodness sake?* He stared hard at the picture on the wall. It was identical to the Banksy painting at the London flat, the one of the monkey sporting a tabard with the slogan 'Keep it real' scrawled across it. Till now Milner reckoned this was a joke – that he might be dreaming. But this wasn't funny. He decided to take it seriously. He needed to switch his mind to business mode, prepare himself to handle difficult people and awkward situations, become alert and aware, tune his senses. Start developing strategies to deal with whatever was presented; if only to get it over with; show he was in charge; couldn't be bested.

Milner perused the briefing papers he'd barely glanced at. He examined the agenda. No surprises there. Different functions spread over five days. He turned his attention to an envelope marked RIDDLES which contained eight pieces of paper. There were no headings or clues as to contents. All except one appeared to be a description of personal attributes. *Are they meant to be about individuals I know?* After studying them for a while Milner decided to shower and prepare for dinner. *It'll become clear, eventually. Hope it doesn't take too long. What'll they achieve with me? I'll be able to deal with whatever they throw at me.*

Dinner was served in a communal dining room, with benches lined up like a monastery refectory or public school. Hera accompanied him and sat on the bench beside him offering occasional advice. *Not sure I fancy this.* Although simple and unfussy, the meal was good.

Waiters attended, for which Milner was grateful. He hated standing in queues to get food sloshed on his plate, something he'd avoided for years. His money ensured it. The difficulty came in getting used to doppelgänger asides. It gave him brain ache to concentrate on what they said, without betraying on his face, or with any other physical reaction, he knew what the person addressing him was thinking.

At the close of dinner, Hera indicated Milner should follow her.

"But I expected a familiarisation briefing. Shouldn't I stay?"

"These people will be briefed together," said Hera. "You, however, are to receive a private one."

"My, my! All this priority and special treatment. You'll make me believe I'm a VIP."

"You are, but you should consider it in relative terms, not the fixed ones you imply. For instance, VIP could mean Very Important Prat."

"All I need. A sarcastic philosophising cat."

"I'm glued to you as well, don't forget. Do you think it's fish and cream all the way for me?"

They arrived at a door pinned with a notice.

Reserved for Milner and Hera
Private Briefing
Knock and enter on arrival

On entry, Milner observed the concierge sitting behind a large leather-tooled desk. This time he wore the costume of a colourful court jester. The doppelgänger on his shoulder had changed into an ensemble more brash and loud than the jester himself – if that was possible.

"Is your outfit change significant?" enquired Milner.

"Flexibility is the key. We adopt multifarious roles. No point allowing guests to become complacent through lack of stimulation or challenge. Sit down please," he said indicating a chair on the far side of his desk. "The purpose of this briefing is to enlighten you about coming events. There are eight riddles in your welcome pack. Have you examined them?"

"I did, but must advise I'm no fan of cryptic clues. I'd rather spread my cards out and be done with it."

"We're well apprised of your likes and dislikes and in tune with your ability to manipulate. As the purpose of this interlude is to challenge your assumptions, you'll need to get used to dealing with things you don't like."

"Always ready to learn something new."

True to form. Delivered the expected diplomatic answer, mumbled doppelgänger.

"Good," said the jester, his face expressionless. "The riddles concern individuals you are acquainted with. As you saw from the agenda, you will attend various functions. Before each one you will read the riddles, then seek to match them with a person or persons at the event you attend. Afterwards, you'll be given the identity of those to whom the riddles apply to see if you guessed correctly. I assume you understand the purpose of this exercise?"

"Reckon so."

"Good, then we'll meet bright and early tomorrow morning."

೮೮ ೮೮ ೮೮

CHAPTER 6

The Stolen Child

Come away, O human child!

To the waters and the wild

With a faery, hand in hand,

For the world's more full of weeping than you

    can understand.

—WB Yeats, *The Stolen Child*

MILNER RETIRED, TROUBLED. *Why has Concierge become Jester? Tarot figures are relevant here, better acquaint myself.* He searched the reading matter lying around and found a tarot pack, together with a brief explanation of the twenty-two trump cards of the Major Arcana. *How convenient.*

"What's does Jester signify, Hera?"

"Not for me to say," she responded. "This is your journey. I'm just along for company."

"He's described as the wild card."

"And? So?"

"Might suggest his role is to challenge complacency. Make us consider the irrational."

"If those are the first ideas that strike you, you should bear them in mind the next few days. Jester intends to brief and debrief you on each activity. Treat him as a sounding board."

"Great. Another obstacle to handle with each charade. Guess I'd better sleep."

The following morning after a hearty breakfast of porridge followed by bacon sandwiches, Milner presented himself to Jester.

"Before we start, fill in this Prophet and Loss Account. You'll do a Balance Sheet later."

"Does money come into this?"

"It's not a financial statement. This exercise examines strengths and weaknesses under the headings Prophet and Loss because you're acquainted with the concept. The balance sheet provides a snapshot of how these work. Note the spelling. Business colleagues call you Mr Prophet and Loss, so it shouldn't be too much of a challenge."

Milner shrugged, rubbed his chin and grimaced. He reached out to take the papers and almost dropped them, overcome by a burning sensation in his arm. Disconcerted, he retired to a quiet corner. He didn't want to hear doppelgänger's remarks, or give himself away to Hera. He'd enough to consider without sarcastic comments. He stared at the sheet. *What should I put down? Bit obvious, ain't it? Reckon the purpose is to humiliate and deliver them a whip hand from the off. Silly game but I'll play along; for now.*

"Why is your first response to suppose the object of the exercise is to humiliate?"

"Is no privacy allowed?" said Milner, rounding on Hera with raised eyebrows and a glassy stare. He was so absorbed he'd forgotten her. "This knowing what people think is hard. Perhaps I should establish whose side you are on. Are you here to help/hinder or challenge?"

"I like to present constructive objective challenges. You haven't considered that in some tarot packs Joker's number is zero. Zeros are significant in financial matters, especially before and after full stops. It's the same with life. Remember zero, while it represents nothing, contains everything. Existence and experience are circular and continuous. You cannot break out. You'll get most from this episode if you examine yourself and your motives honestly. Apply creative thinking/accounting to your circumstances with a sincere attitude. Ask yourself, 'What's a zero between friends?'"

"Very funny – I think. Point taken. So you recommend an honesty policy in drawing up this balance sheet?"

"I do. You might also drop the cynical sarcastic approach. You know – that sarchasm your daughter referred to."

"If you suggest an abyss exists between my sarcasm and the organisers of this jamboree, you're mistaken. Comprehension abounds here well beyond reasonable expectations."

"Pleased you've grasped that. I'm off to forage for a

tasty morsel. See you shortly."

Milner stared at the sheet. *How honest should I be? How best to approach this?* His brain churned and chewed over psychological workplace evaluations. He'd completed them himself as well as examined plenty presented by ambitious young men during interviews. It was an industry grown out of proportion. *I prefer instinct although those questionnaires serve a purpose. Useful to weed out the chaff before it reaches me.*

He wrote –

Strengths		**Weaknesses**
Logical	Innovative	Intolerant of error
Born leader	Career focused	Sentimental
Foresight	Strategic Thinker	
Goal directed	Clear vision of goals	
Assertive	Decision maker	
Intuitive	Self-confident	
Superb networker	Value solid opinions	
Persuasive	Forceful	
Understand and appreciate art		

Only two items for the weakness column. How will that play out? Perhaps I need to work on the weaknesses, except my policy is to ignore negatives in life. You advance by believing in yourself more than the other fellow.

Hera returned, grinning from ear to ear.

"Found something tasty?" asked Milner.

"Sure did. And you? Any progress?"

"Some."

"From what you've written your P&L suggests you persist in treating this as a game? However, if your list of weaknesses is as short as you claim, go for it."

"Onward and upward then."

Jester scrutinised Milner's handiwork.

Only to be expected, said Jester's doppelgänger. *No hubris to deal with here then.*

Milner glared at the doppelgänger and stretched his hand towards Jester.

"Need to make alterations."

"Certainly, take your time," smiled Jester.

Milner reworked the sheet and returned it to Jester.

Strengths		Weaknesses	
Logical	Innovative	Logical	Innovative
Born leader	Career focused	Born leader	Career focused
Foresight	Strategic Thinker	Foresight	Strategic Thinker
Goal directed	Clear vision of goals	Goal directed	Clear vision of goals
Assertive	Decision maker	Assertive	Decision maker
Intuitive	Self-confident	Intuitive	Self-confident
Superb networker	Value solid opinions	Superb networker	Value solid opinions
Persuasive	Forceful	Persuasive	Forceful
Understand and appreciate art		Understand and appreciate art	
Sentimental	Intolerant of Error	Sentimental	Intolerant of Error

"You entered the same in both columns," said Jester, smiling with bared teeth. *Like I said, no hubris. Convinced he'll get one over every time,* said Jester's doppelgänger.

"Precisely," said Milner, trying to maintain a calm voice and not stare at Jester's doppelgänger. "Strengths can be weaknesses that undermine goals."

"Fine," said Jester. "I will, however, offer a piece of advice. Don't squander this opportunity being too clever and assume you've nothing to learn. You regard this as a game. Humility won't come amiss. I haven't asked you to complete the Balance Sheet. We'll begin that at our debriefing tonight. Hera will escort you to the first function on the agenda. Take the riddles. You need to begin matching them to individuals. We'll meet afterwards to examine how you fare."

C3 C3 C3

MILNER AND HERA set off in the pony trap. While the driver gently encouraged the pony with reins and whip, Milner perused the riddles. En masse they meant nothing. Milner recognised characteristics of family members, but the traits belonged to several individuals. He'd no idea who was to be present at each function. *Need to get the general gist of each riddle in my head if I'm to match them with whoever they're supposed to be.*

"There's a notebook and pen in the bag below your seat," said Hera.

"Maybe later. Where are we going? Who'll be there?"

"To a viewing platform. You'll observe yourself taking part in a scene and hear everything said, including the doppelgänger's comments. That's why you must take notes."

"Sounds weird."

"It'll become clear. In the meantime, I'll give you privacy. We all appreciate that occasionally. I'm not here to make this experience deliberately difficult."

"Thanks."

"You're welcome."

C3 C3 C3

THE PONY TROTTED through pretty countryside, Milner overcome by an uneasy déjà vu. Hera dozed on his lap while he petted her. The scenery seemed familiar. Gentle rolling hills filled the middle distance. Beyond that a clear, blue, cloudless sky, brought calm to his thoughts. They passed over a viaduct where, far below, a river gently snaked. *So this is what they mean by a bird's-eye view.* On either side fields were laid to crops. *Pride myself on being a rationalist, not a thinking pygmy. This experience tests me in ways I can't anticipate. Not sure what to expect, or how to prepare.* Leaving the viaduct, they journeyed along a path cut through the hills. Sudden changes in contour and other aspects of the landscape arrested Milner's attention. *How lucky are the folks who live here? To be able to scan such sights every day. One minute in a valley, the next high above. I calculate success with measures and scales, judge results against set/agreed* targets. *This isn't like that. Here outcomes are measured against different parameters.*

They forded a stream and began an ascent. The valley below deepened. The scenery was breath-taking; he was lost in wonder at how quickly a view could change yet remain beautiful. *So many aspects to enjoy. Each as stunning as the next.* They entered the precincts of a small village, where the trap halted before a cliff face. *What's this place? Why have we stopped?*

"We're here. Follow me," said Hera as Milner stirred from his reverie.

"Thought you were dozing."

"Was for the most part. Woke up halfway up the hill."

Milner followed Hera into a massive vaulted chamber, carved into the rock. Although outside was a hot summer day, inside the air was damp and cold. At first he felt relief, then shivered. He'd been handed a pamphlet about the place as he passed through the entrance gate. He stood stunned and amazed. *Entranced after coming through an entrance – there's an idea.* He perused the beginning of the pamphlet. *What's this place called? Have I been here before? Seems familiar.*

"Wait till we get up there," said Hera.

"Where?"

"Look up. You'll see the gallery we're headed for."

"We've to climb up there?"

"Gives the best view."

Milner trudged behind Hera up rickety wooden

stairs. As they climbed, déjà vu kicked in. Memories of a previous visit engulfed him. After a short walk round the first gallery they ascended more stairs, this time sculpted from rock, to reach a further gallery situated above. They were in a medieval church, the ground floor being the nave or apse. Massive supporting octagonal columns carved from stone stretched up through what were originally several floors. At the top Hera instructed him to rest. Milner examined the pamphlet handed him on entry. He was right. He peered over the balcony and remembered the last time he was here. The place was a cave church dating from the eighth century, carved into rock. Benedictine monks in the twelfth century finished it and gave it its present shape although it'd been converted to a saltpetre factory during Napoleon's time. He looked down into the nave, gazing at the baptismal font decorated with a Greek cross and replica of the tomb of Joseph of Arimathea, copied from the one in Jerusalem's Holy Sepulchre Church. It was breath-taking. A sense of history enveloped him. During the ascent he noticed the necropolis, which, according to the brochure, housed some eighty sarcophagi. His cursory glance showed small tombs, and he wondered whether they were children's graves, but the blurb assured him they weren't. *Must look on the way down. Vaguely remember looking at them here before.*

Perhaps it was shortness of breath after the climb, but Milner was thirsty. He shivered when he should be sweating. He rubbed his arms to ward off the cold, fidgeted with his glasses and cleared his throat several times, without success. *Ghosts from the past are here, crowding me, reminding me my corporeal body is a small part of existence – insignificant really – in the great arc of time that went before and will continue after I die.* Milner shuddered as he gazed over the parapet. He blinked – hard. Panic overwhelmed him. He watched himself walk through the entrance to the nave followed by Gronya, Julian and Adelle.

"You aren't seeing double. It is you down there," Hera assured him. "Told you earlier it'd be like that."

"Forgot. Weird the first time. Suppose I better get used to it if it's to happen often."

"Watch the scene play out. Remember, you'll hear yourself and everything the others say, as well the doppelgängers on Gronya, Julian and Adelle's shoulders."

"This'll be a challenge."

"It's supposed to be. Observe carefully. Did you bring your notebook?"

◌ఔ ◌ఔ ◌ఔ

"WE DISCUSSED THIS last night," said Gronya to Milner out of earshot of Julian and Adelle, "but remind me what we're meant to be getting Julian to reflect on today."

"Ethics."

"What's that again?" she asked. *Why treat me like a moron? He's repulsive at the best of times. The condescension in his response makes me mad,* said Gronya's doppelgänger.

"We need to get Julian to reformulate his past – reshape his ethics and morality to cope with the situation we want to put him in," said Milner, trying not to sound condescending.

"In English please?" *Eughhh…. He is so ugly. Whatever did I see in him? Why did I ever let him touch me? Julian on the other hand…*, said Gronya's doppelgänger.

"We must get him to abandon his ideas about how ethical behaviour means he can't sleep with you and desert his wife."

"Thanks," said Gronya. *Why make this so difficult? He agreed I need to be happy so why can't he do it without sounding spiteful?* said Gronya's doppelgänger.

Milner glared at them both and walked away to find Adelle and Julian – *I know Gronya likes to treat fantasy as reality, but she needs to wake up and concentrate. It's all part of her overwhelming sense of entitlement. I mustn't forget Gronya operates more on emotion than brainpower, while Adelle can be variable, sometimes uses brain over emotion; depends how challenged she feels. Hope she's in brain over emotion mode today.*

"Adelle – Gronya is over there. Wants to show you something to do with the tomb."

"Fascinating isn't it? I'll go find her. See what she's looking at." *This is such an eerie place, love the sense of history clawing at my bones. Wonder if the others feel it. So pleased Milner agreed to come. Gronya wasn't keen, but he persuaded her, thank goodness. Sure she'll find something positive in the end. Why wouldn't you? All this history to drown in*, said Adelle's doppelgänger.

Milner watched her walk away. *In a happy mood today, content to be here. Good move to persuade Gronya to come.* Milner located Julian staring at the Greek cross in the baptismal font.

"We'll get a better view from the top gallery. There are two. Can you make it to the highest one? Fancy a climb? I do," said Milner.

"Good idea. Assume we go up by way of those rickety stairs?"

"Looks like it."

Milner climbed behind Julian. *Must use that baptismal font to my advantage. Let's see.*

They reached the first gallery and walked along to ascend the carved stone stairs to the highest gallery. Once there, they rounded a corner to a vantage point and stared down. Milner noticed Julian adjust his trousers with his thumbs. *Does that a lot. Ought to take note. Might be important.*

"You realise how the baptismal font fits into the overall plan from up here, and the significance of the cross emblem," said Milner.

"Wonder when the cross was installed. No mention in these notes. Perhaps it was done recently to add something, like the sepulchre the girls are inspecting." *Where are they? Wonder what they've found. I'll ask Adelle later,* said Julian's doppelgänger.

"The whole area was Richard Coeur de Leon's playground so who knows. Was part of the Compostella route. That's an orthodox cross. Could have been installed when the knights returned from the Crusades. All that knightly chivalric code. You studied ethics. Doesn't the way we practise them today emanate from there?"

"Oddly enough, I listened to a radio discussion on this. The chivalric code didn't give rise to ethical practice as we know it, although nowadays they debate the 'ethics' of the Crusades and how religion allowed Crusaders to imagine they could slaughter Muslims with impunity, while Muslims in turn used religion to justify slaughtering 'infidels'." *Heavy topic for a day out,* said Julian's doppelgänger. *What's Milner's real interest? Oh well, let's go with the flow.*

"I heard that programme. Remember now. They ended up putting it down to the religious politics of the day?"

"Along the lines of one man's religion is another's poison," said Julian, straining over the gallery to locate the girls. *Gronya would stop this discussion. Maybe I should persuade him down to the apse on the excuse of finding them,* said Julian's doppelgänger.

"Succinctly put. Medical ethics are another matter, they stem from the Hippocratic Oath, don't they?"

Julian turned to stare at him. "This place has got you going. What is it? The sense of history? Anyway, you took a law degree. What's the relationship between ethics and law?" *Need to turn this back on him. Don't fancy the way this conversation's developing. Too heavy for me. I want to relax,* said Julian's doppelgänger.

Milner considered this. "Legal eagles say they follow a code of ethics, but law by its nature demands precision, and where ethics and law conflict law wins. Laws can be changed to make better ethics, but that comes out of the practice of highlighting ethical conflicts."

"I suppose doctors are freer in that sense," said Julian. "The overriding principle in medical ethics, as I understand it, says ethics should move away from paternalistic motives i.e. doctor knows best, to autonomy, involving the patient in decisions, since they, supposedly, know what's best for them."

"What about the doctor's autonomy?"

"That gets difficult. The patient is the doctor's first commitment."

"What about 'Physician, heal thyself'?".

"Are you hinting at the notion of public power vs private conscience?" *Must change topic, not sure where this is headed,* said Julian's doppelgänger.

Julian observed the girls climb the stairs to join them. He heaved a sigh of relief that could be heard in Africa. *Thank goodness Gronya is here. Must stop Milner raising the subject with Adelle or those two will prolong the debate,* said Julian's doppelgänger.

"There you are," said Julian ending the conversation. "Want to inspect those sarcophagi going down. Ought to think where to lunch."

"Saw a lovely place along the road near the village

centre. Stairs lead down to a terrace with a fabulous view of the valley. Looked a great spot to eat," said Adelle.

C8 C8 C8

MILNER OBSERVED AND made notes. *Remember now. That was day I realised the idea of autonomy had mileage. Only meant to probe Julian on ethics. Wanted to understand his reasoning. I'll have a lot to debrief to Jester. Had enough. Wonder if Hera can be persuaded to return to the chateau. Need to marshal my thoughts before session with Jester.*

C8 C8 C8

AFTER DINNER MILNER AND HERA located Jester.

"What did you get from the day?" enquired Jester.

"What was I supposed to get?" asked Milner.

"We won't progress if you answer questions with questions. Both old hands at that game. Don't try to outjest a jester."

"Point taken. Straightforward response then. That trip was when I realised I'd to play on Julian's need for autonomy and happiness as opposed to anyone else's."

"Ever the strategist." *Pity he can't see how strategists and manipulators are cut from the same mould, and how people like him would vote for Narnia if they thought they'd be king,* said Jester's doppelgänger.

Milner glared at the doppelgänger. "Strategy over emotion wins every time. Strategy enables you to overcome emotion and make proper long-term decisions."

"It's a way of looking at it," said Jester. "However, since you decided a discussion of ethics was appropriate in your campaign to get Julian to leave Adelle, I'd like you to draw up a Balance Sheet based on the Happiness Principle. You're familiar with the concept?"

"Of course. Bentham's Utilitarian idea that an action is right in so far as it promotes the greatest happiness of the greatest number. Had a big impact on the practise of law, so I'm well acquainted."

"Good distillation. Your Balance Sheet will show your family one side and Julian's the other. As you proceed through your agenda, you'll make notes each day on who gets the greatest happiness from each encounter. At the end of the proceedings, we can decide whether you and Gronya did the right thing and promoted the greatest happiness of the greatest number of people." *Face tells me he doesn't appreciate this challenge. Good. Needs to squirm if he's to understand his actions are like ripples on water, they spread out and have unintended, unimagined consequences,* said Jester's doppelgänger.

"I'll play along for now, if only to get through it. As for 'challenging past thinking', forget it. I never regret what I've done. The only way is forward."

Typical legal/business brain. Doesn't like grey – prefers black and white. Follows the dogma that a man who denies a theory is more correct than one who affirms it, in the mistaken belief it ensures he keeps the magic wand in his hand, said Jester's doppelgänger.

Milner squirmed. He knew he mustn't avoid eye contact or rub the back of his neck. Sure signs of agitation. Rehearsing to himself the physical actions he must refrain from helped him maintain control. Jester sat, unconcerned, staring back. Hera purred and rubbed up against Milner. If Jester knew he had a doppelgänger, he didn't give it away. *Don't like what I'm hearing, but have to pretend I haven't – boy, it's difficult.* Milner couldn't hand over control of the situation by responding to what others thought of him. Didn't make it easy. *Must be continually on guard.*

"Have you studied the riddles? Do any match the individuals today?"

"I've ideas, but as I'm not required to decide until the end, will reserve judgement."

ଔ ଔ ଔ

CHAPTER 7

Ancient Monuments

"SO WHERE DO YOU stand on the matter of conscience?" Jester enquired next morning.

"Mine or yours?" quipped Milner.

Fresh out of starting blocks, said Jester's doppelgänger.

"Damn right," said Milner.

"What?" asked Jester.

"Thinking aloud," said Milner. "You asked about conscience, or rather matters pertaining to mine, I assume."

Smart ass, said Jester's doppelgänger.

"So… do you have one?" asked Jester.

"Like to think so. Difficulty is, given how the world works, I am occasionally required to apply it in a relative fashion – relative to my circumstances. For instance, my instinct could be to behave a certain way in a given situation, but if that went against the tide, or caused more difficulties than it solved, I'd be forced to put it in abeyance, temporarily. For the good of all, you understand."

"So it's a moveable feast."

"When necessary."

"How do you justify that?" asked Jester. "What if you are challenged on decisions that go against your conscience?"

"Like everyone, I make sure I don't get caught, and if I am, can vindicate myself."

"To sum up," said Jester, "you treat it like the Happiness Principle – do what brings the greatest happiness to the greatest number of people, weighting your happiness as of greater value than others."

"Hadn't considered it much, but I'll accept your idea for current purposes."

"Perhaps you could ponder the situation where an equal cohort of individuals would be made happy or sad by the exercise of your conscience."

"Easy. I'll do what's best for me and mine. The rest can sink or swim, they aren't my problem."

"So, faced with a decision that the greatest happiness for your family came from acceptance of sadistic and nasty behaviour, you'd continue so as to seek advantage for them?"

"My family take precedence; their happiness is paramount, whatever the circumstances."

At least that's honest, said Jester's doppelgänger.

"Presumably you've no high expectations of others when it comes to how they treat you?"

"Ain't into self-sacrifice or popularity contests. Here to get the best for me from every situation. If others benefit, fine; if not, tain't my problem. Can't solve the world's problems, only my own."

Suggests he believes everyone acts the same. What he does is justified, but if others' behaviour causes him harm or difficulties, then it's not OK, said Jester's doppelgänger. *Oy. Oy. Things never change. Double standards all round. This guy is happy to outsource contrition to the provinces, where he helps organise pauper baiting weekends,* said Jester's doppelgänger.

Milner glared hard at the doppelgänger as intense pain gripped his stomach. He broke into a sweat, conscious of a desire to punch a wall or table, or anything to release his tension. *Do not react, Milner, keep control, that creature's job is to provoke.* Hera, sitting on his lap, jumped off and purred as she rubbed his leg. Milner, who'd forgotten her, looked down, smiled and felt his discomfort and anger disperse.

"Come on," she said, "let's go before you get more aerated."

"Right, Hera. Good I have you to help keep me calm."

Milner drew a deep breath, stood and nodded acknowledgement to Jester.

"You'll excuse me if I choose not to continue our 'chat' at this juncture."

"Fine. Our conversation will keep. We'll meet later."

As he walked away, nursing the remnants of his dissipating anger, he heard the doppelgänger mutter – *so he can lose it.*

☙ ☙ ☙

"WHERE ARE WE off to?" Milner enquired of Hera once they reached the courtyard.

"Your room. To view a DVD."

"If I must. Lead on."

Milner settled in a chair with coffee and a tarte tatin, took a moment to get comfortable and pressed the remote. *Oh boy, another surreal journey somewhere. Seems wherever we went it was with Adelle and Julian. It's like eating cold porridge. Yup, it's coming back. I remember. Hot uncomfortable, humid day. Gronya in a foul mood. Whinged things not going her way.* He observed himself read rough notes made on his strategy for the outing.

"For goodness sake, Gronya, stop carping on about the heat and how miserable you are. I need to concentrate."

Eugh. I hate this man, even the sound of his voice. Better smile though. Give him what he wants, peace and quiet to think, said Gronya's doppelgänger.

"While you're doing that, I'll check we've enough petrol. When I return you can let me know how to play things today," huffed Gronya.

Milner stared at the screen in a trance. It irritated to hear Gronya's inner thoughts. He wondered how he got through it. *Knew it all along. Hard to acknowledge how much she hated being with me. Wanted to get away. I was loyal to her to the end, tried to help her and was generous. Ungrateful woman. Means I did right by myself.*

On screen Gronya returned and Milner listened to himself brief her on tactics.

"Infidelity. I want to probe Julian on it. Rummage out his opinions on cheating spouses, and if it's something he'd consider."

"What must I do?" asked Gronya.

"Follow my lead. Be more demure than usual but don't over-act."

"What's demure when out and about?"

"That shy, embarrassed, modest thing you do. It appeals to Julian. Adelle trusts you and is so naïve doesn't suspect you'd indulge in underhand behaviour. In other words, flirt, but not so Adelle notices. Got it?"

"Can do it standing on my head. Been at it long enough."

"You have, haven't you? Safe to say you instinctively act that way around Julian. Your stubborn determination to get him is obsessive."

"Not my fault you're emotionally spastic and can't fulfil me?"

Milner blanched. He'd forgotten her painful barbs – delivered in a calm, controlled manner that displayed no anger, to others at least. *Tongue like a wine cork; could open a bottle with it – wretched woman.* What betrayed her was the way her cheeks reddened as she broke out in a sweat. He'd been gullible at the beginning, believed her lie it was 'that female problem'. Others accepted her excuses, but he knew what accounted for her nervousness every time she got within yards of Julian. It was what made her remarks so pernicious.

Milner pressed the pause button.

"What's the matter?" asked Hera.

"As you can read my thoughts you know I find this like eating cold lumpy mashed potato or porridge. If I wanted reminders of the past, I'd be more selective and stick to a review of the good bits."

"Not the purpose of the exercise."

"It's getting tedious. How much more is there?"

"The sooner you concentrate, the sooner it'll be finished."

"Must I watch the whole trip?"

"Afraid so," said Hera.

"It'll be weird inside the car. Like when they use those mounted cameras on film sets. Guess I better get on with it. Let me fetch another coffee first. Any more of those apple pies?"

Duly provisioned, Milner sat down and pressed the remote.

They set off, Gronya driving the Bentley. They collected Julian and Adelle. Milner watched Gronya when she greeted Julian – all that obligatory French kissing – Gronya used it well. *Luckily Adelle was so trusting she was ignorant of Gronya's ambitions towards Julian. Adelle always said she understood Gronya's hot flushes because she had the same 'female problem'.*

It was a beautiful late spring day. The sky was cloudless. Their route wound through several villages, broken by woodland where roads were dappled by sunlight that pierced the tree canopy on either side. On other stretches they passed over bridges beneath which rivers bounced along, around and over rocks. In his imagination Milner smelt that damp, forest floor odour he loved. It was why he enjoyed shooting. They arrived at their destination; a medieval town renowned for building preservation and recreated ancient streets. They parked and wandered the cobblestones, stunned at the amazing houses that hinted of Elizabethan and Tudor styles in England. The place was so saturated with character it was difficult to know when to stop taking photos. Every time they turned another corner they'd emerge into a vista more stunning than the last. Perched on a hillside with a wide panorama, the town basked in an atmosphere created by narrow alleys and crooked buildings with overhangs and glimpses of courtyards that dragged the mind into history.

The aroma of coffee from a pavement café reminded them they'd not had a drink since breakfast. As noon approached, they procured an outside table at a restaurant with a view of the town square. They ordered coffee and asked the waiter to fetch a lunch menu.

"Been reading up about this place," said Milner as they examined various interesting architectural features around them. "Although it dates from Roman times, it became prosperous in the eighth century when Benedictines established a monastery. Fell into disrepair and many original buildings were lost due to remoteness and lack of money. Then about thirty years ago, new roads made it accessible, coincided with some law or other brought in by the government. Lots of funding appeared, so they undertook a wide-ranging restoration. Most of this lot isn't old."

"Done a good job," said Adelle. *Don't care when they did it. Love the atmosphere and history. It's like fairytale land; as if before reconstruction they consulted Disney. Would have preferred not to know. Preserve the illusion. Hope everyone else is enjoying it. Such a lovely day. Despite the crowds it oozes serenity. Must be the way it nestles in the hills. Gives a sense of being separate from the rest of the country. So glad we came before the heavy tourist season,* said Adelle's doppelgänger.

Gronya's phone rang.

"Told you to turn it off," said Milner.

"Ollah is having a crisis. Must take it."

"Shall we wait?"

"No. Carry on. Mine's a salad, so it doesn't matter. Keep an eye on my handbag, Milner."

Gronya wandered off across the square, phone stuck to her ear. From her body language, slumped shoulders, lowered head, tissue in hand wiping perspiration from her forehead, it was obvious she was taking a verbal lambasting.

"These youngsters today," began Milner. "Never consider consequences until the damage rears its head."

"Is it the usual?" asked Adelle. "Drank too much. Slept with a gay man. Now worried about AIDS?"

"Yeah. I know Gronya finds you helpful when the girls have these crises."

"I do little. Just reassure her. Admire her fortitude

and patience. I'd get angry and tell Ollah if she carried on with stupid behaviour, when she knows to avoid danger, it's her own fault and not to bother me," said Adelle.

"I suspect it'll end the way it always does. I'll pay for counselling and medical tests, and Gronya will listen to more phone calls, then we'll all go back to normal till next time."

"Children. Love 'em to bits, but never prepared for the challenges they present, no matter how old we get," said Julian.

Fool. Just throws money at it, like Gronya says. He can't see he makes it worse by not tackling it head on and challenging the girl, said Julian's doppelgänger.

"Darn right. When we got married being loyal to vows meant everything. Today youngsters treat infidelity as a way of life," said Milner.

"Some don't. Take our daughter-in-law. Wanted a traditional marriage with all vows in place, and swears she'll stand by them forever, just like her parents," said Adelle.

"But Sabina, your daughter, she isn't married?"

"No. Says it's a social construct through which the state controls women's lives," said Julian.

"So what are her views on fidelity within a relationship? Does she consider it important?" asked Milner.

How'd we get onto this? It's a day out for goodness sake. Better be careful what I say, don't want to offend with straight talking the way Adelle does, said Julian's doppelgänger.

Milner pressed the pause button as he saw Julian hesitate. His own thoughts from that day flashed into his mind. *It's a nervous tick. Like that habit of hitching up his pants with his thumbs. Because he's sitting down he wants to think before he speaks, so hesitates instead.*

"What's the problem?" asked Hera.

"Just need a moment to congratulate myself," said Milner. "Hearing the doppelgänger in that scene proved I was correct in my assessment of Julian. One up to me, I reckon."

"This isn't about proving you're right," said Hera. "Press the start button and get back to the DVD." Milner did as ordered.

"Only while the relationship lasts," said Julian, stuttering. "She says people change and move on, nobody should feel guilty about failed relationships. They fail for valid reasons."

"There some sense to that I suppose," said Milner. *This'll be easier than I supposed. Need to get into Sabina's good books somehow. Wonder what help I can offer. She's obviously the person to bring on side.*

"Sorry. You were saying?" Milner returned his attention to Julian.

"I was remarking it's a big open debate these days. Like most things we've swung the pendulum from rigid ideas of fidelity and trust to an acceptance of anything goes," said Julian.

"Where do you stand?" asked Milner.

"Don't know. Always needed to be with Adelle. Can't see that changing. On t'other hand, staying in an abusive relationship because you made stupid vow years ago isn't healthy either. I agree with Sabina; people experience guilt when relationships fail. The idea these days is to help individuals get over imploded relationships and guilty feelings and make new lives. Be positive, don't rehash the past, emphasise future success instead of past failure, move on, don't look back."

Milner watched himself on screen stare at Julian. He'd forgotten how it felt to be flustered, how it was years since he allowed such a weak emotion to take control. He remembered the thoughts that flooded his mind. *Concentrate, Milner. Get a grip. Don't let this sudden revelation upend you. This'll be easier than I reckoned. I need to fathom the hold Adelle has on him. Lots to consider when I get peace and quiet.*

Back on screen, Gronya returned to the café, flustered and annoyed.

"Problem solved then?" Milner heard himself ask.

"Sort of. Ollah will fly over and join us so she can rest."

Oh God, said Julian and Adelle's doppelgängers.

"What?"

"Told her you'd book and pay and we'd let her know what plane she is on by email this evening. We'll collect her from the airport tomorrow."

"Why?"

"She was hysterical and I don't want to go home to

sort her out. Better to get her here, sedate her and put her to bed to sleep it off."

"Mercy me. All we need is for Hattie to copy her."

"Let's hope not," said Gronya, tucking into her salad.

Milner pressed the pause button on the DVD again.

"Come on, Hera. We went home not long after. Can't I be spared that journey?"

"OK. We're running late. You can contemplate what you've seen over lunch. This afternoon we're off to rubberneck gastronomic celebrations. Make sure you bring the riddles and keep puzzling who is who."

"I've taken photos. They're on my phone. Thank goodness I can charge it. Funny though. There's a charger in my room but no signal to allow calls."

"Feeling not quite in control, huh?" said Hera, muzzling his hand.

ରୁ ରୁ ରୁ

HERA AND MILNER set off on the pony and trap after lunch. Milner studied the riddles, oblivious to the countryside they passed through. The bouquet of a fresh spring breeze carrying a hint of herbs failed to penetrate his senses as normal. Without realizing it, the rhymes obsessed him. A couple made sense, but the more he mulled them over, the more he wondered if he was anywhere near solutions. *Hate mysteries. My brain won't relax till I solve them, just like in business. Maybe that's the intention. Need a strategy and don't rest till I find it.* The people he dealt with in business were straightforward. He knew their motives and, over the years, had fathomed their weaknesses. It was possible to keep them compartmentalised and at arm's length. Family were different. Emotion reared its head with them and that curious thing he never got to grips with and wanted to abolish – love. His kids were part of him, but they dogged him daily; it was painful to dwell on their idiosyncrasies. They were a problem he couldn't resolve no matter how he tried. That was one reason for his extensive work schedules; why he delegated everyday problems to Gronya. His excuse to himself, and them, was it was essential he earn lots of geld to maintain them in a style that befitted their overwhelming sense of entitlement. *Perhaps I am guilty of creating unhealthy expectations. Gronya insists I do, loud and often. Says it's my fault. Doesn't accept any blame. Some might call it a Catch 22, but I enjoy work. It's not an avoidance tactic.* It was how he kept Gronya in the manner she expected and made her dependent on him while he needed her. If he removed her privileges, like that eight-hundred-pound handbag he bought last birthday, she'd moan. It was just somewhere, he wasn't sure where, he'd reached a tipping point and wondered how much was too much.

Lost in these thoughts, he became aware the pony trap had stopped by a car park. Milner saw Gronya had parked the Bentley. He observed Gronya and himself climb out of the front while Julian, Adelle and Ollah emerged from the rear. Julian did the thumb/trouser hitch.

"Come on," said Hera. "We'll follow. Don't forget to make notes."

He and Hera followed as the party strolled along the main village street where a large evening market was underway to celebrate some drink or other around which the local tourism committee created a legend. It was good marketing; the streets were packed. Milner had booked a table at the Hotel de France, which served the most amazing seven course meal. Overcome, Milner pressed pause. He could smell and taste the foie gras he remembered from the menu. It'd be torture watching them eat. Mouth watering, he relived every savoury morsel. What he wanted to forget was what happened afterwards. *I hope we fast forward at that bit, don't want to see it again.*

There were too many people for the restaurant to do its usual impeccable waiter service. The gardens were full of extra tables. Theirs was under a lovely tree that offered welcome shade from the evening sun. Dinner was a hot buffet which meant you could help yourself to seconds of every course while there was any left. At regular intervals more and different dishes appeared. Milner revelled in it, enjoying the food. He remembered the sublime Cahors he chose from the wine list, how it excited his palate and complemented the meal. They supped at five bottles between the six of them. Since Adelle and Julian never drank more than half a bottle each, four got polished off by himself, Gronya and Ollah. Ollah drank the most which explained what happened.

Milner watched as Adelle and Julian visited the buffet and Ollah took the opportunity to have a go at him.

"Why are they here?" Ollah demanded in loud imperious tones.

"Because your mother and I like their company."

"Can't see what you've got in common. They make me uncomfortable. Adelle judges me, and Julian dislikes me."

"In your imagination," said Gronya. "I'll thank you not to be rude. They're my guests."

"Yours? Not Dad's? He's the one paying, isn't he?"

"His as well."

"Are you sure? Julian makes you squirm. Can't imagine why. He's an uptight prat who I can't see fitting in anywhere. Hasn't he other friends to eat with?"

"They're the reason we come here. We like to be with them, so pack it in," said Gronya, tears welling up.

"Why? Tell me why. What you have got in common? Nothing." insisted Ollah, her voice getting louder. "Fill my glass," she demanded holding it out.

"You've had enough," said Milner, "perhaps you should give it a rest and eat. This wine is to be drunk slowly and appreciated." *What sixth sense almost made the girl give the game away? She came close that night.*

"Had several helpings of some dishes. Get me my own bottle of something not so good if you don't want me to drink your hallowed stuff. Give me money as well. Want to buy a carved frog from that market stall," demanded Ollah.

"Don't you have any? I paid to fly you here, and I'm paying for your dinner. Oh… go on then, here's fifty. Bring me change."

"Ollah going to get something?" asked Adelle. *I wonder she can stagger anywhere, she's so drunk,* said her doppelgänger. *If I drank that much I'd be ill. Gronya puts up with a lot, so patient. The girl is so rude and overbearing. Know she dislikes Julian and me. If she carries on, the feeling could become mutual. Perhaps we better not do stuff together while Ollah's here.*

"Gives us a few moments' peace. She'll be back soon," said Gronya. *Hope they didn't hear what Ollah said. If she's going to be like this with Julian, I'll make sure we don't bring her in future. It'll be easy to persuade her to stay in bed and sleep till she goes home,* said Gronya's doppelgänger.

They ate in silence, enjoying the food. Too soon, Ollah returned with her prize.

"Got my change?" asked Milner.

"A couple of Euros. Bought the big one."

"Hand over whatever's left."

"For goodness sake, Dad. Don't be stingy. You can afford it. After all you're paying for this lot tonight, guests and all. Surely I can keep a bit of change."

Milner squirmed as he watched. He remembered his embarrassment. He longed for this observation to end.

"Please, Hera, I want to go. No need to see the rest."

"OK. We'll make our way back to Belldeep. The sooner we meet Jester for your debrief, the sooner you can retire."

CB CB CB

"IS IT NECESSARY for me to relive this in such great detail?" Milner demanded of Jester.

"Take it you find reviewing failure uncomfortable."

"Don't like seeing my family in distress."

"Do you mean you don't want to acknowledge Adelle and Julian witnessed Ollah's self-induced vomiting before you went home?" asked Jester.

"Why do I have to be reminded?"

"You think admitting failure tarnishes your image?"

"Don't play semantics with me, Jester. I won't accept a conflation of events with Ollah's difficulties that purports to show the whole picture. Haven't failed my daughter. Everything done for her has been out of love. It's just we haven't solved her problems yet."

"Fine, but the notion of failure will be examined at some point. We're here because you decided you found the answer to your unhappy relationship with Gronya. Do you think the way you solved that problem helped resolve Ollah's difficulties, or Hattie's come to that?"

CB CB CB

CHAPTER 8

Moulin Rouge

"IS IT WRONG to embark on a course of action, knowing it will cause heartache?" asked Jester.

"The point of the question being?" asked Milner.

"Do you believe it right to pursue one's intentions in the knowledge it will bring profound misery to others?" *Expect a slippery non-committal answer,* said Jester's doppelgänger. *Don't forget this guy always puts responsibility for questionable outcomes on other's shoulders.*

"Grief is personal," responded Milner, as he curled his hands into fists then straightened his fingers. *Got him,* said Jester's doppelgänger. *He's struggling to control irritation at my assessment of his character and motives.* Milner glared at the doppelgänger then looked Jester straight in the eye. "Individuals experience it in different ways. I can't be held to account for others' reactions."

"That's not the proposition," said Jester. "I asked if you've a right to intentionally cause grief." *Pin him down,* said Jester's doppelgänger. *What's the betting he'll slither out of the direct challenge?*

"If I take advantage of individual weaknesses, it

doesn't make me responsible for their misery. It's their fault if they fail to guard what they'd hate to lose."

There you go. What did I say? said Jester's doppelgänger.

"So, would it be fair to suggest you don't concern yourself with the results of your actions on any level?" said Jester.

"That's harsh. I protect my own from suffering, or take steps to relieve their misery to the best of my ability, but can't be responsible for people outside my family if they suffer unforeseen loss or are careless with what they value."

"Interesting," said Jester. "One for further discussion."

ᬊ ᬊ ᬊ

"So where are we off to, Hera?" asked Milner, disconcerted by Jester's challenge on grief. *That idiot makes a game out of provocation. Mustn't respond otherwise I lose advantage.*

"Be careful referring to Jester as an idiot," said Hera. "It's not like you to underestimate opponents. Suggests chinks in your armour."

"If Jester reckons he's rattling me, he is, but the situation is temporary."

"As you wish. Don't let your ability to dominate and win be what you rely on. This is about more than winning. But to business. Since gastronomy was a big part of your outings, we're off to a restaurant. On the way, think about the time Adelle's mother came to stay, and you treated them to Sunday lunch."

"Is that our destination? The Michelin-starred heaven where they served divine food and had the gorgeous waitress who simpered fit to die for?"

"Yup," said Hera. "Meanwhile, study the riddles and recall what you can of the meal. Concentrate on what happened so you and Jester have sensible discussions tonight."

"Doubt our chats will be rational while I struggle to ignore his doppelgänger's second guesses of my motives."

"Why? Is doppelgänger too close to the bone in his assumptions?"

"Aren't you on my side, Hera? I've never shown you anything but affection. Can't you help me a bit more?"

"My task is to guide and keep you company. If I ask difficult questions, it's because I'm trying to assist."

"I believe you, thousands wouldn't," said Milner, a smile playing around his lips.

The rhythmic trotting of the pony mesmerised Milner as his mind reminisced on the occasion they were to relive. In keeping with that day, the weather was auspicious, the sky blue and the breeze fresh. The mottled shadows cast by the leaves on the trees excited feelings of communion with nature in Milner, like those captured in Impressionist art. It was why he admired Monet and his contemporaries.

Milner remembered how he took to Adelle's mum straight away. Her face was a map of her life, on which you read sadness and a sense of humour, mixed with a faint suggestion of mischievousness. His own mother was always exquisitely and expensively made up. Never exposed her true self, only what she wanted you to see. Come to think of it, he couldn't remember seeing his mother without makeup. Adelle's mum, on the other hand, refused to use cosmetics and was proud of it. What you saw was what you got. Milner envied Adelle her mother's open, trusting nature and down to earth, practical attitude. *How wonderful it must be to have someone who takes whatever life throws then finds the positive in every situation. Wonder why Julian doesn't like her. Gives the impression it's because he judges her a bit simple.*

Milner's mother never approved of what he did. *Was always ready with hurtful remarks. Criticised what she called my 'congenital ability to underachieve'.* Despite his long business career spent building a fortune, she failed to acknowledge his efforts. *Her expertise was in relocating goalposts.* Whenever presented with an achievement, she'd dismiss it, imply it was unimportant; insist the next goal was the one that counted. She'd hint at his uselessness and inability to get anywhere no matter how he tried. Over the years he questioned her on how she valued success, but couldn't get a straight answer. So he accepted whatever he attempted wouldn't be good enough. Despite that, Milner loved her dearly and kept trying to discover ways to win her approval. *It didn't help when Dad died. If anything, she expected more. Perhaps I'll never succeed in pleasing her.*

CB CB CB

WHEN HE AND HERA arrived at the restaurant, she led him to a quiet corner to observe the party arrive. Milner remembered his annoyance how after Ollah went home, Hattie, not to be left out, persuaded Gronya to get him to buy her a ticket, so she could descend and be nursed by her mother. He should have expected it. The girls took it in turn to demand attention. Their habits were as predictable as Swiss clockwork, expensive, innovative and precisely balanced as to their oscillations.

Milner watched as he directed everyone to a seat in accordance with his plan. He'd reserved a spot on the terrace that overlooked the old mill wheel turned by a stream which then meandered past them. Milner found the gentle murmur of the water as it flowed downstream idyllic. A herb garden stretched away on the further bank, its smells wafting towards them. The scene was rounded off by bees collecting herb pollen to infuse their honey with a delicate, delicious flavour. He'd read somewhere how contented bees hum in middle C. Not being a musician, he'd no idea if it was their pitch, but they sounded happy. He occupied the head of the table, Gronya the bottom. He placed Adelle and her mother either side of himself. At the far end Gronya sat with Julian and Hattie either side of her facing each other. He'd invited French friends from the village to sit opposite each other in the middle. He briefed Gronya to exploit the situation but realised Hattie might cramp her style. Still, he couldn't do everything for Gronya, she'd to make some effort herself. He had misgivings with Hattie there, but she insisted on attending, and, as usual, he and Gronya let her have her way. *Anything for a quiet life. Trouble was, although Gronya coped at first, it didn't last. It started as soon as they sat down.* Milner watched the interactions unfold.

"What's so good about this restaurant?" said Hattie, inviting stares from all quarters. "Can't eat half these things, especially that dreadful foie gras."

"Keep your voice down, Hattie, there's plenty to choose from. Let us help. Julian, what do you suggest?" Gronya appealed to Julian with a desperate stare.

Poor woman, said Julian's doppelgänger. *Must be awful to have an adult child who needs constant managing. Would exhaust me. Thank goodness my youngsters are sensible and on an even keel. Let's see what I can suggest.*

"Several starters look appetising. I fancy lobster, followed by monk fish for main," said Julian.

"I'll have those too. How about you, Hattie?" said Gronya.

"Whatever. Just order for me. Make sure you get lots of water. Don't want wine, too many empty calories." *Why did I come out with these fools?* said Hattie's doppelgänger. *Tedious and a nuisance. Dislike Julian. Ollah is suspicious of him. Reckon she's got a point.*

Milner watched the French exchange glances. Madame made her own foie gras – delicious, it was. He enjoyed it many times at her table. He remembered being anxious. Willed Gronya to get Hattie to tone it down before she embarrassed him and his guests. *Wish we'd left her at home. Has to be centre of attention every time.*

Meantime he concentrated on enjoying a chat with Adelle and her mum. Adelle showed a genuine interest in his work, unlike Gronya, so he was never short of subjects to divert her. The unexpected thing he discovered was, like himself, Adelle and her mum were avid readers. He was surprised at how widely read Adelle's mum was. *I thought there must be a reason I liked her soon as we met. My instincts weren't wrong, and it wasn't the last surprise she had in store.* Absorbed in chatting about books, he remembered it relaxed him more than he had been for ages. Until Hattie decided she wanted all attention on her.

"For goodness sake, can't eat even a mouthful of this muck." Hattie pushed aside the lobster. "Makes me nauseous. Must be badly prepared from rubbish ingredients."

The French guests drew deep breaths; Milner noticed Madame blush. Gronya broke into a sweat and looked at Julian, imploring him for help.

"Perhaps you'd like something else," Julian suggested limply as he turned to look at Milner. *It's your daughter for goodness sake,* said Julian's doppelgänger, *you might consider intervening for all our sakes. Not sure how much Gronya can take.*

Milner, recognising danger, rose and walked along to whisper in Hattie's ear. After a couple of minutes she left the table with him. *Belittling me and trying to get me out of the way,* said Hattie's doppelgänger. *Make him pay, I will.*

"Excuse us," said Milner as he led her away.

He returned a while later, alone.

"Hattie is unwell and resting in the Bentley. I'll run her home and pop her in bed. Should only be a while. Please carry on with your dinner."

He was back in twenty minutes. He consulted with the maîtresse d'hôtel as he left, who agreed to slow down table service, so everyone was part way through their main course on his return. *It was seamless, excellent service. That gorgeously attired lady head waitress did more than simper.*

"I agree. The waiting staff dealt with it brilliantly, didn't they?" said Hera.

"What's the point of these observations?" Milner asked.

"To remind you of the day. The most important part came after. We'll follow them back to the house and afternoon tea, which is where you called in the cards you dealt over lunch," said Hera.

"Fine. If we must. At least I can reminisce about the marvellous meal for now."

CB CB CB

ON ARRIVAL AT the house the party scattered themselves

about the garden under trees and by the pool. Hera led Milner upstairs to view the scene from an overlooking window. Milner watched himself, memories of the afternoon assailing him.

"Tea all round, I reckon," said the Milner in the garden.

"Excellent idea," chimed in several voices.

Milner remembered preparing it, how instinct took over. His intuition told him Ollah and Hattie having contact with Julian and Adelle could upend his plans. Strange to have that confirmed by Hattie and Julian's doppelgängers earlier. It was more eerie to realise how he used the situation to his advantage. He watched himself talk to Adelle.

"Must apologise for Hattie's behaviour."

"Not to worry," Adelle responded. *Glad it's not my child. Where Gronya and Milner get the patience to deal with her, I don't know. Amazing how young people learn to manipulate with food,* said Adelle's doppelgänger.

"We've exhausted all angles with Hattie's eating disorder. Sometimes we progress, other times we go backward. She's well for long periods, so it's disappointing when she has repeated crises."

"Must be difficult. Hope it resolves in time for her to take her exams."

"We're worried. Gronya is grateful to you and Julian for your support when the girls have difficulties. What would we do without you? Other people don't understand like you."

"Just pleased to help," Adelle responded. *Glad it's not me facing it every day. I suppose all I can do is encourage them. Good to know they appreciate our input. Trouble is I'm so useless,* said Adelle's doppelgänger.

Milner watched himself wander off to give Julian tea. Gronya and Julian were seated away from the others by the pool which Milner noted as encouraging.

"Must apologise for Hattie's behaviour," Milner said, putting the tea tray down.

"Not to worry," Julian responded. *Must feign politeness. Can't stand the girl. Opinionated, selfish brat,* said Julian's doppelgänger.

"We've tried everything with Hattie's eating disorder. We make progress and then she goes into reverse. Been well for a while. It'll be a shame if another crisis is on the cards."

"I understand. Must be worried with exams on the horizon."

"Gronya and I are grateful for your support when the girls have difficulties. Gronya doesn't know what we'd do without you."

"Glad to be of help," said Julian. *Big joke, the child's an incurable nuisance,* said Julian's doppelgänger.

Milner watched as it dawned on him why Jester questioned him about grief. This was the day Milner tackled Julian on the subject. Milner wished to establish if Julian could be persuaded to leave Adelle, or if he would be swayed by Adelle's grief. Milner needed to be prepared in case Julian's resolve weakened if Adelle's anguish at losing him was a price he couldn't pay.

"I'm concerned because Hattie's close to her grand-parents. My dad's ill and we're never sure if his next crisis might be the last," said Milner. "Wonder how Hattie will deal with it, whether her difficulties make her more vulnerable, or if we could do groundwork to be pre-pared."

"Grief is individual," said Julian. *Oh boy, another weighty subject, and on such a lovely afternoon,* said Julian's doppelgänger. *No wonder Gronya finds him emotionally inappropriate sometimes. Wondered what she meant – now I know.*

"I'm aware in some people it's more extreme than others. Must be something in their personality makes it harder to bear loss," said Milner. "Knowing Adelle and meeting her mother, I admire their healthy attitude, treat it as something to deal with practically because it can't be avoided."

"You're right. Adelle will cope, it's in her nature to take it on the chin and move on. Often says you can't blame life because you lose someone. If you did, you'd lock yourself up and hide, and even then there's no stopping decay – you're dying from the minute you're born."

"So you aren't too worried how she'll manage if you go first?" said Milner.

"No. She's energetic, determined and will survive, despite her protestations she is inadequate on occasion." *Need to end this conversation, excuse myself and leave*

Gronya to her own devices, said Julian's doppelgänger. *Come back when he's gone.*

"That must be comforting. Hope I can help Hattie appreciate the same when the time comes," said Milner.

"She has a loving mother, father and friends," said Julian standing up. "The support is there. That's half the battle. The fact you're considering it now, means you'll be ready to do what's necessary when it happens. It's all you can do. Excuse me. I need a word with Adelle."

"Don't forget your tea," said Gronya. "Take it with you."

"Thanks," said Julian, giving her a smile that encouraged Milner.

ભ ભ ભ

MILNER DIDN'T RELISH his debriefing. On their journey back to the chateau, dark clouds bubbled up, brewing a storm. The dampness penetrated his nostrils, and Milner was sorry he hadn't brought a warm jacket. As they approached the gates, raindrops fell – big heavy ones – and his arms stung as the wind lashed them against him. Soaked through, he was thankful to be spared too long in the rain and took advantage of a hot bath and clean, dry clothes as soon as possible. While he did so, Hera disappeared to the kitchens, claiming she'd get warmth from the ovens and dry off there. This gave him time to himself. He was glad of the reprieve. He wanted to think without worrying about Hera sharing his thoughts. It was astonishing how the storm changed the atmosphere, made it broody and moody.

After his bath, Milner paced, glancing sidelong at the door, anxious for Hera to return so he was not alone, but at the same time wanting solitude. He listened for her approach, then realised it was useless; she was a cat and padded around quietly. He flicked through the riddles, tried to concentrate on the words. He was exhibiting the physical symptoms of unease – he'd trained himself to recognise and control them. Tonight he was in difficulty and struggled to work out a strategy to deal with Jester.

"So you spent that day questioning Julian about grief because you wanted to find out how he might handle Adelle's loss of her marriage. Did you have any conscience about it, or were you trying to make sure you had all bases covered?" asked Jester.

"What bases?"

"You know what bases."

"If you spell them out for me, I'll address them one by one. Which 'base' do you wish to discuss first?" asked Milner.

Won't say more than necessary, said Jester's doppelgänger. *That hoary old trick – only reveal your ideas on a 'need to know' basis. The tactic never failed. The idiot in front of you being ignorant about what they need to know doesn't ask the right questions.*

"If your plan succeeded, and Julian left Adelle for Gronya, despite your unhappiness with Gronya, you were bound to experience grief from loss of companionship and shared experiences. You'd been together more than forty years, just as they had. You wanted to establish whether Julian would feel the same. Whether he would feel guilt over Adelle."

"Latterly, my 'shared experiences' with Gronya were unpleasant and our desire to separate was mutual. I assumed if Julian left Adelle, it would be the same for them," said Milner.

"There you go again, avoiding the issue. Did you consider you'd no right to deprive Adelle? That you were judging her by your reactions? To assume makes an ass of you and me. You've said it often enough. Why make an exception in this case, especially as you'd persuaded her you were her friend?"

"I can't see this getting us anywhere," said Milner raising his eyebrows and scowling.

Got him, said Jester's doppelgänger. "Fact is," said Jester, "you accused Gronya of being stubbornly obsessive about getting Julian for herself. You were just as guilty, just as determined to have your way. You were so committed and obsessive you lost sight of what was appropriate for your family as a whole."

"Rubbish," responded Milner, trying to remain expressionless.

"Methinks he protests too much," said Jester smiling. "You never considered Adelle's loss of hopes, plans or dreams, or how she would cope with a lonely old age. All you saw was Gronya believed Julian would make her happy, and persuaded yourself getting her what she wanted, at whatever cost, was what had to be achieved.

That way you eased your conscience and earned the right to happiness for yourself."

"Flights of fancy," responded Milner with what he hoped was a sarcastic dismissive tone, his hands locked into fists.

"I'm right because the next 'base' you actively considered was Adelle's loss of financial support. You refused to consider her loss of social, emotional or intellectual support. Those are not measurable in any way you recognise so you dismissed them. You concentrated on manipulating Julian over the financial stuff."

"I've had enough," said Milner, scowling. "You'll have to excuse me. I'm off to bed to nurse the headache you're giving me."

"Sweet dreams," said Jester. "Or as Adelle's mother used to say – 'good night, sleep tight, don't let the bugs bite'."

଼ ଼ ଼

CHAPTER 9

Kingfishers

"WHAT PART DO NEED AND LOVE play in the achievement of happiness?" Jester asked.

"Can I sit first?" said Milner, who frowned and rolled his eyes at the ceiling. "Prefer to get comfortable and catch my breath before the onslaught. Breakfast was rushed this morning for reasons I can't fathom. Porridge was lumpy. Perhaps you'd speak to chef."

"By all means. But tactical delays won't stop my questions." *Idiot should realise I'm acquainted with his tricks and have plenty of my own,* said Jester's doppelgänger.

"So I'll employ different ruses." Milner rotated his head to ease tension in his neck and shoulders. *Must sleep if I'm to be on my toes. Last night was a real bummer. Hardly any shuteye.*

"Sorry?"

"Nothing. Thinking aloud is all."

"Fine. When you're ready. Is it necessary to repeat the question?"

"No. My response is both play a part in the search

for happiness. They're closely aligned. Individuals in love have emotional/physical needs met through quid pro quo. In other words, people fulfil needs through love and vice versa."

"Have you considered one can be mistaken for the other?" asked Jester. "That an individual thinks they're in love, but are in need."

"If I understood the purpose of your question, I might be able to answer," said Milner, crossing and uncrossing his arms and sighing. *Don't do that again. Control your foolish body.*

"Why is it necessary to understand the point? Why can't you respond without telling me what you calculate I want to hear? Why do it? Why base responses on your need to control the situation or me? Give a genuine instinctive answer. You've nothing to lose. No bonus or prize. You can consider it and advise me if you deduce anything later today. How's the balance sheet?"

෴ ෴ ෴

"JESTER WAS CURT and rude," Milner said to Hera as they arrived in the courtyard to mount the pony and trap. "What was that about? He's supposed to be in control. Betrayed weakness in my book."

"I'd guard my words. There's a different driver this morning," said Hera, flipping her tail towards the cart. "Let's hope he didn't catch your comments."

"Not worried if he did. Who is it? Since you're aware of my thoughts, I'll say it. It's a battle of tactics between me and Jester. Thinks he can outsmart me. No chance. Needs to develop another supposition if he does."

"He has rattled you. I'm the only one privy to your inner ruminations. By moaning out loud you give the game away to anyone within hearing distance."

Milner turned his attention to the cart, disconcerted to see Jester in the driver's seat dressed in his concierge outfit.

"Run out of staff today, have we?" said Milner as he climbed up, sat Hera on his lap and stroked her. "Hope this doesn't mean tiresome philosophical debates all the way to wherever it is we're headed."

"Why? Tired of having to think on your feet to produce tactical answers?" enquired Jester.

"Something like that," mumbled Milner.

"Fine," said Jester. "I'll talk, you listen. Would be good if you did. Then you can marinade my ideas and offer helpful responses at our debriefing instead of those guarded stock replies you are programmed to spurt out."

"Great. You ramble on, I'll tune in or out, dependent on how boring your prattle proves to be. Am I allowed to know our destination?"

"You'll find out when we arrive."

CƷ CƷ CƷ

THE PONY TROTTED through the forest, past the ancient oak Milner was curious about. *Been so occupied, forgot to ask Hera about that tree. Its bark is so evocative, all them whorls and knots. Isn't that Adelle's face? Wait on, there's another image higher up. Resembles Sabina. It is them. Their expressions are sad and tortured. Barely recognisable. Never seen either of 'em look so miserable.*

Distracted, Milner was taken aback when clipboard man emerged from behind the tree, dressed in his expensive suit, handmade black brogues and bowler hat, with umbrella and doppelgänger in attendance.

"This gentleman has information for you to ponder in addition to the riddles, which I trust are about your person," said Jester.

"They accompany me everywhere on my phone." *You never know when I may get a signal and a sensible conversation with someone from the outside.*

"Good. Sign to acknowledge receipt. Perhaps you can photo the documents so you don't need a paper copy."

"Thank you, sir," said clipboard man as Milner signed. *Still a prat,* said his doppelgänger. *My guess – hasn't had his ego pricked one bit yet, is arrogant as ever.*

"I know what you're thinking," said Hera. "Remember I'm the only critter who hears your inner dialogue. Communication with me is private. You'd be sensible to accept clipboard doppelgänger's implied criticism." *Why?* Milner said in his head.

"You'll face a final trial before you leave, and opening your mind along the way will make it easier to live with the outcome."

Milner opened the photo gallery on his phone to scrutinise the information handed him by clipboard man. He read, 'You're required to put meanings to the following – Litheropaedion and Moral Dyslexia'.

Jester interrupted his thoughts. "Won't find the phrases in any dictionary, not yet. The word I made up. The phrase I came across and realised – according to its definition – applies to you. I want to debate them with you once you suggest meanings."

"Does that mean you'll give me peace and quiet the rest of this journey, or do you plan to prattle on regardless?" asked Milner.

"I intend to talk. You accused your wife of having a tongue that could open a wine bottle, but you should recall we recognise others habits because we indulge in similar behaviour. Psychologists call it 'Projection'."

Oh boy, would be nice to shut him up. Perhaps he could die of some nasty complaint connected to his verbal diarrhoea. Nothing funny about this Jester.

"Now, now," said Hera. "Graciousness is called for if you want to maintain dignity."

"Yes, yes, I'm aware of that, it's hard though."

Milner donned the metaphorical headphones he'd used over the years and stared at the riddles and new material. He sat rigidly and turned his body away from Jester, head tilted over his phone. He ignored Jester in the hope he'd give up and finish the journey in blissful silence. No such luck. Jester droned on. Milner picked up odd phrases and deposited them in his grudge bank to chew on later. They could await the next briefing. Holy Grail... honour... piety... love... needs... alter egos that transmogrify from truth-tellers to liars... *Deus ex machina,* were some.

Wish I could concentrate. Milner stared at the word Litheropaedion. *I know a Lithopaedion is a calcified, dead foetus. Results from a pregnancy outside the womb that the mother's body hasn't expelled. Gronya had a friend who had one. Horrible and sad, it was. Affected everyone. Is the ero in the middle a short form of something – Eros perhaps? Babies/mother love? Is he referring to love/passion? Maybe trying to make up a name for a stone love child? Why? What idea is he attempting to formulate? Moral dyslexia. That should be easy. Dyslexia sufferers see letters/words in the wrong order or back to front. Can't visualise things the right way round however hard they try. Is he proposing that happens with morals? Does he mean ideology or morals? Interchangeable things these days. Individuals who claim to be moral sprout ideological ideas, without first interrogating the ideology. The phrases sound good so they blindly accept them. Glad I don't get caught. It's what gives me the edge and leaves me in control when dealing with idiots and the situations they end up in. No progress on riddles. Every time I reckon to have pinned one down, it morphs and applies to another person. All I'm sure of is they're about me, Gronya, Julian, Adelle and our children.*

Milner looked up as they approached a large town. Jester guided the pony and trap into a field and jumped down.

"Hera will escort you from here on foot. I've my own agenda this afternoon. Watch out for me. My appearance holds clues as to our discussions tonight."

Milner and Hera set off towards the heart of the shopping district. En route, Milner noticed advertisements for a mime pageant. This provoked reminders of the last time they visited such a festival. Then the party consisted of himself, Gronya, Julian and Adelle who were accompanied by Sabina, who'd come with her partner to visit her parents. They took a day out to enjoy lunch in a tree-shaded courtyard, where Milner could rely on getting a splendid meal. He briefed Gronya to flatter Julian every chance she got. He'd to find a means to make Julian accept the idea that compromising himself by taking Gronya as his lover was the only path open to him – fate had intervened over his head and he couldn't help himself. He deserved personal happiness at whatever cost. What Milner needed to achieve was to persuade Julian to justify to himself the outcome Milner chose for him.

Hera stopped beside a stone seat in a small square. Milner looked around and realised, as he suspected, he'd been brought to observe proceedings in the courtyard restaurant they dined in that day. He salivated as he remembered the wonderful dishes, the superb wine and the amusing banter. Gronya played her part well. Julian was more accepting of her flattery. She found ways to impart it without arousing Adelle's suspicions. Adelle had her daughter to distract her so it'd been the perfect occasion.

Milner watched the party wait for the starter and

remembered how he'd observed the interactions between Sabina and her partner. He was sure the girl would be crucial to his manoeuvrings and searched for evidence to support his instincts. *Did well that day, I did. Took full advantage. Here comes one of pièce de résistances.* Milner smiled inwardly as he listened to himself control the conversation just as he planned.

"Don't you just love the way French women have simpering down to a fine art," said Milner, looking at a couple seated at a table on the opposite side of the courtyard. Sabina and Gronya followed his gaze, looked at each other and smiled.

"Are you thinking of the head waitress where we took Adelle's mum?" asked Julian.

"The one and only. Love to eat there regular. Simpering worth the cost of the meal. Considered going without food but pay the bill just to enjoy the way she's made an art form of it," said Milner.

Gronya blushed and looked at Julian, who smiled back, then surreptitiously reached out to pat her hand under the table. *Encouraged me that did, remember thinking was getting somewhere at last, wish he wasn't so slow to take bait.*

"Wish I'd been there to see," said Sabina's partner.

"No longer possible. Hot bed of intrigue, that restaurant, I hear tell," said Milner. "Local scuttlebutt is she was the wife of the owner and head chef, but deserted him to run off with some wealthy old bloke."

"Good luck to her, if it makes her happy," said

Sabina.

Everyone turned to stare.

"Life's too short to spend it unhappy. Recognised in training for counsellors and psychologists these days. The best way to deal with breakups is not to dwell on negatives, go for quick acceptance and look forward. Never blame yourself if your wife/husband/partner fails you. Not your fault. Don't take it personal. Tell both parties the same."

"Is that a reason you won't marry?" asked Gronya. "Not being nosy. Just interested as my daughters are ambivalent about marriage."

"One of the reasons. Another is it makes it easier and cheaper if you want to end a relationship."

I could've enlightened her on that idea, but it suited my purposes not to, thought Milner. *Her comments made her partner squirm, poor chap.*

"In a way, I reckon it forces couples to work harder at keeping it together if relationships can collapse quickly and be sorted without hassle," she said, looking at Adelle. "Unlike the stupid notion marriage is based on that once you got the man legally bound, he can't escape."

"What if little ones are involved?" asked Adelle.

"Children will accept it if parents stay positive, don't deal in blame, and remain friends."

"Sabina should know, being a psychology PhD supervisor an' all. But the subject is too serious for such a glorious day. Seems there's a mime about to start over there," said Milner, nodding towards the square, "so I suggest here endeth the lesson." *Girl after my own heart. A real ally.*

"Hear, hear," chimed in several voices.

Main course was served as three actors of a peripatetic mime unloaded stage sets from a small cart and prepared to begin. Milner remembered how he welcomed it as a further deflection from the simpering discussion he just watched himself steer to its conclusion. *Had a right to gloat. Thank you, happenstance.*

In the restaurant, they finished their main dish, and waited for puds while they watched the goings on in the square. The mime scenery suggested the venue for the story was a lush green valley with a castle in the distance and lake in the foreground. The performance commenced. Two actors revealed through mime they were disabled. They sat down to fish, while a third character rode up on a child's hobby horse, dressed as a medieval knight. Through an entertaining performance he indicated he wanted to learn about the castle. In a flash the words he imbibed while only half listening to Jester on the journey here made sense. Milner recognised the mime and the role of the character on the hobby horse. It was *The Fisher King*. Milner knew the character of the knight could ask to stay in the chateau/castle or whatever. *Part of the chivalric code, wasn't it?*

The next scene inside the castle confirmed it. Everyone assembled for a banquet in the great hall. Seated at the top table were the fishermen from earlier robed as presiding knights. Milner was familiar with the legend.

The point of the fable was the visitor failed to understand the significance of the Holy Grail and the part he must play in healing *The Fisher King*. So, as the mime ended, the lords/fishermen limped away, still disabled.

Milner remembered pondering how fate sent him that mime. He was amazed at the good fortune it represented. There was Milner manipulating Julian to follow a future Milner decided should be his, and here was a story of fickle fate involving mediaeval metaphors for sexual impotence. Milner's opportunity came at the end of the meal when Sabina and her partner went off to shop. He suggested to Adelle and Gronya they fetch stuff for dinner while he and Julian finish their coffee and liqueurs. It fell into place in perfect order. *Lady luck was there for me.*

"Do you know the story of *The Fisher King*?" Milner said to Julian.

"Not really. Something to do with courtly virtues connected to honour, fertility, healing? Never considered it. There was something on the radio. I half listened to it a while ago. Enjoyed the mime. It was performed well." *Wonder what point he wants to make. Hope it's not too heavy, lovely lunch, don't want to spoil it. Wish Gronya was here, she'd put a stop to too much philosophising,* said Julian's doppelgänger.

"Believe it's to do with impotence and fertility, sexual fertility in particular."

Will let him prattle on, he may get embarrassed and give up if I go silent. He's slightly sozzled anyway. Time to summon an imperious look; put him off, said Julian's doppelgänger.

"Wondered if you'd be interested. I know you are aware Gronya told Adelle about her fantasies of taking a lover to find someone better endowed than me. It's what women do, make us feel small by suggesting we are inadequate/impotent. Keeps going on about the difference between need and love, tries to suggest they aren't the same. I'm sure Adelle suggests similar to you."

Curse these women and their intimate conversations. Can't they keep anything to themselves, said Julian's doppelgänger.

"Ever reckoned to take a lover to spite Adelle? I have. Encouraged Gronya to see if she can find better elsewhere. Then she might realise she has steak at home and hamburgers are no substitute. Wish she would. It would settle the matter."

He's drunk, said Julian's doppelgänger. *How to shut him up?*

"Ever felt fate controls life more than you credit? I contemplate fate as imitating the theatrical notion of deus et machina, you know, in Greek tragedy. The play goes along towards a dead end, then an actor representing a god drops onto the stage from a machine, in a fortuitous happenstance that upsets the way it was heading; then before you know it the performance arrives at a more palatable ending."

What is he going on about? said Julian's doppelgänger.

"Might go and investigate if the girls have been successful finding goodies for dinner," said Julian. "Interesting idea, God in the machine. Never considered it too deeply, but will give it head space."

"Good idea. May tempt you to try a radical change in life, hey."

Milner watched as he and Julian settled the bill and strolled off to find the girls. Hadn't Jester used that 'deus' phrase this morning? *Wasn't paying attention, tried to ignore him. Maybe should have listened.* If Jester had, he was one step ahead again. *Better get my ducks in a row before debrief tonight. Hope Jester doesn't travel back with us. Need to think without endless prattle.* As he and Hera made their way out of the square to locate the field with the pony and trap, Milner saw Jester disappear around a corner with the troupe of mime artists they'd watch perform. *Was Jester there that day as well? No – don't want to consider the deus ex machinations if he was.*

CB CB CB

"WE'LL START WITH a review," said Jester.

"Oh yeah?"

"How is the Balance Sheet? Have you listed each event and recorded happiness or loss to your family, then given equal consideration to the consequences for Julian's?"

"Work in progress is all I'll admit to."

"It will be examined before you leave, so don't neglect it."

"How can I forget when you issue regular ultimatums?" said Milner. *He won't let it go. Better put some-thing on the damn thing. Another game playing exercise.*

Hera, sitting on his lap, purred loudly and flicked her tail. *Don't bother with the reprimand, young lady. I'm about to get grilled anyway.*

"Time for cards on the table," said Jester. "Tried the subtle approach. Doesn't work. So I'll ask outright. Are you as self-obsessed, selfish and intent on insisting yours is the only way as your behaviour suggests?" *Let's see him wriggle out of this one*, said Jester's doppelgänger.

"I've no intention of wriggling out of anything, any-where, in case you're curious," said Milner sitting on his hands to stop wringing them. "I fail to see why I'm here, pleasant and unpleasant as the surroundings and memories are. Am I on trial or can I leave any time?"

"You aren't on trial, but can't depart till the exercise is complete, the purpose of which is to make you consider your past conduct, and prepare you for what is to come. In your determination to pursue your own interests, you never acknowledge actions have conse-quences; consequences you had no right to visit on others, particularly as you claim to have philosophically worked this through and justified it to yourself."

"I've stated I cannot be responsible for others."

"Is that so? You may choose to ignore it, but living in a community makes you just that. The way you live affects everyone no matter how private or secluded your life. We've considered questions of ethics, conscience, whether you have the right to cause grief, if love or need is predominant in your decisions. Each time you dodge or deflect the issues with the justification you cannot be 'responsible for others'."

"I don't have to answer to you."

"No. You must answer to yourself. Have you worked out what moral dyslexia is?"

"I've some notion, but I suspect you're about to enlighten me."

"Morally dyslexic individuals are in thrall to a personal ideology that sanctions a belief they are morally superior to everyone else. They skew facts to fit their beliefs and promote their version of them no matter how much overwhelming evidence to the contrary exists."

"You suggest I'm deluded?"

"No, but you are intentionally blind to the misery you cause, and give the impression you feel no regret or shame for your actions."

CB CB CB

CHAPTER 10

The Goblin Market

MILNER STARED INTO his breakfast bowl. *Always enjoy porridge, but this resembles something someone threw up. Sugar doesn't improve taste. Why did I stir it in? Don't like it, bad for me.*

"Smarting from your parting with Jester last night?" enquired Hera.

"I am."

"You tossed and turned a lot in your sleep."

"Arrogant creature. Thinks he has a right to challenge me."

"He can and has. It's why you are discombubulated."

"Discom…. what?"

"Unnerved."

"Ah…"

"Why don't you follow his advice? Embrace the process. He can't be bested," said Hera.

"I never give way. May retreat to review tactics, but won't surrender."

"Ever heard the one about pride before tumbles?"

"Doesn't apply."

"Famous last words, I reckon. Given your mood, you'll be pleased to learn Jester decided not to brief you today. Will meet you after completion of agenda items to look at riddles and balance sheet. You'll be escorted from the premises the day after."

"What blessed relief. Suggests he's retreated. Means I can wade through the rest without justifying myself. Forgive me if I don't pay attention. Let's get on with it. Where are we going?"

"A market and art exhibition."

"Something I might enjoy for a change?"

"You wish. Will note your question in my dictionary of remarkable final remarks," purred Hera.

⚃ ⚃ ⚃

MILNER ALIGHTED FROM the pony and trap. The surroundings looked familiar. Crowds jostled amid produce-laden stalls in front of an *abbaye*. He picked Hera up to protect her from the crush. All those shuffling feet. As he meandered towards the throng, a figure dressed like Jester accosted him and pushed a pamphlet, pen and notepaper under his nose. Milner contemplated refusal, but realised he couldn't. *What a nuisance. Must locate a bin to dump this rubbish?*

"Don't be so quick to discard it. Jester arranged for you to be given a list of questions to put to stallholders," said Hera. "That's probably it."

"Hoped I'd be let off easy today. What's this about?"

"Read your instructions."

Milner found a café, ordered a coffee and almond croissant and half-heartedly studied the pamphlet. It instructed him to look for stalls displaying the names 'Cloud Cuckoo Land', 'Avalon', 'Shangri-La', 'El Dorado', 'Irkalla', 'Sodom and Gomorrah' and 'Pandemonium'. At each one, he was to ask –

What's for sale?

Why?

How much?

What's the returns policy?

How is success measured?

Examination of the notebook showed a page for each stall with the questions listed and space to record answers. *Crude attempt to manipulate. How boorish. Can see through it no problem.*

"Don't like being manipulated, do you?" said Hera.

"No. Believe that's my prerogative despite being trapped in this wretched place against my will."

"So you're allowed to engineer situations, but won't tolerate others doing the same to you."

"Damn right."

"Why?"

"Because Y is a crooked letter and you can't make it straight," Milner spat out, grinding his teeth and baring them at Hera.

"Jester has annoyed you. Did you consider he might be proffering help?"

"Don't need it? All he achieves is to remind me how much I wish to leave."

"You'd do well to remember your usual tactic is to learn what you can, then use it later. You've forgotten you throw away advantage by hasty actions."

"Thanks for the exquisitely timed hint," retorted Milner, offering Hera another bared-teeth smile.

Milner surveyed the close packed stalls loaded with fruit and vegetables, meat, fish and other sundry items. He spotted odd booths dotted amongst them with large placards displaying the designations he was to look out for. He made towards the first one, taking a moment to revel in the lush smell of strawberries, tomatoes and melons along the way. He opened his notebook at the page labelled 'Cloud Cuckoo Land'. *Surely loud garish stands with obtuse names make other stallholders uncomfortable? Although they don't seem fazed. Not paying attention – too busy with customers. Have they noticed them even? Weird. Possible I'm the only one who has. Me and Hera, that is.*

As Milner drew near the stall, slung with blue tarpaulins covered in painted white clouds, he noticed the stallholder standing on a box; a short, dwarf-like creature with a big bust, tiny stunted legs and long pointed ears. Its large hands and feet were out of proportion to the rest of its body. Dressed in a tight pink jumpsuit, decorated with gold embroidered emblems he could only guess the meaning of, the figure made him pull up when the face that stared back at him resembled Gronya. Blonde hair strayed from under a spiky, ill-fitting, grotesque helmet tied under her chin. *She looks like a ghastly, nasty goblin.*

Maybe not far from the truth.

"Goblins are out in force on the stalls you are to visit," said Hera.

"Suppose it was too much to wish for a peaceful, enjoyable last outing. Jester hasn't given in."

"Told you you wouldn't best him," purred Hera.

"Better start this ridiculous exercise. If I finish in time, I'll treat myself to another coffee and tarte tatin at my favourite patisserie."

Milner swallowed hard, shook his head and curled his lip. He avoided eye contact as he posed questions and jotted answers, glad of the protection offered by the stall table. *Don't want to get near the horrible monstrosity.* Desirous to end the interview without delay, he adopted a curt, business-like stance. He accepted whatever answer came, tolerated no discussion or dialogue, and ignored any attempt by the goblin to expound. Hera purred as he made notes.

Sale items? Cherry pie, peaches and cream, banana bread.

Why? To attract a man with a lusty appetite so I can give oral, moral and between decks satisfaction.

Cost? Nothing as long as consumption meets four criteria. Effect of eating is neutral. Consumed not for being delicious but good for my lover, who is convinced my wares are supremely wonderful at whatever price. My lover accepts no bad side effects ensue. If they do, they don't outweigh positive outcomes.

Returns? My perfect man is a glutton who squats with me in perpetuity and gives satisfaction by eating at my stall and not stopping even when sated.

Outcome? As long as I'm happy and fulfil my cost criteria, that's all the success required. Want my natural rights so have no difficulty taking them. My wares are the most beautiful and wholesome that can be bought – with or without money.

Milner jotted down her answers and turned away overcome with nausea. As he did so, he observed the Pandemonium kiosk opposite. A glance confirmed a goblin manned it, standing on a box with items on display in front of him. Dressed in workman's clothes, he brandished a tool belt about his middle. His headgear was a back-to-front baseball cap, and he wore a tabard embroidered with the emblem of a staff or rod entwined by a snake. Behind the goblin was a notice. 'Carpenters are good tongue-and-groove men'. The tarpaulins on this stand sported pictures of houses in various shapes and sizes with titanic-sized demons that appeared to struggle to shrink to a size that would squeeze into the buildings. *Weirder and weirder. Better take a photo of those murals. Need to understand what they signify. OMG this goblin looks like Julian. Big ears suit him, always thought his resembled an elephant the way he sits and listens imperiously to everyone else and says little or nothing. Perhaps they match the big dick Gronya claims he sports. Let's hear his answers.*

Sale items? Already sold my entire stock. You bought these building materials together with drills, hammers, screwdrivers, vices and similar tools. They are to build the mansion you designed as architect of this project; one that far surpasses any other in its glory. I understand the plans incorporate a studio for me to sculpt and model in.

Why? To install the woman we bartered over. That's the deal, isn't it? I source materials, tools and construction expertise in exchange for the plans and the woman. Then I spend the rest of my life sculpting and modelling the perfect future for her.

Cost? Quid pro quo. You instate her in the building and I get to mould her forever. It's natural and right. I can fulfil both your and her needs with my talents. No one else is affected by our bargain, and if they are, will soon consider the benefits outweigh the disadvantages.

Returns? None. No going back for either party. Once executed it'll work because it's the perfect solution to satisfy all involved.

Outcome? Happiness all round. Everyone gets what they want. The power of emotion set us in motion with no reason to doubt the consequences for anyone outside the three of us. It's one of those win-win scenarios you preach about.

Wonder if those demons squeezing into the houses on his murals represent his ego?
Milner closed his notebook, nodded to the goblin and walked away. *Has the world gone mad? How much*

more of this nonsense? Must hand it to Jester, he knows how to provoke. Better find the next stall.

Milner strolled down a side street, his senses assaulted by the smells from a variety of delicious foods. He wondered why he'd to waste his time searching for a loud, inappropriate placard and goblin. He would rather contemplate where to procure a good lunch.

"Are you taking this seriously?" asked Hera.

"It's so ridiculous I'm struggling. Wonder who the next goblin resembles and how they are attired."

Milner didn't have far to go. A larger than average stall covered in gold tarpaulins grabbed his attention. The placard indicated this was El Dorado. Behind the items offered for sale stood a goblin, dressed in gold. *Gold usually enhances what it comes into contact with, but this is garish and way over the top.* The goblin looked like Sabina, but was more grotesque in build and adornments than the two already encountered. Milner drew a long breath before he tackled her with his questions.

Sale items? As you can see. Golden apples, figs, grapes and cherries, studded with gemstones. Ornaments to grace any home.

Why? I consider them the Holy Grail of wise investment. Gold holds value and as an economist you know the world's currencies are set according to the gold standard. *How does she know I studied economics? Don't ask. Don't want to find out. Keep your stiff upper lip in place.*

Cost? How much can you afford? I'll check your

credentials. Only sell to individuals with the wealth to make it worth my while.

Returns? You quibble over returns? You're the sort who buys after undertaking full cost/benefit analysis. Look at you. You don't randomly purchase. Nor would you buy because someone else had similar items or ideas about their worth. You make acquisitions based on the merit of the investment. What would be the point otherwise? You're an astute businessman. Acquire from me and you won't regret it.

Outcome? You've got this far. Success is when you toddle off happy with your purchase from El Dorado, then become a repeat customer. You'll never end up washing dishes and will always ensure you have means to tide you over.

Milner turned away as he slammed shut the notebook.

"Not sure how much I can tolerate, Hera. Despite the fact I usually avoid it, need a dose of caffeine before I face anymore."

"Don't dawdle. You must visit all the stalls before lunch. Four remain."

"Does Jester think he'll wear me down with this iniquitous form of torture?"

"He succeeded, if your annoyance is any indication."

؃ ؃ ؃

MILNER DRANK HIS COFFEE deep in contemplation.

Guess the other characters will be a challenge. Hope they aren't too grotesque. It'll be hard seeing my family as goblins. I curse them for goblin attitudes sometimes, but it's difficult to experience that transformed to weird semi-reality.

The next stall he encountered over the bridge beyond the strawberries and melons and the cured meats nestled among the leather goods and household items stands. It displayed the placard 'Sodom and Gomorrah'. Two disfigured goblins stood on stools behind the wares for sale. *Goblins are usually grotesque, but this pair trounces anything I've come across today.* As he approached, the hairs rose on the back of his neck. The creatures, whose mutated features resembled Hattie and Ollah, screamed at each other. No tarpaulins covered the frame of their stand and anyone within earshot could witness the spectacle. He attempted to ignore the ranting as he inspected their fripperies, ornaments, necklaces and chains. He wondered why the tat was arranged around two outlandish ugly stone gargoyles. He recorded this in his notebook, scribbling an asterisk next to the word gargoyles. His inspection caused a cessation of bellowing as they sullenly turned attention on him. This proved a temporary diversion. Irritated that he appeared to be taking his time, one of them lost patience, reached under the display stand, extracted a bag of food, and began to gorge. The other watched for a moment, pulled a face, climbed down from her upended box, retired a short distance, stuck two fingers down her throat and threw up into a rubbish bin. *Why aren't they attracting more annoyed glances? Don't tell me nobody has noticed. Perhaps other stallholders are being polite and hoping they'll pack up and go.* Vomit over, the goblin remounted her crate, and the shouting resumed. Absorbed in attempts to secure the last word, they didn't notice Milner wipe his forehead with the sleeve of his shirt. He wanted it over, to walk away, find a tree to rest beneath. He inspected the items for sale more closely and recognised them as presents he'd bestowed on Hattie and Ollah over the years. *Won't show wounded pride. This is low of Jester.* Milner banged the table with his fist and without drawing breath asked his questions, writing fast to record their responses.

Why? Decided on a clear out. Get tons of this stuff, want to turn it into hard cash. The fool what hands it over is generous with spondoolies and gifts. We tangle and twist his emotions every-which-way every day. Thinks he solves our problems handing out money or presents. Just creates a problem of how to get rid.

Cost? What do we charge? Easy come, easy go. Just want rid. You suggest a price for whatever takes your fancy. Idiot who gives it doesn't know we're here, so what's the diffs? If he discovers, we'll wheedle and he'll hand over more.

Returns? You jest? We want it gone. Give us cash, any cash, just take it off our hands.

Outcome? Never to see you again.

Rattled, Milner hurried off. He needed to locate the

next repository of challenge and misery and get it over with. *Can't stand much more. Need to keep my cool. Not let Jester think he has upended me.*

After a short walk along the riverbank, he located a flower stall, bedecked with the name 'Shangri-La'. It looked colourful and harmonious. He hoped for a better experience here. The tarpaulins were decorated with representations of flowers that reminded him of impressionist paintings he admired. He observed a goblin leaning over a table assembling a bouquet. As she straightened up to give him her attention, he recognised Adelle's features and thought how this goblin's body seemed to be in comfortable proportions. Perhaps it was the modest, appropriate outfit. Suggested she was at ease. Her ears were round, not pointed, and she had a lovely smile with eyes that danced in tune.

Sale items? At his request she listed the flowers on display. Red chrysanthemums, forget-me-nots, honey-suckle, double red pinks, violets and red roses. She went on to list *alstromeria* and *statice* and suggested these might be better known to him as Peruvian lilies and sea lavender or marsh rosemary. She explained they represented her theme for the day; love, loyalty and devotion. Today she had a special offer and select customers who purchased flowers would be given, free, a wooden box containing a keepsake. Milner asked to inspect it and was handed an exquisitely carved contain-er, lined with lush velvet. The object sitting in the middle caused him to recoil; a carved curled foetus. He sought explanation. "Why, it's a stone love child," she responded, "a Litheropaedion." Despite his determination not to question more than necessary, this intrigued him so he listened intently to her explanation. "Love resembles a child conceived in a woman's body and sustained through nurture. Hurts cause it to shrink and small areas turn to stone. When abandoned entirely by its creators, any active parts that remain become sealed in a stone womb and expelled in great pain. You need to decide if you want one as finite supplies make it a limited offer."

Why? To spread the message that love yields a bounty to enjoy as long as we work to sustain her. Go against that and everything turns cold and hard.

Cost? If a purchaser shows empathy and is chosen to receive the free keepsake, they will be offered the bouquet at a discount.

Returns? No returns on flowers due to their perishable nature. Tended, their life is prolonged. Neglected, they perish fast. The Litheropaedion is non-returnable. Its purpose is to warn of the unrelieved pain of abandonment which fades to a dull ache you learn to live with, but never dissipates entirely.

Outcome? To remind you love is fragrant when cherished, but fades or turns to stone without care and attention.

Two more to go. Jester hasn't spared me with this exer-

cise. Hope I've seen the worst, but if his enactments so far are representative, sure I haven't. I'll stroll back over the bridge. Try the other side of the river. Perhaps the final stalls are there.

A tarpaulin decorated with a fruit tree design, each branch laden with a bounty of shiny red apples, drew his attention. The name 'Avalon' caught his eye. The goblin in charge sported a blue suit similar to those used by surgeons in operating theatres. This was topped by a personalised scrub cap covered in images of the Lithero-paedion offered as a gift on the flower stall. Emblazoned on the pocket of his scrubs jacket was that rod with the entwined snake he saw on the Pandemonium stall. *Wish I could remember where I've seen that symbol? The surgical scrubs are a clue. Maybe it's that Greek logo the medical profession uses? But how do Avalon and apples relate to doctors?* Milner scribbled down a reminder to research this. *Since I'm doing the rounds of mine and Julian's family, this must be Daniel. Don't know him well by sight but Adelle talks about him a lot.*

Sale items? Milner noted the items on display; an elaborate decorated sword, surrounded by surgical tools, scalpels, forceps, probes and retractors. There was a framed copy of the Hippocratic Oath and another listing a code of ethics, beneath a depiction of the rod and snake emblem. Milner was told it was the Rod of Asclepius. *One puzzle answered. I was right. Did see it in medical connection.*

Why? These instruments relate to my work. I remove

Litheropaedia from souls that have experienced traumatic loss or abandonment. It happens when loving relationships are abandoned and hearts turned to stone. Such organs need removal and replacement by ones able to beat again. The Rod of Asclepius denotes the basis of ethics. My books and pamphlets offer guidance on social and moral virtues; how to develop and maintain ethics in private and professional lives to avoid the growth of Litheropaedia. My family had such surgery, which tore it apart, so I want to cease providing solutions for the end result and concentrate on prevention.

Cost? You want to buy these items? You couldn't afford them. I give them away to anyone who wants to accept the metaphysical cost of the sacrifice needed to maintain ethical practice – once you demonstrate you understand it. They can be displayed as reminders of the destructiveness of selfish and unethical behaviour.

Returns? No returns policy. I expect those who take them to stick to ethical principles and do no harm.

Outcome? My reward – to achieve better standards of behaviour.

Milner snapped his notebook shut. *Bit of a simplistic idealist, that guy? And they accuse lawyers of being unable to deal with grey areas. One to go. Hope Jester hasn't save the most irksome to last.*

He didn't have far to walk. The final stall was located along from Avalon. It was hard to miss. The tarpaulins were black and painted with seven braziers; three along the back, two either side. Each brazier disgorged fierce flames onto the canvas. A lighting effect made them look as if they were actually burning. This was Irkalla. *That's a new one. Never heard of the place. More research.*

Milner approach and looked for the goblin. Displayed were three pictures, which provoked a gasp and jerk of his head. His skin tingled and heart pounded. His brain went into paroxysms, sending mixed messages to his limbs. The end result was rigid legs. He looked down and glared at them, as if by doing so he could force them to move, but realised he stood in a puddle. *Perhaps it's spilled superglue. From the way my limbs are stuck fast it probably is. Another underhand ploy to push me to play these ridiculous games.*

"Careful," said Hera. "Your eyes are bulging and will pop if you don't breathe."

"I forgot you were following."

"Mingled and observed is all. Gave you space to make notes uninterrupted. Tried to be conspicuous by my absence. You were so absorbed you didn't notice. Should I be offended?"

"Those comments and this stall are below the belt. I thought you were my friend," said Milner.

"I'm your guide, not your mentor. All my actions are without prejudice," purred Hera.

The pictures for sale were his Banksy monkey wearing a tabard sporting the words 'Keep it Real' and the picture from the London flat of the man walking down a hill. Third was a portrait of a dwarf with a chimpanzee on its shoulder. Replicas of these images adorned the tarpaulins. At that moment a goblin lifted a side panel and climbed onto his stool. Dressed in a tailored suit and tie, with manicured hair, the creature was a replica of himself. *Do I laugh or get angry? Hand crafted tailoring on that distorted body. Bears no resemblance despite the likeness of the face. Better get on with this. Best way is not to react, keep cool and professional.*

Why? The goblin stated he'd undertaken a clear-out after meeting seven advisors on a recent journey. Each one guarded a gate where they stood warming hands at a brazier. They invited him to pass through each one in turn. Inside each entrance, he'd been offered different and increasing amounts of freedom from ties and issues that dragged him down for forty years. They helped him take decisions on what to discard and cast into their respective braziers once he emerged. These pictures he'd kept to sell. Had to make some profit from years of acquisitions.

Cost? Not bothered. Small profit acceptable. Already paid a price and enjoyed them as much as possible. Time to move on. Make me an offer.

Returns? None. Don't want sop who takes them thinking he can return 'em. If they decide not to keep can choose whether to discard or sell on for a profit.

Outcome? Personal happiness and contentment. No punishments or rewards just a sense of relief and a clear unhindered path ahead to what I hope will be contented boredom from loss of shackles.

CR CR CR

"Need lunch. Need the comfort of quality, well-prepared ingredients accompanied by a good Cahors to wash away the taste in my mouth."

"You pushed Jester to the limit with your intransigence. What did you expect?" asked Hera.

"Don't lecture me! Must think. Must fill in that wretched Balance Sheet before final joust with Jester."

"I'll leave you in peace. I'm off to find some delicious fish to devour. See you later."

"You will be off if you come back stinking of fish."

"Ha! Ha!"

Milner enjoyed his meal in a lush courtyard. He'd dined here before and would enjoy any dishes on the menu. He felt his equilibrium being restored the moment he enquired of the waitress whether they had a bottle of his favourite Cahors. The year he asked for produced an impeccable vintage. He savoured every last drop before he pulled out his notes and the wretched sheet he'd to complete regarding the effects of his actions on both families. *Can't face this now. Will complete at château before dinner. Maybe this afternoon will bring enlightenment.*

Hera arrived looking satisfied. They set off for the abbaye where a *vernissage* was being staged. *Hope I get to look at some decent stuff at this exhibition. Something soothing and enjoyable.*

"You'll be pleased to learn they secured the loan of a few Impressionist paintings," said Hera. "Not many, but a good core. Invited local artists to contribute; asked them to copy the Impressionist works to hang next to the originals to show the exemplary skills of the masters. Brave of the local artists I thought, but an excellent idea."

"Some people will do anything for a few moments of attention," said Milner.

They arrived and Hera installed Milner on an unobtrusive seat in a passage above the main viewing area. Milner watched himself and Gronya arrive, followed by Julian, Adelle, Daniel and his new wife. He recalled his surprise that day at his enjoyment comparing the originals and copy paintings. It gave him lots of excuses to probe Julian's thinking and challenge his rigid ideas. Then he was reminded of the incident that almost upended him. He spotted a mutual friend walk into the gallery. The friend drifted over, anxious to communicate some local gossip.

"Heard about Mrs Simper from the restaurant?" he asked Milner, Julian and Daniel who were inspecting a painting of Gare Saint-Lazare.

"Spill then," said Julian.

"You know she abandoned her chef husband for the rich old codger?"

"That was the rumour," said Milner.

"Turns out he wasn't so wealthy. Came to light because she was only with him eight weeks, when he had a heart attack and died. She's fallen on hard times as they say."

"Won't she get a hefty divorce settlement?" asked Milner.

"Eventually, but for now her lover's family kicked her out and her husband won't help her, on account of he's quite upset still."

"Don't know this lady," piped in Daniel, "but sounds like she met her nemesis. If you act without considering consequences, you must accept the outcome. Rough justice, but there it is. The other week I learned of another woman who married her lover of many years. He abandoned his wife and seven kids for her. Six months after the wedding he had a massive stroke. Now a cripple and she's his nursemaid."

"Enough already, Hera," said Milner, who stood and brushed her off his lap. "Won't listen to anymore. Let's get back to the château. Must prepare for last session with Jester."

CႽ CႽ CႽ

THEY MET IN the same room as their first meeting; Jester behind his leather-tooled desk with doppelgänger on his shoulder. Milner noticed doppelgänger wave a wand surmounted by a replica of the Litheropaedion he saw at the Goblin Market. *Intent on rubbing it in, is he? Got my response to this ridiculous farce here. Thinks he can best me, does he?*

Hera purred and flicked her tail. "Congruence of stubborn minds, huh."

"Right, young lady. Where'd you learn such big words?"

"Been around you too long."

"Maybe I'll christen you the Catastrophic Cat in honour of the way you provoke."

Milner handed over his Balance Sheet. Over one column he had written 'My Family (and other animals)'. Over the other was 'Julian's family (The Seething Pot)'. The columns were empty.

"Determined to be arrogant to the end," responded Jester, a smile playing about his mouth.

The doppelgänger curled his lips in a smirk. *No need for me to comment. He's letting it hang out without remorse or shame.*

"Determined to be annoying to the end," responded Milner.

"Where are your riddles? Have you solved them?"

"Have my answers. Take it the market and stalls were meant to be clues. Crude, low tactic, which I judge to be beneath you."

It takes someone who indulges in low tactics to recognise them as such, said doppelgänger.

"You have shown reluctance to examine the consequences of your actions at every step of this process. I'd no other recourse to get your attention. That's what happens when you treat others with contempt."

Curse the wretch. Using the 360° tactic.

"I told you there was no besting Jester. The most you can achieve is stalemate," said Hera.

Thanks, but I worked that out for myself. Stating the obvious no help at this point.

Milner handed over his list of riddles with names appended. Jester took his sheet and entered Milner's answers onto a master copy. He handed it back Milner who saw two columns next to the riddles, one with his attempted answers, the other the correct ones.

"You can study them in detail later," said Jester. "For now, you must acknowledge that despite your boasts about understanding characters and personalities, you could not determine which riddle related to which character. Didn't even recognise yourself."

"Made your point. I see nothing to be gained in prolonging this meeting. I've taken part in your puerile exercises and wish to be excused, sir," said Milner, who stood and offered a mock salute.

"As you wish. Permission to leave granted. Perhaps I should have brought you here later in this process after you've lived with the consequences for a while."

"It wouldn't matter when I came. I'm not responsible for grief experienced by anyone other than my family. That I can control. Will do so for their own good. They might not understand it, but life thrust the role on me, which I took on and bore. I never regret actions, never consider failure. Not concepts I recognise. If faced with unfavourable circumstances, I don't label them failure; I reassess, pick myself up and move on. Out of bad odds I create success by employing superior tactics."

Bases his idea on the notion that everyone is as capable

as him. Doesn't accept others aren't cold-hearted and calculating, muttered Doppelgänger. *Complete empathy failure. Bet he would deny validity to such concepts.*

"Finished?" asked Jester.

"Quite."

"Good. Dismissed. Tomorrow morning you'll be escorted to your Bentley to continue your journey."

"Praise be. Can't wait. Want to dismiss all memory of this place asap," said Milner as he opened the door to leave.

"Enjoy your last dinner with us, by the way. We have something special prepared."

"How very gracious. Missing you already," said Milner as he pulled the door shut – firmly.

႘ ႘ ႘

CHAPTER 11

Milner's Inferno

H E HAD TO ADMIT they served a magnificent *dîner.* All his favourites. *That fresh foie gras was superb, and the steak done to perfection. The French are the only ones able to cook Bleu with precision. As for the Cahors. Words inadequate to describe its qualities. Same with the cheeses. If the meal was intended as compensation for what I've endured, all is forgiven. Shall ignore the other annoyances as tomorrow can get on with my business, thank goodness.*

On arrival in the dining room, Milner had been disconcerted to be led to a secluded spot in a corner of the communal eating area, his waiter for the night – the concierge. Milner's irritation rose when he spotted Jester's doppelgänger perched on the concierge's shoulder. *What is Jester up to? What's the game? Trying to get the last word? Miffed because I refused to play? Who knows?* It was unusual for Milner to have a private table with waiter service. Previous nights he'd shared benches with guests; meals served buffet style. *Never liked help yourself although tolerable at Hotel de France on La nuit du Spardos. That was exceptional in every way. Prefer to pay to be waited on. What good is money otherwise?* He decided not to talk except to indicate his order. No banter or chatting with concierge or Hera. He hated being undermined by doppelgänger's comments. Eye contact was a no-no. As a result, he ate fast enough to leave early, but slowly enough to savour the dishes and avoid indigestion. Towards the end of the meal he felt at liberty to look about, but then regretted it. His table was situated in an alcove adjacent to an ancient chapel. From the stained glass and icons painted on the walls, Milner surmised this had been part of a monks' refectory. He studied the images and motifs. They weren't the usual array of saints. Curious, he scrutinized them. How had he missed it? The windows were tightly arranged with eight panes forming the base, then two ascending rows of seven, making twenty-two in total. His lips parted, and he squinted as he leaned forward. *Need my specs. Something fishy about them.* He searched his trouser pockets for his glasses case, conscious his impatient sighs attracted annoyed glances from neighbouring diners. *Not there, damn it! More haste, less speed. Stop, don't let this spoil your dinner, Milner.* Ignoring his own admonition he jerked his jacket from the back of his chair. The case clattered to the floor, drawing more stares. He bent to retrieve it, but was beaten by his waiter. Jester's doppelgänger gave Milner a facetious grin as they both reached for the offending object. Milner wrinkled his nose and snatched it from the concierge who got to it first. Glasses installed on end of his nose, he blinked. *Surely not. Should've paid attention.* The figures were the Major

Arcana from a Tarot pack. As he stared the facial features in each pane began to distort like reflections in rippling water. *The oak tree bark in the forest did that. Ignore it. Too late to be excited or wonder at it. Don't allow yourself to be distracted. Concentrate on your food.*

Milner finished his meal, but what was left turned to sawdust in his mouth. The Cahors went sour and his overwhelming desire was to escape to the privacy of his room. As he passed under an archway towards the stairs to his quarters, he looked back. He spotted the couple from the car in front of his when they entrained at Folkestone. *It's those kids.* Before they disembarked along the tunnel, they'd argued over what to watch on their tablets. He remembered gizmos hadn't solved the problem of rug rats arguing on journeys. *I was right. See them now – glued to their phone screens, each at liberty to choose and still rowing over the best things to watch. At the dinner table too, tsk, tsk. Parents have no idea. Wait a minute. No doppelgängers. How did I not notice? Is it a signal Jester is no longer interested in tormenting me because I ignored the one on the waiter's shoulder? What a relief! Never thought I'd find something to irritate more than Gronya's constant debilitating grumbles. But why the windows? Don't dwell on it. I'm leaving and won't allow loose ends to annoy.*

Milner revelled in the sanctuary of his room. He poured a whisky, slouched into his favourite comfy chair, coaxed Hera onto his lap, unfolded the riddle sheet and read.

	Milner's Solution	Correct Solution
Once entwined with honour – now entwined with dishonour Once delivering healing and compassion – now attracting anger and hate its poison diverted not to search for Wholeness but to Maim, Destroy and Incapacitate. His totem should have remained sheathed in its scale headed helter-skelter Impotent to cause harm imbued instead with power to disperse peace, healing and understanding	Daniel? Julian? Is this the Rod of Aesclepius?	Julian
Who publicly affects to digest the past but forgets he is not omnipotent or able to dispel remnants of discontent Who publicly affects to face problems with courage but capriciously exploits weakness making cat's paws of victims Who publicly affects to sooth worries but relies on selfishly acquired gains without understanding the inadequate, ineffectual nature of his tools	Me? Julian?	Milner

Who feigns cleanliness and
innocence
but wallows in a muddy waterhole
Who crawls into beehives to steal
honey
and howls when stung
Who exudes chasteness
but is as empty and deceptive as
froth
Who pretends to have no bristles
but disingenuously stirs settled dust
Who wants to warm an already
warm bed
then slyly and contentedly lick clean
their whiskers

Gronya?
Hattie?
Ollah?
Me?

Gronya

Who sports a synthetic blindfold
enhanced by a spirit level
while claiming impartiality
Who sleeps with danger
unbalancing the scales
then indulges in feigned wan hope
imperiously declaring innocence,
fear and regret

Gronya?
Hattie?
Ollah?

Ollah

Who believes they are the sun
around which planets revolve
Who, if a planet wanders from their
sphere
petulantly manipulates gravity until
it is forced to return
Who constantly calculates, processes
and reasons
with waspish glee
how to turn the pudding sour
even when made in their honour

Gronya?
Hattie?
Ollah?

Hattie

Whose anvil was intellect
on which questionable aims were
forged
Who quietly reasoned away
obstacles
in the search for a truth
obtuse, painful and difficult to
manoeuvre
Who succumbed to the temptations
of Babylon
and became steadfast in upholding
ambiguous ideals
with an intermittent and destructive
roar

Julian?   Daniel
Daniel?

Who thinks they know everything
but knows nothing
Who forges words into steel blades
honed to conceal double meaning
Who superciliously believes they are
a distillation
of perfect balance and taste
but decanting their vessel reveals
rancid overtones
which anosmia means they cannot
detect
Who, seeing their reflection in the
mirror of life,
sees no vanity
but prudence holding sway

Sabina?   Sabina
Daniel?
Julian?

Who saw only good in those they
believed friends
and expected no harm from those
they trusted
Who naively judged others
to have honesty and integrity
Who believed hot water never came
from cold taps
and learned 'I mean you no harm'
and 'I want only the best for you'
were misleading duplicitous lies

Adelle   Adelle

"Why am I so tired, Hera?"

"Long days. Lots of challenges. Little relaxation."

"Jester's riddle trick worked because all personalities have bits of each characteristic he highlights. When you see the solution, it's obvious. He highlighted how I must hone my people skills."

"Do you never climb down?"

"Can't. My strategy is to pull 'em up or knock 'em down first."

"Suppose it's one way of doing it. I'll leave you to enjoy your whisky. I'm off to say goodbye to my kitchen friends."

Milner struggled to concentrate. *Need matchsticks for the old eyelids. Why this tiredness?* He dozed. Startled by a noise, he roused himself and moved to lie down on the bed. He'd no energy to change into night gear. Milner fell into a doze, disturbed by a sensation that his arms and legs had divorced themselves from his control while his brain whirled him to another dimension. *Hold on. Why am I sitting on a forest bench? How the devil did I get here? There's the oak tree and clipboard man who jumped out from behind it on my journey here. The faces in the bark are talking to each other and me, distorting and changing constantly. How am I meant to keep up with what they're saying? Can't think. It's a babble.*

Milner glared at the tree trunk, aware of two men sitting either side of him.

"Do you recognise us?" they asked in unison.

Milner gasped. "You look like Warren Buffett and Steve Jobs."

"How astute, although for these purposes you can call us The Wizard of Omaha and Master of Innovation. We have another friend coming. We call him JR or Smartmouth."

"What's this in aid of?" asked Milner.

"We're taking you on a journey through the inferno you created. Trouble is unlike the one in the *Divine Comedy* there's no *purgatorio* or *paradiso* to ascend through once you get to the bottom. That's where you stick. No escape."

"Why is this necessary? What will it take to spare me this nightmare?"

"Nightmare is your description…," said Wizard.

"… and we cannot be bribed," said Master.

"Boy, you're just one dumb ole cowboy, ain't you!" piped in Smartmouth who swaggered up behind them.

"Your half-hearted cooperation in examining past conduct," said Wizard, "means you get to relish the consequences."

"You refused to acknowledge mistakes," said Master, "now you find out where the blind power of lust leads and the passionate intense emotions you set in motion through Cupid's bow and error…," said Wizard.

"… that you blithely encouraged him to fire," finished Master.

"They got you," said Smartmouth. "They know you never tell the truth when a good lie will do."

How long must I listen to this lot finish each other's lines and make idiotic quips?

"As the Master of Invention I condensed the number of circles in this version of the comedy. Dante had nine; you'll visit six virtual ones. I've preserved some of Dante's original features, but have incorporated some up-to-date gimmicks you'll appreciate. My design geeks have devised a tablet, with buttons on the screen so tempting you'll want to lick 'em. First are two spheres covering the inadvertent sins of lust, gluttony and greed. These you had in your control, but chose not to keep them in check because you rate the rewards from manipulating them too good to pass up. Then you cross a drawbridge over a moat to the three enclosures dealing with premeditated sins; heresy, violence then fraud and treachery combined. Last you get to take your place in the lake where souls are submerged to different degrees."

"Like my daddy always said: if you can't go through the front door, just go round the back," chimed in Smartmouth, "or, in your case, dream your way in."

ೞ ೞ ೞ

MILNER STRUGGLED TO ROUSE himself. He forced his eyelids apart. His eyes were scratchy and clogged. Fuzzy black spots danced as he rolled them side to side and up and down. *Focus, man, focus,* he muttered as if it would make his pupils obey signals from his brain. He tried to shake his head and limbs but got no reaction. His insides swirled and whirled and his jaw clenched, but his skin stayed dry and anyone looking on would have glimpsed a heavy, placid body. *Wonder if the wine was tampered with.* Panic overtook him as he willed his arms to push himself to sit up. They ignored his brain's demands. *Am I tied down? Can't feel restraints.* His legs were there, he sensed them, but the muscles didn't respond to the commands pushed the length of his body through the nerves and tendons or whatever it was made them work normally. *This is like a water-bed. Jelly wobbling under me with nothing solid to grip. No way I can lever myself into control. Roll over. Don't drift back to sleep, old man. Damn them.*

His extremities refused to cooperate. Milner's mind battled to maintain consciousness and banish the dream or vision or whatever it was. He lost. His eyelids drooped then snapped shut. He'd no power to coerce them to stay open. He succumbed to a fitful doze. He found himself, with his companions, standing at the head of a valley, stripped of vegetation by a vicious wind. Tumbleweed drifted and bounced between rocks, with individual tufts occasionally sticking to a rock until a sudden gust forced them to dance in the wind again. Bleak tree trunks reached to the sky, their branches ripped and torn. In the distance rocky crags riddled with caves stood desolate; too far away to offer shelter. There was no escape from the tearing, howling sound whipping about them. *At least I can't hear the jibes of the three monkeys, and with no Hera either my thoughts are private.*

"You reckon," said Smartmouth.

At this point a dust devil spinning counter-clockwise began circling the valley floor. Milner saw heads trapped within it buffeted back and forth. As it drew nearer, he recognised the faces from the Goblin Market. It was Gronya, Julian, Hattie and Ollah. The dust devil arrived at the spot where he stood. It twirled in front him while the heads took it in turn to emerge one at a time and shout.

"See what getting me a bit of rough has done."

"Fool. Thought money bought solutions to problems, did you?"

"What a liar and manipulator you turned out."

"Reasoned you were clever. Just a greedy, interfering idiot is what you are."

"Proud of the hell you summoned up and put us in, are you?"

"You'll be in here with us soon."

"No idea what miseries you've created, have you?"

"Hope you can't escape and get stuck like us."

Milner couldn't distinguish which face shouted what. The anger and frustration of their features lodged with the words in a jumble in his mind. The abuse stopped when the dust devil spun away to swirl along a route around the edge of valley unable to break free of its confines. As he watched it move back and forth, his companion's remarks and observations began to penetrate his thoughts.

"Arrogant twit. Didn't know the difference between being in need and being in love. None of that lot capable of making sacrifices necessary to secure love. Never understood what it was. Believed money bought love and loyalty. Never appreciated money buys loyalty as long as it lasts, but when it runs out, forget it. Sex and lust destroy friendships and trust. You engineered that. If they escape that whirlwind they'll get caught up in something else; be restless and aimless the rest of their existence. Serves you and them right."

Milner tried to block out the voices and words. Looking for a way to leave, he examined the tablet hung around his neck. He pushed a button that showed he should head towards a cave entrance along a path through a bog. His companions followed. *Why can't they shut the hell up? Why did I use that word? Is it where I am, a kind of hell?*

The relief of escape from the wind and dust whipping the exposed parts of his body, quickly dissipated as a foul stench assailed his nostrils. In front of him stood a notice mounted on an easel. Beneath a direction arrow were the words 'This way to the bog of Gluttony and Greed'. The sign was inscribed in large letters impossible to miss. Milner attempted a retreat, but was prevented by a chain formed across the path by his accomplices. He tried to push past, but they blocked him and indicated he must proceed. Milner glared at each in turn, crushing down the insults he wanted to hurl, conscious Smartmouth could read his thoughts. Smartmouth smirked at him, "Control your temper, don't let it get the better of you. Some mantra – if it works. Clever dick."

Milner held his nose and ventured carefully along the trail marked by bollards and chains woven through the centre of the bog. Ahead in the distance he saw the cave entrance lit up. *The cave may also be a tunnel. Let's hope so. Must get there; avoid the boggy bits. Better get on it with it. Can't be any worse so I'll push on.*

In the gloom he found his attention drawn to creatures that lay about either side of his path. Half snake, half worm, large parts of their bodies were immersed in the foul slush of the bog. Sightless, their glazed-over blank eyes indicated blindness.

What are these vile things?

"Werpils," said Smartmouth, "a particularly nasty subspecies. When they rest to digest, they embed their noses in the slush and wave their back claws in the air, if they can get 'em up that is."

It was hard to see. Milner was forced to lean towards them to secure a better view. The stench was overpowering and Milner struggled to overcome disgust. When he got close enough to examine them, the inspection didn't last long. He jerked backwards and heaved the instant he recognised the faces attached to the monstrous bodies distorted into horrible shapes by stuff they'd swallowed whole. The goblin heads on the hideous brutes bore the likeness of Hattie, Ollah and Sabina. Milner groaned. *What's the point?* "Every point," his companions echoed in unison. "Subtlety hasn't worked, nor has reasoned debate. Hammer and anvil are the only choices left." Around the Werpils lay mouldy food, containers filled with prescription pills, bags of illegal drugs, syringes, bottles of alcohol, heaps of bricks and mortar, wood and money. These were shovelled into the creatures' mouths with webbed paws adapted to ensure maximum intake. Blindness made them unaware of fellow gobblers, but if they sensed an item they wanted to purloin being claimed by another, they began clawing and screeching until one or the other gave it up, whereupon the loser returned to the pile, reached out and took something else; the winner stuffed the prize into its mouth. The Werpils had no idea of the size of surrounding mounds. Large beetles, working in teams like a conveyor belt, resupplied the piles, while the Werpils kept gorging.

"They'll explode eventually," said the Wizard. "Maybe need to find some means to adapt their digestive systems," piped in the Master. "The way I see it, they're sailing on the Titanic while they can. Bound to go down in the end and boy, will they sink fast!" said Smartmouth.

"Heard enough," said Milner. "Can we proceed?"

"Sure thing," giggled Smartmouth. "Press the next button."

"So pleased I provide amusement," snarled Milner.

"So pleased you are enjoying your angst," said Smartmouth, "coz you follow the golden rule of conscience. You treat it like some do a boat or a car. If you feel you need one, you rent it, with no penalties on short term return."

Milner headed towards the lighted cave entrance in the distance. A dimly lit path indicated the way through. He emerged from the darkness, blinked and looked about. He found himself stood on a drawbridge over a moat surrounded by a stretch of land bounded on its far perimeter by a stone wall. A portcullis marked Exit was visible. Spread around were frame-like structures on which large spiders spun webs. As Milner pondered the reason for webs being woven on frames instead of the usual places, a group of goblin prisoners marched out of a side building escorted by a troop of guards. Milner recognised one of them. It was the goblin with Julian's features. Milner watched as each prisoner was led to a frame, stripped naked and strung on the web. Some struggled, but most accepted the procedure. *What is the purpose of this nonsense?*

"The purpose of this nonsense, as you call it, is to hang 'em out to dry, because they hung ethics out to dry," said Smartmouth.

"Need more information to understand," said Milner.

"You are destined for further down in the Inferno, otherwise you'd be joining this lot. Like you, these professionals blurred the line between public power and private conscience. They allowed power to override scruples when dealing with people close to them; exempted themselves from the rules. They forgot to apply them to themselves, reasoned they were above it all."

As Smartmouth finished speaking, another door opened and several komodo dragons emerged. Milner watched horrified as they attacked those suspended, tearing off chunks of flesh, which they played with while their victims howled until a replacement piece grew.

"See. Groundhog Day for these sowers of discord. They come out daily for four hours to experience this delight. Aren't you glad you're spared this one?" asked Smartmouth. "What grows back is never as tasty to the dragons, so they avoid that until they've had a go at fresh bits, then return to the regrowth to degrade it more. The other problem these guys have is the closed drawbridge. No escape. Can't go back or forward. The guy who looks like Julian, I heard him pleading his case. Said he never meant to betray his wife and family, but Gronya got hold of his balls and made him want to relive his youth to gratify sexual whims. Said Gronya appealed to his passionate side. Trouble is she couldn't satisfy the spiritual and dignified part of him and now he is tortured because he's trapped in this miserable existence."

"Enough already," said Milner. "Can it get any worse? Let's go through the exit portcullis."

"OK, but you do know each circle gets worse, not

better."

"You jest. And here I am trying to hurry through this damn nonsense."

"He's realised, hasn't he," piped in the Wizard. "It's when the tide goes out you discover who's swimming naked."

"Another of my sayings is risk comes from not knowing what you're doing. I knew what I was doing."

"Sure, are you?" said Wizard.

Milner pressed a button. They headed towards the portcullis. As they neared, Milner heard rusty cogs and wheels grind over each other as the gate lifted. *Someone failed in their duty. Didn't oil that lot. Wouldn't happen in my business. Keep wheels well oiled, I do.* Another of those inept notices on an easel caught his attention. This way to 'Hell of Violence'. Milner determined to give nothing away to his companions. He resolved to remain calm, nod his head, agree, register no emotions on his face, think neutral thoughts. It would be hard, but he must do it. He closed his eyes, breathed deeply and put on those metaphorical headphones he'd mislaid, but relocated. If they got no response they might not detain him, but proceed to the next circle. Always worked with Gronya, the kids and that fool Julian. Should work now.

Smartmouth pulled one of the earphones away and shouted in his ear. "Want to hire a Kevlar umbrella? Necessary item for your jaunt through this circle."

Milner tried not to sneer. *Careful, old boy. Fill your head with neutral ideas. Don't entertain or express negative ones. Ask lots of questions. Think inane thoughts. Anyway, why does this guy reckon I need a brolly?* Milner surveyed the landscape. Fiery flakes rained from the sky, landing on a surface of quicksand, pockmarked with craters of boiling blood and fire. He saw a woman with children huddled on a small island under a makeshift shelter that offered limited protection from the rain. *Who are they? Who would leave defenceless women and children here? Surely not.* He turned up the volume on his metaphorical headphones, but was unable to block out the sound of his companions' discussion. Partial phrases rang in his ears. "Those victims of his... Their shelter isn't made from Kevlar... Said he never worried about others... Only took care of his own... If he looks round the corner he'll see his grandchildren under a Kevlar hut... Not like Adelle and her grandchildren... Thinks his lot were safe and exempt... In same kind of hell as Julian's family... Bit more protected, but still in turmoil... He should be in one of them pits with no cover... Yeah, but got a better punishment for him further down this inferno."

Milner resolved to take matters into his own hands and hurried away along the low, wobbly bridge that lit up when he pressed another button on the tablet. It led to a doorway in a wall a short distance ahead. The distressed crying of the woman and children penetrated his headphones. Whatever was the other side couldn't be worse. "Oh, yes, it is," sang his companions in unison. "Oh, no, it can't be," Milner threw back over his shoulder at them. "Oh, yes, it is," they chorused. *Sounds like they're at a pantomime. Get your ducks in a row, Milner. I told you not to respond.*

"What's next then?" Milner asked.

"If you look at the door you are stood in front of, it tells you. You are headed for the circle of Fraud and Treachery."

"Such terms are harsh. Not used in diplomacy these days. Never been a criminal. Maybe bent the rules and encouraged others to do things in my interest, but fraud and treachery?"

"Here we call a liar a liar and a manipulator a manipulator. You betrayed family ties. Against your own was bad enough, but you decided Julian would betray his at your command. His family had no choice; you imposed your will on them for your gratification. Want it spelled out any clearer?"

"No thanks. Let's just get on with it."

Milner pushed open the door. A cacophony of screaming and loud raucous music assaulted him. A party was underway in a barren landscape pitted with lakes of faeces and boiling pitch. Large crowds milled about between the pits dressed in designer outfits with logos on their backs saying 'Panderers', 'Flatters', 'Hypocrites', 'Thieves'. Some partygoers had their heads on back to front. They were trying to read the labels and one group were negotiating to swap.

"Why the negotiations?" asked Milner, intrigued into breaking his no comment rule.

"Because the label assigns them to a head first in pit or feet first in pit," said Smartmouth. "They get to spend three hours each morning and afternoon in their pit. During immersion they are whipped by demons swinging a cat o' nine tails. Depends whether they want it around head and neck or ankles and feet. Great choice, huh!"

Milner pushed fists into his ears and forced a route through the partygoers. He didn't want to see if any of the revellers had faces he recognised. He avoided falling into any of the pits, but failed to block out the stench and noise. He reached the shelter of a doorway labelled 'Emergency Exit' beneath which was another sign in large letters. 'Abandon hope, all who pass beyond this door.'

Milner turned to look at his companions. "Wasn't that displayed in Limbo in Dante's Inferno?"

"It was," said the Master. "I told you I made innovations and improvements. Decided this was the most appropriate place for you. Fact is, you aren't getting out once you get in there. No reprieve for you or any of the people you plunged into this nightmare."

"Ah, got you there," laughed Milner. "This is a nightmare. As soon as I see what's behind there, you'll let me wake up, won't you?"

"That's for us to know and you to find out," chorused his companions.

"I'm going through. The sooner I do, the sooner I can escape."

Milner opened the door and fell onto a frozen lake. As the ice parted to swallow him up to his neck, he saw a balcony above. On it stood his and Julian's family leaning over and shouting down at those trapped below. He was being arraigned with a list of the charges each of them wished to level at him. In their hands they waved large fans that sent cold air towards the ice which ensured it did not melt while they recited their litany.

Horrified, Milner forced himself to consciousness. His eyes opened. He found himself stretched naked on his bed, uncovered and exposed, unable to control his shivering. Beside him lay the tablet handed him by the Master in Limbo, the screen emblazoned with the words –

Julian was a psychiatrist and Gronya his patient.
How could you?

ෆ ෆ ෆ

PART 3

The Accounting

CHAPTER 12

Le Bouffon et le Chat

"ENTER," CALLED JESTER in response to a knock. The door swung open and Hera padded in.

"Ah. Hera. Come share my company and ruminate."

"Nothing untoward I trust?"

"Depends on your point of view."

"An answer that lives up to your name. I'll be more specific. On who and/or what? Or is it the usual – my earth family?"

"Exactly. How long since you joined us full time and only visit them in spirit?"

"A while. With time measured on different scales here, I don't keep track. It's painful watching the shenanigans, but it's been enjoyable haunting Master Milner. They talk about our nine lives and he is always content to see me. He attributes my presence to one of those lives being in a spiritual dimension. Spends ages in his favourite chair with a whisky chatting to me. I think he sees me. Was ever perceptive that way. Guess it comes with his wizard skills. None of the others are aware of my presence."

"Your relationship with Milner is why I summoned you. I don't believe he ever reflected deeply on the challenges we presented to him. Never revisited the riddles and his failure there. Did pull his neck in for a while, planned things with more caution, but seems to have relapsed and is once again lauding it over everyone. We need to reintroduce him to reality."

"Not the train thing again. You tried to set him on the right track last time, but do we have to run him along the same lines? Although enjoyable, the trip took a huge effort, but seems to have derailed, hence my summons. Anyway, he won't return to France since we hijacked him. Any alternative?"

"Certainly. Hoped he'd leave sleepers lie, but being Milner, can't resist rerouting and railroading."

"Enough. I'll never better you in the pun arena. I'll retire gracefully?"

"Thank you."

"How do you propose to bring further enlightenment to Master Milner?"

"Through various TVs and computers dotted around his house. I plan to show him a series of episodes from reality. He often drowses in front of a screen with a whisky in his hand. It'll get our message across and be less demanding on resources."

"Does this mean I'll stay longer than usual? I was comfortable there and will enjoy my old haunts. Never liked the new place Mistress took me when she moved in with that Julian character. He hates cats. Put up with me because she's besotted with our species. Talked in his dreams about how he loathes us, how we dug up his garden and left mess everywhere. Detests us more than the rabbits that plagued his vegetable patch in France. Close run thing which he despised most. Persuaded himself to feign love for me for my mistress's sake. Now it's going pear-shaped he no longer pretends. Complains to himself how we scratch furniture, pee on carpets and climb on kitchen counters. Says he doesn't understand how she puts up with it, considering the OCD she claims is the reason she can't go shopping, push supermarket trolleys around or travel on underground trains."

"He turned out a flatterer who sought benefit at her expense. Couldn't keep it up when she saw through his charade."

"Seems his Fiddler's Green got infested with weeds and the grass died. Then they lost the tuning fork, so the violins sound like shrieking hyenas."

"Or to put it another way, he haunts the grave of his dreams."

"*Touché*, Jester. We've been distracted. I thought we were discussing Master Milner and the labyrinth he needs to be guided out of. What are the starting points of his visions to be?"

"The riddles. We need to show him how the years since he united his wife and Julian in their longed for paradise has affected everyone."

"Could be painful."

"Undoubtedly. To mangle Catherine Aird's words – 'Each individual will be a good example and a horrible warning'."

"Or to use another analogy, he makes a lot of beds for others to cry and die in, and doesn't offer them tissues!"

"Quite so."

ଔ ଔ ଔ

SO HERA SET off to join Master Milner to guide him through incidents concerning the subjects of seven of the riddles. The last riddle related to Milner himself, for which Jester had a special occasion planned.

CHAPTER 13

The Howler

Who believes they are the sun
around which planets revolve
Who, if a planet wanders from their sphere
petulantly manipulates gravity until it is forced to return
Who constantly calculates, processes and reasons
with waspish glee
how to turn the pudding sour
even when made in their honour

HATTIE FORCED HER EYELIDS apart to survey the room. It seemed an eternity since 'that man' enticed Mum away and destroyed her family. *He claims to be a psychiatrist and a professional. I read in the GMC stuff he's supposed to practice ethics. Can't remember if I asked Ollah about it. It's a muddle.* She turned over; half-plumped her pillow and lay back. Made no difference eyes open or closed. Reality wouldn't go away. Dad's house echoed emptiness. *Although Mum comes from the love-nest most days, it's not the same, she doesn't live here, isn't available every minute I need her.* Yesterday was ages ago. Hattie knew Mum gave lots of time to nurse her, but resented it when she left for Ollah's or to get home as 'that man' had dinner ready. Despite fussing, Mum didn't get it right. She put Hattie's glass of water on the wrong spot or made her sip soup. Hattie sipped, but after a couple of spoonfuls complained of nausea. It was Mum's fault she'd to force food down. Mum lost authority to criticise her eating habits when she left them in the lurch. *My anorexic crisis is down to 'him'. Had it in control till he came between Mum and Dad. I'll never forgive him shattering my family.* Hattie hated how Dad had been humiliated, having to buy Mum a house and lend her his Bentley to drive 'him' all over. Reckoned her dad a fool, but then if Dad hadn't appeared to humble himself Mum might not fuss around to prove she loved them. *From all accounts 'that man' hardly ever visits his lot and doesn't see his ex. Seems she's unreasonable and blames Mum and Dad for her family collapse. Never was it Mum's fault. 'He' persuaded Mum she could have it all, get me and Ollah in control, then persuade everyone to accept Mum and him had a right to be happy. At whose expense?*

Hattie's fitful sleep left her exhausted. She wanted to exercise, but if anyone was home and heard they'd stop her. She'd been a prisoner in her room a few days, where Mum insisted she rest, unconscious, as much as possible. Hattie didn't want to. Her stomach pangs didn't signal hunger; their message was she was worthless, inept, incompetent and incapable of being loved. She deserved it, needed to punish herself for her failings. Those who suggested her thinking was distorted, that she was capable and adorable, lied. They said it to trick her into eating, but food was a poison. It made her obese and ugly. The nonsense about her looking thin proved it; why was she the only one who saw her fat? Anyway, if she was lovable why had everything gone wrong, why did her parents' marriage fail, why couldn't she keep a boyfriend? *I'm a good catch, why do I always pick losers? Drat. Forgot to switch my phone to silent.*

"Ollah."

"Hattie."

"Spoke to Mum. She's coming to you first. Don't keep her. Want her here."

"She'll stay as long as I need."

"That may be longer than you imagine."

"What's that supposed to mean?"

"You'll find out."

"Don't be mysterious, Ollah."

"Like I say, don't detain her too long. I have my own crises."

"Before you go, did I ask you about the GMC stuff, the ethics bit?"

"GM what?"

"Don't plead ignorance. The General Medical Council. Can't remember if we spoke about it. Anyway, you're a solicitor, you must've come across 'em."

"Heard of 'em. Why waste time on that?"

"Because standards of behaviour are part of my curriculum, believe it or not."

"Oh yeah! Solicitors are supposed to have an equivalent."

"Don't be sarkie, Ollah. Stuff like that spiralled to the bottom of your priority list, same as me. Given my attention to physiology, symptoms, drugs and treatments. Those were the reasons I reckoned medicine would be good, healing sick bodies etc. Never thought about standards and ethics until 'that man' did what he did. Didn't you begin your career with ideas of achieving something other than earning big bucks?"

"Can't honestly say one way or t'other. Dad persuaded me into law. You got more choice than me."

"Don't start that again."

"It's true, whether you like it or not."

"Anyway, since a purported medical professional broke Dad's heart, I can't ignore it. I sorted through the mountains of paper I get to read for uni. Physical healing ain't enough. Patients need to trust their doctor and he/she needs to practice ethics to earn it. That's what I read."

"You have been mooching it over. Swallowed the manual. Thought you weren't eating. Where'd you find the energy?"

"Don't extract the michael. Just answer."

"OK. I'll concede they make similar claims for law and solicitors."

"My point is some example 'that man' turned out."

"And you only just got there?"

"Give over. Hoped you'd agree on whether we

should do anything."

"Not now. Too late. If there's waves to be made, let others make 'em. Sure Dad would say the same. You don't want to be labelled a whistle-blower before your career starts. Don't go sinking the boat before it's launched or shoot the bird before it's in the air or whatever. Apart from which, you don't want your street drug history dragged up, do you?"

"How'd you hear about that?"

"Dad told me."

"Traitor. Why should it be? It's nothing to do with 'his' behaviour."

"Really! I understood 'that man' wangled treatment to get you off 'em. Dad paid him to make the problem go away quietly. Told Dad he destroyed the records, but provoke him and he might discover he still has 'em."

"Point taken."

"Remember, Dad is happy if Mum is. It's not for you to take the high ground. Dad's reputation is also at stake."

"Enough! I'll send Mum over when I've finished with her."

Hattie laid back and thought about the assortment of general practitioners, psychiatrists and psychologists had dad paid over the years to offer solutions on her anorexia. In lucid moments, she understood control over symptoms was the best outcome; there was no 'cure'. *Never stopped me pushing though. Always another boundary to test. Dad was always a pushover – money wise. Affection was different, for that I'd to stand in line behind Mum and Ollah.* Hattie hated the cat fights between the three of them while Dad walked away or solved problems with bribes. She overheard Mum and Dad talking once, not long after 'that man' took Mum as a patient. He told Mum to tell Dad they must present a united front – how she and Ollah used food to manipulate to get the upper hand. Dad insisted it was fanciful nonsense and got angry. His girls wouldn't do such a thing. Hattie didn't listen to the rest. She started to cough and panicked. Anyway, she wasn't sure she wanted to learn more, so crept back to bed to lie awake for hours, regretful at losing her nerve and wondering what else 'that man' said that she missed. Didn't take note of him then, except he was a psychiatrist and annoyed her.

Hattie woke to knocking on her door. Mum poked her head around.

"Sorry to wake you. Can you come downstairs? Dad and I need a chat."

"What about? Can't you come up here? What's wrong? You bin crying. What's up?"

"Just come downstairs – please."

Hattie sat up, then flopped back against her pillow. Something was up. Was it what she longed for? Would life return to normal? Had Mum and that creature's relationship collapsed? Was it payback time? Hattie didn't give a hoot for 'his' family, only her own. None of what happened was Mum's fault. What a piece of work 'that man' turned out? How could he? What possessed him? He obviously groomed Mum during her years of therapy. *He's the reason I relapsed and am in bed at Dad's house instead of at uni. It's what's happened since Mum left that undermined my confidence, made me feel worthless. He's more important to her than we are and it ain't fair. We should be her priority; especially me as he's responsible for my symptoms being out of control. Maybe things will come right again.*

Another knock.

"Come on, Hattie. We're waiting."

"OK. Coming."

Hattie descended the stairs lightheaded but confident. *Must get my thoughts in order, not appear too triumphant when Mum announces it's over.*

Milner pointed to a seat at the dining room table where she should sit. *Why are Mum and Dad opposite?* Her grin dissolved as she looked from one to the other. Mum's eyes were swollen and red – wouldn't look Hattie in the eye – kept her head down – slumped onto her chest. Hattie noticed Mum bite her lip.

"We need you to stay calm, Hattie," said Milner.

"Why? What's up?"

"There's been an accident. It wasn't Mum's fault, but Hera is dead."

"No... No... Not my precious, wonderful, loving, gorgeous Hera. She can't be."

"She is."

"Who murdered her? That creature you live with, Mum?"

"No one murdered her. She ran into the road and was hit by a car."

Hattie went numb. Her brain said scream, smash things, but her arms and legs ignored the commands. She stared at her parents, but their faces blurred. Everything went into slow motion. Dad talked at her, but she couldn't make out the words. Uncontrollable rage welled up from her middle regions and registered itself in sudden excruciating pain in her hand. She looked down to realise she'd smashed her fist on the table although wasn't aware she moved her arm. She wanted to hit Mum. She jumped from her chair, which went flying. Milner moved to place himself between her and her mother. Hattie sensed she wouldn't achieve her objective and collapsed in his arms, her strength exhausted as she gave way to tears.

"Will you calm down so we can have a rational discussion?" asked Milner.

"Rational. You expect rational? You allow the man who destroyed our family to murder my cat and then ask for rational?"

"No one murdered Hera. If you listen, Mum will explain. She's as upset as you. You forget when you brought Hera home as a kitten, it was Mum who took on her care, loved her as much if not more than you."

"Then why take Hera to live in a strange house with that creature? You never asked if I agreed. You decided it between you. Mum promised Hera would be safe, but she wasn't. I haven't seen Hera for ages because I won't set foot in that wretched place."

"The same thing could've happened here."

"No. This was Hera's home. If she was on a street outside the love-nest, it was because she was confused, wasn't happy, was trying to get home."

"You're hysterical, Hattie. You need to calm down."

"Why should I? Bet that creature let Hera out deliberately. I don't live on Cabbage Stalk Lane. He doesn't like cats. Pretended to like them to lure Mum from us."

"Will you calm down and listen to your mother?"

"No. I'll never forgive her for deserting us to live with a cat murderer. All I can see when I look at her is Hera lying injured and in pain under car wheels."

"Right. Enough," said Milner. "I took the precaution of booking an extra session with your therapist. Get upstairs, shower and compose yourself. I'll take you to see her."

Hattie retreated, lay on her bed and sobbed. Hattie knew all along 'that man' would bring grief. Ollah agreed. They discussed it often; how Ollah believed he feigned friendship with Mum and Dad so he and Adelle could sponge off her parents while he seduced Mum. Ollah said Mum and Dad had nothing in common with them and told Hattie she challenged Mum and Dad on why they tolerated them hanging about. *Ollah told me Adelle told Mum we'd no right to question her friendships. Don't know how Ollah found out. Stupid Adelle didn't realise the reason for sponging off Mum and Dad in the first place was so 'he' could groom Mum to desert us. If she understood she might not have sucked up. Eugh, the idea makes me ill.*

Hattie reckoned Ollah was right about Adelle. She was a tiresome, conceited woman, always on about how she found her rock when she married 'that man'. *Big joke – look how easily he left her for Mum. Not so smug now, I bet. Only had to put up with her twice that I remember. Ignored her as much as possible. There was the incident at the Moulin restaurant in France when I had a wobble over second year exams. They sat me next to Mum and opposite 'him'. Eugh! Also had to endure Adelle's dreadful relatives. What was Dad thinking?* The occasion at home in London was worse though. Hattie never understood what possessed Mum and Dad to have them to dinner that night. *They must've been uncomfortable. Went all quiet when I turned up. I was in one of my well phases; everything fine. Mum was keen for me to eat and prove I was happy. From something she said I guessed she wanted 'him' to see how the tactics he taught her to deal with me had positive results. I played along, didn't say no, but didn't swallow much either. Despite what 'that man' believed, Mum knew I was unhappy with her entertaining intruders.* Hattie hoped they got the message she gave off loud and clear.

A knock on the door interrupted her day-dreaming.

"Come on, Hattie. You need to get ready for Dad to take you to your appointment. Can I help?"

"Don't want your help. Hera had your help. Look what happened to her."

"Hattie, please. You're hurt and angry. Let's deal with what is, not what we want the situation to be."

"Thanks for the advice, but I'll rely on others from now on. You betrayed me and Hera. I won't forgive you."

Hattie watched her mother shut the door and thought she heard a muttered 'maybe I'll get some peace for a while then!'

03 03 03

"So, HATTIE. YOU had distressing news today?"

Hattie eyed her therapist and tried to fashion a convincing sneer.

"Might say that."

"Do you want to talk about it?"

"Isn't that why I was kidnapped and brought here?"

Hattie examined her therapist's face. *Come on – show something in response to my outrageous statements.*

"It'll help to talk. I know you know that. Where shall we begin?"

"Reckon I'll make a good doctor when I qualify."

"That's some way off. But if it's where you wish to start, tell me why."

"My illness and experience with 'that man' give me a thorough understanding of patients' needs and the standards a physician must maintain. It's why I'll specialise in psychiatry. At first I considered surgery, but psychiatry is more up my street, don't you reckon?"

Harriet searched the face opposite. *Ah... was that a*

*Mona Lisa-like ambiguous smile that crossed her lips or was
it a scowl? Am I getting to her?*

"It's good to speculate on a speciality, but you must
qualify first. Can we concentrate on today?"

"If you must. Of course if Mum really loved us – as
she pretends – she wouldn't have gone off to live with
someone else. Can't understand why Mum is infatuated
with 'him'."

"You're very angry, aren't you?"

"A little."

"We discussed anger before. How it is negative and
affects self-esteem."

"You told me so – often. I repeat your mantra not to
let anger at others' behaviour control me. But this
situation has overwhelmed me. Taken away my certainties."

"How can we restore them?"

"We can't. Hera died 'cause Mum was selfish. I must
be worthless and useless as well, otherwise she wouldn't
have gone off with 'that man' and taken Hera."

"Let's not dwell on Hera but concentrate on you."

"Why, what good would that do?"

"You're allowing what happened to undermine your
progress."

"Mum and 'that man' are responsible."

"But you can take back control. Your resilience is low
due to your anorexic crisis, but you can fight it. Remember your 'crisis' questions. 'Who in your life have you
lost, or might lose, because anorexic rules demand so

much of your time?' Did you think that's fair?'"

"I need to refocus attention on recovery, don't I?"

"Right. Be positive. Don't alienate support. Your mum made a mistake, but I suspect she regrets it more than you. Don't lose her support because you're angry with what she did, not who she is. She loves you."

"You're right. Fact is, he's the professional but his family is the one falling apart. He's the one who should answer questions like 'Who's suffered because you had sex with Mum and stole her from her family?' Does he reckon it's fair to anyone?' Does he care about his lot at all? My family for all their faults stick together."

"Banish 'him' from your head. Consider yourself and what you need to recover and get back to uni."

Cg Cg Cg

BACK HOME, HATTIE reflected. She'd recover from this bout stronger. The therapist helped her refocus on positives. Uni helped. Studies brought rationality – helped her understand and disperse cloudy preoccupations. She'd suffered treatments, in and outpatient, understood behavioural therapy and the challenge to her notions of 'fatness' and distorted reasoning. They gave insight to self-help manuals and exercises she'd attempted. Problem was, they were based on the false premise of 'normal' that everyone aspires to. *I'm not normal, I'm ugly, and fat and worthless. Otherwise why would Mum leave me for a man who means nothing? Stop it. You aren't supposed to think that, Hattie. It's easier when you're in a therapy session. Thing is I can't escape the idea it's not my thinking that's distorted, it's theirs. Stop it. My brain is tired. How do I square this circle?* She'd read about biological causes of eating disorders. Wondered if they caused her relapse, not bad family dynamics. Perhaps it was abnormalities in her brain's serotonergic and dopaminergic systems due to inborn genetic vulnerability. She'd read it up and pondered if there was mileage in the argument that when Mum and Dad criticised or argued with her while she was ill, unstable biological changes set off the illness. Whatever the truth, it wasn't her fault. 'That man' caused the problem. *When I'm well, I trust Dad when he tells me how clever and bright and gorgeous I am. It's when I can't cope and feel fat I think he's lying. The therapist calls it emotional resilience? Where's mine gone?*

Exhausted, she swallowed a sleeping pill. Sleep might stop the jumble of ideas running riot in her skull. She read the bottle label, but couldn't recall what her formulary said about side effects. Did it matter? She wanted to be unconscious, but stomach pain prevented this. Hattie gulped down the tablet. Some hours later she woke. Had she dreamed or hallucinated? The creatures she spent time with while unconscious were vivid, half snake and half worm, large parts of their bodies immersed in a foul, slushy bog. Glazed blank eyes suggested blindness. Someone named them Werpils, a nasty subspecies who, when they rested their mouths to aid digestion, embedded their noses in the mire, then waved their back claws in the air – if they could get them up.

Hattie remembered leaning towards them for a better view. She was overpowered by the stench. She jerked her head and heaved the instant she recognised her likeness attached to one of the monstrous bodies distorted into horrible shapes by what it swallowed whole, prescription pills, bags of illegal drugs, syringes, money. The Werpil that resembled her shovelled stuff into its mouth with webbed paws adapted to ensure maximum intake. Blindness made the Werpil unaware of fellow gobblers, but when it sensed an item it wanted to purloin being claimed by another, it clawed and screeched until the other gave it up, at which point the loser returned to the pile, reached out and took something else, while the winner stuffed the prize between its jaws. The Werpils had no idea of the size of the surrounding mounds. Large beetles, working in teams like a conveyor belt, resupplied the piles, while the Werpils gorged.

Haunted by these images, she remembered something she meant to do and reached over to check in her bedside drawer. She'd been given two BMI calculators by a drug rep. He offered one, but she begged two, one for her, the other for Ollah. *Rats, they're gone. Mum must have cleaned the drawers out.*

CƷ CƷ CƷ

THE IMAGES ON the screen faded. Milner shivered. Although his lap felt warm the rest of him was cold to touch. Was he awake or had he been dozing? He thought he tried to reach out and blank the screen several times, but something glued him in his seat. He looked down to see Hera looking up.

"What you doing here, young lady?"

"Jester sent me."

"Jester? Why?"

"He'll explain. He's discovered an app that allows him to do video conferencing and thought he'd try it out on you for starters."

Milner turned to the computer.

"Welcome, Master Milner. Seems this app thingy does work. How good to see you. I trust you are well?"

"All the better for seeing you."

"Do I detect sarcasm?

"Wish you'd leave it be, Jester. Don't want to see this stuff. It's like eating cold, lumpy mashed potato."

"Really?"

Milner stared at the screen, wishing away Jester's image.

"Really. Why can't you desist?"

"Is it because Hera's death upset you? Or because Hattie is happy, content and knows what she's about? That everyone else in this saga is doing as well as her?"

"Sarchasm still your strong point then, Jester?"

"An excellent word your daughter appropriated. Describes the situation well. Alternatively, you might consider me a therapist getting you to focus on what a joke your meddling turned into."

"Are you suggesting therapy is a joke?"

"Your interpretation, not mine. I heard laughter is the best medicine; he who laughs last laughs longest. Can you laugh at the outcomes?"

"I won't trade polemics with you, Jester. I want to be left alone."

"I'm here to remind you that you consider yourself to be the ultimate game player. But games don't go according to plans. You entered unchartered waters when you embarked on this journey with risky outcomes."

"Are you suggesting I should've plotted a better course before I began?"

"Would have helped. No. Your problem was you'd no chart to start. You believed your skills able to handle whatever happened. If you'd developed a chart, with proper consideration, you'd have realised the only outcome would be you'd run aground, but you carried on regardless."

"I'm sick of exchanging clevernesses with you, Jester. I'll turn off my computer. That'll shut you up."

"You could try. But my powers are greater than yours. You'll be apprised of the outcomes of your meddling one way or another. Those cards are in my hand. But for now I'll let you go. Sleep tight, don't let the bugs bite!"

ᔑ ᔑ ᔑ

CHAPTER 14

Begging a Stone to Talk

Who thinks they know everything but knows nothing
Who forges words into steel blades
honed to conceal double meaning
Who superciliously believes they are a distillation
of perfect balance and taste
but decanting their vessel reveals rancid overtones
which anosmia means they cannot detect
Who, seeing their reflection in the mirror of life,
sees no vanity
but prudence holding sway

S ABINA OPENED HER EYES. *Look at him lying there. What is it about selective memory?*

"Hey, can't you hear the kids?" she said, kicking Adam. "Ignoring it won't make them disappear in a puff of smoke. It's the weekend and feigning sleep won't help either. We agreed. Get up and do your duty."

"Are you suggesting I don't? I do. Tain't my fault I leave home early all week and come back late. In case you forgot, it's where the money comes from."

"Did I criticize? It's your turn this weekend on the schedule we worked out. You work long hours, but so do I, only mine involve getting the kids up every morning and into nursery before I begin the day job."

"Don't start that demented rant again. I told you – telling me over and over what a martyr you are doesn't make you one. You might fool yourself you're the exception, but here's the latest: you aren't!"

"There you go again. You rant – I state facts. Postpone this one till after you've seen to the kids, who need food before they tear more strips off each other."

"Sure. Madame Right About Everything Never To Be Contradicted. Your wish is my command! And to think I only get three hundred and sixty-five chances a year to obey."

Sabina pulled the duvet over her head. The bed shook as Adam got out. She listened to him descend the stairs and wade into the children's fight. She tried to tune out as the children vied for attention while he emptied the dishwasher looking for clean plates, then opened cupboards at Ben's direction to find what he said he wanted to eat. Then came the struggle to get Ben to sit at table. Adam's frustration oozed up through the floorboards. "OK, if you don't want cereal now what about an egg and/or toast? Your sister ate hers. You haven't touched anything. What's the matter? Isn't what I make good enough?"

In the hope it would be more effective at blocking out noise than the duvet, Sabina pulled a pillow over her head. It didn't work. She heard everyone troop out of the kitchen to the front room where the TV started up. The children fell silent, bewitched. *Which is worse, screaming kids or mindless cartoons? Do I care? Why am I so tired? The kids are a handful. Ben refuses to eat, Katy to sleep. They push my buttons for sure.* It'd been ages since Sabina remembered a satisfying, full night's sleep. For yonks she slept with Katy so she didn't spend the night up and down between her bed and Katy's cot, but then they had the terrible battle of wills to get the child to sleep alone. Thank goodness Dad helped pay for someone to come and help sort the problem.

What a miserable time they'd had. The upheaval from Dad's decision to leave Mum and make a new life with Gronya proved relentless. So much had gone on. It'd been hard deciding who deserved her loyalties, but Dad persuaded her she was right to award them to him. Her relationship with Mum always was precarious. Sabina agreed with Dad: Mum was Borderline Personality Disordered, emotional and unpredictable.

Sabina was astounded when, not long after Dad left, Mum complained to Adam that Sabina gave her the constant cold shoulder, made it clear she didn't want to talk to her, grunted in response to every attempt at communication and stared at her with blank eyes in sullen silence. Adam told Sabina he asked Adelle not to give up on her, with his dad so ill and Katy not sleeping, Sabina had a lot to cope with. It was natural everyone was tired. But Mum continued to probe and showed no patience or tolerance. Sabina wouldn't admit to Adam how Dad said he'd been miserable for years, which was why she couldn't trust Mum or speak to her.

Boy oh boy, did Mum wallow when Dad left. All her guff about how she won the lottery when she married him. Mind you, I suppose she did, he was forgiving and tolerant and put up with her insecurities. Why did I want to take care of Mum and Dad when I grew up? Must've been as deluded as her. All their lives Mum's difficult behaviour had been a problem. It made sense after Dad explained: how he'd shielded Sabina and Daniel, taking the brunt of it. How he tolerated it, Sabina couldn't imagine. Dad's patience was worthy of sainthood, and Sabina would have nominated him for one, only she didn't credit such nonsense. Dad said Gronya gave him strength, helped him appreciate life with Adelle had been a sham, that Adelle bullied, manipulated, and exploited his loving kindness. What a revelation, finding someone who understood and wanted to make him happy. *Told me he regretted fooling himself all those years his marriage was worth saving.*

Sabina thought about that first Mother's Day after Dad left her. *Why did I bother to ask her for lunch?* Mum gave Sabina some nonsense about being unhappy; said she didn't want the kids to see her break down or be like Banquo's ghost at the feast – so for everyone's sake suggested she keep away. *I told her not to talk rubbish, she must be there.* Mum insisted she wouldn't come, so that morning Sabina took Ben and Katy to Mum's flat with their presents. *Hoped if I surprised her she'd change her mind and come. She'd obviously been wallowing for hours and was in a terrible state. Trouble was, Ben ran up the stairs ahead of me and Mum opened the door to him on his own.* He was so terrified he threw a tantrum. When Sabina reached the top, the damage had been done. *Why couldn't she control herself? What was wrong with her? How dare she upset Ben?* Mum apologised, said she felt wretched and wished Sabina had given her time to prepare. *Told her straight off – I wouldn't play her games. Of course, she chose to misinterpret my words.* Any vestiges of sympathy or respect Sabina entertained for her drained away. *If I think back, I probably never respected her. Time makes it difficult to remember sequences.*

Why did Mum insist Dad owed her an explanation? He didn't; that he tolerated it for years was enough. Dad accepted responsibility, told Sabina he was sorry her relationship with her mother was damaged, suggested he should have stayed and put up with it to contain her bad moods so the family might stay together, but he couldn't take it anymore.

Sabina dragged herself from the bed. It was the only way to distract herself. Her legs felt like lead as she descended the stairs. She was grateful the children were occupied by the cartoons and didn't notice her. She hoped Adam would leave her alone, but after a few minutes he joined her in the kitchen.

"Been brooding again. Don't head shake and grimace. You can't hide it. It's written all over your face."

"You've no right to question me."

"Never change, do you? Never want to be questioned, always defensive. How do you expect anyone to help if you won't open up?"

"Oh boy, here we go again."

"Damn sure. Explain how, if Adelle was such a terrible mother, you took her to Barcelona as a surprise for her fiftieth. How come you wrote and published that book about her grandmother and your great grandmother together? Doesn't she have any redeeming features? She displayed generosity, especially the way she helped my mum and dad. Then she gave you a car. Surely that shows someone with compassion and empathy."

"Don't you ever listen? She has a PhD in manipulation."

"And you never manipulated anyone in your life, did you?"

"You got room to talk."

"Just saying."

"Mum was the arch-manipulator. Dad told me she did it to fool us into believing she loved us. But really it was a bribe because she's terrified of being alone in old age, terrified of her body being found years after she dies, decomposed in her bed."

"We're all afraid of the end of life. Why is it wrong for your mum to voice her fears?"

"I don't care anymore. Her self-fulfilling prophesy will come true. She offered me nothing my whole life. She may have paid to educate me, but my skill and talent got me where I am. She may have offered your parents a flat to live in, pretended to love her grandchildren, but it was all a sham. I owe her nothing."

Adam shrugged his shoulders, bowed and walked off to watch cartoons with the children. Sabina sat staring at her tea and the remains of the children's breakfast. *Mum was right on one score: They were all in pain. Mum let us all down, not accepting Dad's need to be happy making Gronya happy.* Mum's misery was self-inflicted; it came from her betrayal of everything a mother and grand-mother ought to be. Dad said so and he should know.

ᗶ ᗶ ᗶ

"COME ON. WE gotta go if we're gonna get there."

The kids dawdled while Adam loaded the car. It was Ben's birthday, and they were off to visit Adelle who was hosting a birthday party for Ben. Daniel, Natalie and Alexander would be there, and Ben and Katy were excited about seeing their cousin. Sabina dreaded it, but yesterday's events gave her a lot to tell Daniel and Natalie. Sabina strapped the children into their car seats then patted the camera and lenses to reassure herself she'd not forgotten them. Lots to photograph today.

After the usual tedious journey spent arbitrating the kids' arguments they arrived at Adelle's. The others were there, and the children lost no time spreading toys around. Natalie was supervising a painting session with Alexander while Adelle made tea and coffee in the kitchen.

"How did yesterday go?" asked Natalie.

"Dad arrived late for Ben's party."

"Why?"

"Had to spend hours hanging about because Gronya was at Milner's trying to console Hattie."

"What over?"

"Apparently Hattie's cat, the one living with Dad and Gronya, got run over and killed outside their house the day before."

"No."

"Yeah. Keep your voice down. Dad didn't want to leave Gronya who came back from seeing Hattie in a state. Gronya said she couldn't be at Ben's party as planned, but let Dad come so Ben wasn't disappointed at not seeing his granddad on his birthday. Mum's not supposed to find out. Don't want to give her anything to gloat over."

"Why should she?"

"Because she won't be able to help herself."

"Careful. Here she comes with the drinks. I'll phone tonight then you can spill."

"Sure. I need to get shots of the kids and everyone. Excuse me while I fix the lenses."

ᘓ ᘓ ᘓ

"DID YOU GET LOTS of pictures of the kids?" asked Adam later than evening.

"Yeah. Sure did. I'll upload them tonight."

"I'll bath the kids then. We'll look after they're in

bed. Must have some good ones. You took a lot."

"Right."

A few hours later, Adam retired. Sabina spent so long sorting the photos he said he'd leave her to it, they'd keep for another time. Sabina kept at it and a while later emailed her dad.

'Turns out to be easier to show you photos. Here is link – tell me when you've got what you need and I'll delete them. The blurry one with pics on a board – I think the top middle is Uncle H and family and the bottom left might be your grandmother. Also not pictured are graduation pics for uni; Shakespeare pics, trees pic, Mackintosh prints, a Miro and the Tunis pic – woman with shawl. I'll send more of furniture and stuff later.'

03 03 03

"YOU WERE AGES sorting the photos. Must've taken a lot."

"I did. Dad wanted some, so I sent him a whole load."

"Thought it went well, considering the grandpa party got messed up the day before. Feel sorry for Gronya losing the cat. Must've been horrible. Did you speak to Natalie?"

"Yeah. Something else to deal with here though. Mum sent this legal document for me to sign. Can you go through it and tell me what you reckon."

"OK. We'll discuss later."

The document in question concerned the flat Adam's parents occupied in the village. Some years before, when Sabina secured her lectureship at the university, she persuaded Mum and Dad to join her in investing in a flat for Sabina's use during term time. It saved her a commute or being forced to stay in horrible bed and breakfasts. Then they owned the property in thirds. Since then Mum and Dad had invested more and now owned three quarters. After Sabina's university post became permanent she and Adam settled themselves in the village and the family agreed to let Adam's parents live in the flat because of their difficult circumstances. Adam's dad was ill, didn't have long, and everyone wanted to support Adam's mum. At least that was the reason Adelle gave. Sabina was now convinced it was all manipulation on Mum's part. The document Mum wanted signing was to show the changed ownership percentages.

"Do you realise what this document in its current form means to your mum?" Adam asked later that evening.

"Yup, but I want you to confirm it for me."

"It means she gives up all right to her investment because this document gives you full control over when and how it is sold."

"Right. Dad has been told the same."

"So your mum, at a time when she is struggling with the end of her marriage, is signing documents like this. Do you think she knows what she is doing?"

"She says she's trying to protect your mum's right to live there no matter what happens."

"But the document is more than that. Does your mum understand its exact implications?"

"I don't care."

"That's obvious."

"Mum owes Dad and me for what she put us through all our lives. This document gives Dad and me control because once they divorce, Dad will side with me on everything. I'll make sure he doesn't suffer, but Mum will."

"Has this got anything to do with you tapping your dad for help with nursery fees?"

"No. That's different. You should be grateful he's willing to help. You know how expensive those fees are. I told him we want to be responsible for ourselves, having decided to have a second child, but now he's working again, having left Mum, we could do with temporary support if there's flexibility in his cash situation."

Adam walked away. Sabina heard him mutter 'demented'.

"So glad you felt free to mutter that. It's not good to let things fester," Sabina said to his back.

Adam turned.

"I'd try for one of your withering stares, darling, but can't manage them as expertly as you. My face wouldn't stay emotionless, but distort, and ugliness was never my forte."

C03 C03 C03

AFTER ADAM HAD gone upstairs, Sabina read the legal document, signed it and readied it to post to the solicitor. *How dare he call me demented?* Sabina was glad this document would make certain the money stayed in her control. Mum's ignorance was her own fault. Mum didn't deserve it; Dad's efforts earned it. All her guff about running Dad's private practice for years, making sure business flowed in and bills got recovered. Mum was nothing without Dad, his brains and efforts. He gave everything, she exploited his talent. She chose to alienate herself from Sabina, chose to play the martyr 'for the good of the grandchildren'. *Pretends to be grief stricken. False tears is all they are, designed to paint me bad. Her personality disorder would've been impossible to treat by any of the clinicians I work with, too hard-boiled and intractable. The car she gave me and her investment in the flat were all attempts to buy me. Now she's signing it away and is so stupid she's no idea what she's doing. Why should I watch out for her?*

CƷ CƷ CƷ

THE PHONE RANG as Sabina got in from hockey practice. Adam had put the kids to bed and Sabina wanted to shower and have dinner.

"I need to discuss an email that ended up in my email account," said Daniel.

"What email?" asked Sabina.

"I think it was addressed to Dad, but because there's a mistake in the characters before the .surname.org.uk part, it has diverted to my admin box."

Sabina grabbed an unopened letter lying on her desk and began to fan her face. She began pacing and Adam, who appeared at the bottom of the stairs, mouthed at her 'What's the problem?' 'Nothing' she mouthed back. She put down the envelope, bent over and tugged one-handed at the laces on her boots, then kicked them off. Sabina noticed Adam disappear into the kitchen. A few minutes later she was forced to slam the kitchen door shut to cut out the distraction from the pot banging going on.

"So why spy on Mum and take pictures for Dad?"

"Why do you think?"

"Don't know. I'm asking you. You're the one with the PhD in psychology, and Dad's the psychiatrist. I only put people to sleep."

"Convenient way to avoid talking to your patients."

"I'll ignore that. What I want to know is have you considered the ethics of what you did?"

"Mum deserved it?"

"Why?"

"Mum forced us to it. She's unreasonable to divorce Dad. He promised to take care of her and look after her. He worked hard to provide for her, but she wasted his efforts, and bullied him as well."

"But that's between Mum and Dad. Not our business."

"You're wrong. Mum forced Dad to ask for his share of everything through the solicitor. He shouldn't have to.

It was his by right. He provided it for them through his hard work."

"Wow. Must ask if you'll take the same attitude if you and Adam separate. What if he says he did all the work and is entitled to keep it all?"

"He won't because he knows I contributed half of everything."

"And Mum never contributed?"

"No. Dad told me she exploited him. I didn't want to accept it, but now I do; Dad explained to me. He needed my help, and I gave it. You need to decide where your priorities lie."

"My experience of Mum lately is she's been good with Alexander. She's just very sad."

"Watch out, it's all manipulation. She's trying to control you."

"I still consider your behaviour unethical. Whatever has happened, Mum doesn't deserve this."

"Think what you like. I won't discuss it. You've no right to judge me. No one has."

Sabina slammed the phone down as Adam appeared at the door.

"Dinner's ready. Hot spicy curry with lots of chilli. Hope you're hungry."

 CB CB CB

THE NEXT DAY SABINA received an email from Adelle, copied to Adam.

'Sabina. I am very unhappy and want answers. I hope

you'll give me some. I hope you'll find the compassion to grant me that. I have only one question. Why? I cannot understand what I did to deserve such treatment. I want to know if Adam knew what you were doing and colluded with you and your father in this underhand behaviour. The stuff in my flat was agreed with your father. He arranged for it to be moved here and helped deliver it. He has taken lots of stuff from the French house for which he has not sought my permission. This was being negotiated through solicitors. Why did you feel the need to interfere? Your father had the manifests. Why couldn't he consult those? Why did you do it? Your behaviour suggests you do not want me in your or your children's lives. Is it because you judge me by your father's standards and don't accept me as a mother who only wants the best for her children despite her failings? If I am not to be part of my grandchildren's lives I will accept that, but surely you must agree I deserve the courtesy of an explanation. Equally, if you do want me in your children's lives, you must see as your mother, I am entitled to be treated with respect.'

Sabina responded.

'We tried to support you as best we could in difficult circumstances (it has been a difficult year for all of us) but the unpleasantness now associated with Ben's birthday party (which was held for you) demonstrates spending time together is counter-productive at the moment. It does seem lashing out at me (or others) in response to negative events in your life is a pattern of behaviour to which I am now sadly accustomed and I do not want it around the children at such a formative age. I suggest while the divorce negotiations remain ongoing between you and Dad we use the space as a positive to reflect on how family relationships might be better in the future. I would welcome email contact, but ask you modify your language so it is not so aggressive or accusatory.'

ℭ ℭ ℭ

"ARE YOU REALLY going to send that to your mum?" asked Adam when she showed him.

"Sure am. She needs putting in her place."

"What about Daniel? I assume he told her about your emails to your Dad."

"I'll decide how to deal with him later."

Adam turned to walk away, and as he did so Sabina heard him mutter 'demented'.

Sabina stayed up long after Adam and the children had gone to sleep. She couldn't sleep. If Daniel had been standing in front of her she'd have slapped him. *Where'd he get the gall to phone me and say I behaved badly towards Mum? How dare he? He needs to consider his child and the danger she is to him. He doesn't realise she manipulated us into tolerating her unreasonable behaviour.* How Mum held down jobs all her working career Sabina had no idea. Must have lied about how employers valued her, exploited those she worked with by inflating her abilities. How she managed five years in one and ten in another

Sabina found hard to understand. One woman boss even begged her to go back when they heard she might be going to live near them again. Poor deluded soul.

Then there was Mum's intolerance of Hattie and Ollah's eating disorders. Sabina knew eating disorders to be destructive, but Mum tried to suggest they were mislabelled, they weren't eating disorders, but attention-seeking disorders, and said how Gronya's girls competed with Gronya for Milner's attention. Dad put the kybosh on that interpretation. Had to. It was another example of the difference between how the world is and how Mum wants it. *I was shocked when I realised Gronya was his patient.* They hid that one, but now Sabina understood why Dad did it. Sabina didn't blame him, even though it distressed her. Sabina spoke to someone at work who told her dad's behaviour was unethical, that it would lead to upset and misery. *What did they know? Dad reassured me he had it all in control and was entitled to pursue his own happiness after years of heartache with Mum.*

Sabina had no doubt about her support for Dad. Mum got worse after Dad left. She behaved despicably towards Gronya lots of times. Dad told Sabina about Mum's anger when Gronya texted him, especially that day he met Mum to go over their affairs and share the money out. Dad told Sabina Mum had a tantrum and demanded he switch off his phone and not read texts from his whore every five minutes, who must be attention-seeking because she felt insecure. *How thoughtless and nasty. Didn't she realise she confirmed what*

Dad said about her? Despite Dad's generosity, Mum carried on being unreasonable and ghastly.

Mum lost weight. *Another ploy to manipulate I bet. I'm in pain because she was my mum. When she asked why I betrayed her, I was right to defend myself, protect my children. All the years she made Dad suffer, now it's her turn. It's true you reap what you sow.* Sabina couldn't have someone so unpredictable around. She thought to distract herself by beginning the book review she'd to submit for a psychology journal. She searched the papers on the desk. *Drat, wonder where that's gone.* She turned to the bookshelves where stuff got shifted by Adam if he used the computer. She riffled the piles, moving some to the desk. As she did so the books and journals behind revealed themselves. Sudden tears welled up. Standing innocently among the lined up volumes was the big folder Mum prepared for her grandchildren; the one that contained the family history full of birth, death, marriage certificates and other documents she and Mum spent ages gathering before writing up the biography. It'd been a rollercoaster of a project, working to uncover her great-grandmother's past. Mum's early years came under the spotlight as more and more information surfaced. Some if it was gratifying to learn, but some surprises shocked. They worked well together and tying it all up proved satisfying. *Where are my tissues? Why do I cry every time I think of her? I know I don't need her in my life, I don't miss her, I don't. I must talk to Dad. Maybe he'll still be up if I phone now.* Sabina dialled his number but was diverted to his message service.

Wish I could rid myself of that image I came across the other day. Sabina didn't remember where it came from, perhaps she dreamed it, or maybe saw it on TV, but it stuck in her mind like an earworm. Every time she closed her eyes she visualised creatures, half-snake and half-worm, large parts of their bodies immersed in a foul, slushy bog. Sightless, they gazed with blank, blind eyes. *Someone said they were "Werpils", a nasty subspecies of something or other. When they rest to digest, they stick their noses in the slush and wave their back claws in the air if they can get them up.* Sabina didn't understand why she could smell their stench when they were creatures from imagination. The Werpils lay amidst mouldy food, containers, bags, bottles, piles of bricks and mortar, wood and money they shovelled into their mouths with webbed paws adapted to ensure they got the most in. Blind, they were unaware of fellow gobblers, but if they sensed an item they wanted might be claimed by another, clawed and screeched until one or the other gave it up, at which point the loser returned to the pile, reached out and took something else, while the winner stuffed the prize into its mouth. The Werpils had no idea of the size of the surrounding mounds. Large beetles, working in teams like a conveyor belt, resupplied them, while the Werpils kept gorging.

Why would I remember such a nasty scene?

 G3 G3 G3

CHAPTER 15

The Lion's Den

Whose anvil was intellect
on which questionable aims were forged
Who quietly reasoned away obstacles
in the search for a truth
obtuse, painful and difficult to manoeuvre
Who succumbed to the temptations of Babylon
and became steadfast in upholding ambiguous ideals
with an intermittent and destructive roar

DANIEL RAISED AN EYELID to undertake a surreptitious recce. Sounds from downstairs suggested everyone was in the kitchen. Daniel didn't want to face the world. They were driving to Dad's later to stay overnight, although Natalie wasn't keen. The first visit they made Daniel suspected Natalie went out of curiosity to inspect the love nest. He presumed this trip was to assess Gronya's progress with her plans to 'make it theirs'. Given Natalie's antipathy towards Gronya he surmised her interest was voyeuristic; to glean gossip. It was all too tangled. A few more minutes under the duvet wouldn't hurt. It was painful; he struggled to accept Mum and Dad really had broken up. Even more incredible was the misery that started with such cataclysmic intensity.

He appraised his surroundings. Meticulously hung handmade curtains, quilted bedspread with matched cushions; all harmonious, homely, loving, warm and cosy. Their home displayed Natalie's talents to perfection; a *place for everything and everything in its place.* The dressing table with pots and creams, pictures on white walls; all arranged like cogs on a wheel, each item the right size and shape for the space it occupied so life ran with effortless smoothness. He often wondered if he'd alighted in a fairy tale land where a magical twitch of Natalie's nose or wiggle of her ear, made each thing slot in perfectly and where dust never dared settle. Friends envied him, praised Natalie as a wonderful homemaker, with the bonus of being a stunner in the looks department – all a sensible guy wanted and needed in a wife. *Why aren't I content? Why this sensation of being boxed in and stifled?*

Natalie's family oozed loyalty. Not like his. Emotional turmoil was all he had to show for his lot. It came out of nowhere. One moment he'd a steady, caring family in which to rear his son, the next it was shattered; his idea of the perfect clan dissolved in the ether. Comprehension evaded him. Mum and Dad the ideal couple, devoted and steadfast; then with alarming speed they betrayed every value ever taught him. He wanted to be a doctor same as Dad since he was small. Didn't fancy psychiatry, but other parts of humans needed care, and after med school specialised in anaesthetics. 'What's the difference between a gas man and a heating engineer?' he would joke when meeting people socially. 'One saves lives by putting 'em to sleep, the other keeps 'em warm.' He never understood why people who weren't anaesthetists didn't get it, until Natalie enlightened him.

Happy, busy sounds drifted up the stairs. Natalie had made bread. The machine beeped to indicate a complete baking cycle. He listened to Alexander drag his chair-cum-stool across the floor to help Mummy open the lid. He heard Natalie insist Alexander don his apron and oven gloves that hung on a special hook below his and hers in the kitchen. The noise of taps and water signalled the hand washing ritual before the loaf got decanted to stand on the cooling rack. Natalie timed it to perfection. It would be cool enough to slice for breakfast. *Natalie and the kid will enjoy it. These days it tastes of sawdust to me.* He ate like an automaton to keep up strength, but hated mealtimes and all that pretence at family togetherness.

He sighed heavily, jiggled his nose between his finger and thumb, and then rubbed his eye sockets and forehead with the heel of his hand. He turned over to face the middle of the bed. He laid his fist on the warm spot Alexander occupied after he woke early and Natalie let him snuggle up in a groove between their pillows while he played on her tablet. Anosmia rendered Daniel unable to distinguish the baby smell Natalie went on about. Perhaps he was lucky. Before a heavy cold did its job he'd associated smells with pleasure, but the last few years robbed him of that joy. Daniel sensed Natalie allowed Alexander to sit between them and play in the hope he'd wake and join in, but he doggedly pretended to be asleep. They gave up in the end; left him to it. Natalie moaned at his missing precious first years, how they loved him, and how much he'd to live for, but it washed over him. As an adult he should be able to deal with Mum and Dad's break up, but it'd been bitter and angry and Dad told him things he didn't want to hear. Mum tried to do the same, said she'd to defend herself, but it was like being in a whirlwind, unable to escape, one minute he believed Dad, the next Mum. The few bits of evidence as to what really happened proved contradictory and confusing.

Natalie disagrees, but I'm pleased I've work to bury myself in, means I can avoid the issues. Suppose I'll have to get up. Thank goodness it's the weekend and I'm not on call. He looked at the cup of tea on his bedside stand. They put it down earlier, but he kept his eyes closed and feigned sleep. Alexander poked him, but got shushed away back downstairs with Mummy to prepare the meal and lay the table. Alexander was good like that, ready to help his mother with chores then tidy up. Knew where everything belonged and was meticulous in making sure it all got put away properly.

Daniel sat up and gulped down the lukewarm tea. It

broke his thirst. Alexander called up the stairs to signal breakfast, so he dragged back the covers and hoisted himself out of the warm space. Natalie had laid his dressing gown over the foot of the bed. He pulled it on and wandered out of the door to stand at the top of the stairs. A cold draught from an open window made him shiver. As he descended he glanced at the photos that lined the staircase. Among pictures from bygone days gaps had appeared; ones that featured his family. Did Natalie remove them because they no longer represented an harmonious whole? Should he blame her? He was ashamed of the way his parents' marriage disintegrated. *Why feel guilty, it wasn't my fault?* Natalie insisted she wanted Alexander to grow up in a loving environment, untainted by the nastiness she came across in families whose children she taught at school. Why had his parents let him down?

Daniel seated himself at the table. Natalie gave Daniel a look of reprimand, he assumed for making them wait, but was past caring. Alexander helped himself to the fruit and toast Natalie laid out beside his special bottle of homemade preserve. He carefully extracted a spoonful to put on the side of his plate and picked up his knife to spread it. He wanted to do everything himself and was proficient, but had the occasional mishap. It didn't matter with jam, but liquids proved problematic. When he spilt things, he wouldn't be persuaded to continue until Natalie wiped up the mess.

As Daniel contemplated the toast in front of him, a

foot appeared beside his plate.

"Stop that at once, Alexander," he bellowed as he grabbed the child's foot and pushed it beneath the table. Alexander howled with pain as Daniel observed Natalie flinch mid munch of her toast.

"Alexander," said Natalie, "that's no way to behave. You don't want to upset Mummy or Daddy do you? Please stop."

Daniel observed Alexander cast a glace from him to Natalie then back again. With a fixed gaze straight into Daniel's eyes, Alexander pushed his chair back to raise his foot and place it carefully on the table beside Daniel's plate. *I will keep my temper, but this brat will not get away with it.*

"Perhaps 'Mummy' could explain to Alexander how to behave, as he has clearly forgotten what she told him."

"Sarcasm won't work. Perhaps you might take your toast to your study while Alexander and I finish breakfast together and discuss table manners."

"Your endless patience isn't working. You better get him to stop, or I'll discipline him, then he'll be sorry."

"We'll discuss it later, if you don't mind."

"I want to discuss it now."

"Really? I thought you said as I was the teacher you'd leave it to me."

"I have, but your tactics aren't having the desired effect."

"Very well. I wasn't going to say so, but fact is, Alexander only does this when you decide to grace us with your presence at table. Perhaps you'd reconsider your decision to discuss this now and postpone it to later as I asked."

Daniel snatched his plate and with an angry snort left the room. He trained to doctor, she to teach. That was why he let her deal with disciplining Alexander. Till now. *Was I wrong to leave it all to her? Not sure where the boundaries have shifted. Her calm patience is as annoying as Daniel's naughtiness. Oh, Dad, why have all my certainties been flushed away? Am I proficient at anything I do? I always relied on you for guidance and reassurance. Natalie is disappointed with how things are. How did we get in this mess?*

Daniel finished his toast and listened as Natalie helped Alexander wash and dress after which all went quiet. He wandered into the kitchen. The table had been cleared and dishes disposed of in the dishwasher while Natalie and Alexander were nowhere to be seen. A note propped up on the dresser said – 'Gone to Mum and Dad's. Enjoy making love to your PhD. See you later. We're all packed and ready to go to Julian and Gronya's.'

Daniel did his ablutions. He wandered back to his study and sat in front of his computer to stare at his algorithm. His thesis came from a temporary secondment looking at patient safety issues. It proved hard work, but gave him an excuse to ignore the emotional turmoil. Cold numbers and statistics on the screen that made pretty graphs out of catchment areas could be controlled and manipulated. Didn't matter if they didn't like what he did to them, he moulded them into facts to help medical administrators develop policies to control patients.

Concentration proved impossible. Daniel opened his email inbox. He hadn't looked since last week after Ben's party at Mum's. He'd been tired and too busy at work. One email caught his eye. The name before the .surname.org.uk was a jumble. As administrator he often got these emails. He'd open them to find the intended addressee, readdress and send them on. Mostly it was junk mail. He stared at the screen with wide eyes then blinked rapidly. He struggled to breathe as light-headedness crept over him. He phoned Natalie.

"Come home now? I need to show you something. Leave Alexander with your parents?"

"What's so important?"

"Just come. Don't argue."

He paced the room, tugging his earlobe, looking at the clock. *How long does it take to drive a few miles? Why so slow? What's wrong with her? Why isn't she here?* Natalie's key grated in the front door. He shouted from the top of the stairs.

"Get up here. I need you to see this."

Natalie took the stairs two at a time.

"What's so important you dragged me here in a panic?"

"Look at this email."

"What email."

"The one on the screen. Are you blind? Can't you

see?"

Daniel stared as Natalie perused the screen. He watched her eyes widen and the colour drain from her cheeks. *What's wrong? Why's she taking so long? Is she too thick to realise what it means?*

"C'mon. Say something."

"What can I say? I'm stunned. Can't take it in. How could they? Whatever Adelle may have done, this is below the belt, way below."

"Now you understand why I wanted you here fast."

"Sure. But the more important question is what are you going to do?"

"Don't know. Need to think."

"You'll have to talk to them."

"Don't tell me what to do. I don't know what to do. I feel sick."

"I'll make tea."

"You do that. Your answer to everything. What else did I expect?"

"Don't adopt that tone with me. To imply I'm stupid or inept may make you feel good, but convinces no one. I'm stunned and can't begin to imagine how betrayed Adelle feels if she knows. If she does she must be absolutely wretched. Are we going to your dad's tonight? This makes it awkward."

"We'll go, but I won't discuss this with him till I've spoken to Sabina since she generated the damn email. I already planned to talk to him about other stuff. This on top will make it too difficult."

"OK. But it'll be uncomfortable and tense all round."

⚃ ⚃ ⚃

DANIEL AND JULIAN shared a whisky after everyone had gone to bed.

"C'mon, son. You've something on your mind."

"Tell me about the time we didn't talk for the year right before I met Natalie."

"What do you want to know?"

"Why you and Mum treated me the way you did."

"As I remember it, we were packing the house and moving to France and we needed you to take your stuff from the attic."

"Yeah."

"You came and took it, then wrote and said you were fed up. Said we kicked you out of your home so you had nowhere to go if you needed. I understood, but Mum said as you were over twenty-one and fully vaccinated and you'd been to Australia for a year, had come home, was working and renting your own place she didn't understand your attitude and got upset."

"So?"

"She composed the reprimand about how you'd shown us disrespect; how we'd spent all our lives giving you everything; how we were doing something for ourselves and wondered why you questioned our right to do so. Then she made me write it and send it from me."

"I remember. Didn't get why you wrote and not her.

And you went along with it?"

"You've experienced her dictatorial moods. I got no choice. Anyway, you replied with what she regarded as more hurtful comments, and that was that."

"Still don't understand why you did what she said."

"Mum insisted you be punished for the way you hurt her and told me I wasn't allowed to speak to you."

"Like I say, why do it if you didn't agree?"

"She insisted we put on a united front, teach you a lesson. Daren't go against her. I was scared. Then she spent every day after crying pretending she missed you. All sham. You know how she manipulates."

"I guess you've always been the tolerant one."

"Like to think so. She used to say she hated rule by committee as nothing ever got done. That was why it happened her way or no way."

"Did she say that?"

"Not in so many words."

"Yeah. Never forgave her for embarrassing me that time at school when she waded in to tell the teachers off when I was being bullied. Made it worse."

"Pretty typical behaviour for her."

"Don't reckon she did it because she cared. Just wanted to throw her weight around."

"Something like that."

Daniel retired. Confused thoughts obsessed him. So Dad wasn't responsible for that miserable year. Now made sense. The things Mum said when Dad left her weren't true. Dad explained Mum catastrophized every problem, would shout and rant and make life unbearable. No wonder Dad was sad when he came to visit Daniel. Had Mum been like that the whole forty-five years they spent together? Mum was forceful, but surely Dad hadn't been that henpecked; otherwise why put up with it? Was Dad so patient? Daniel was sure he'd never forgive Mum.

But then what about the other stuff? Mum visited regularly and was good with Alexander. They played for hours. Mum couldn't do enough for him. While Dad seemed to withdraw from Alexander, Mum got closer. Dad came once or twice, but turned up as a passenger with Gronya driving her husband's Bentley. When Natalie asked Mum why, she said Gronya did it to display him in a Bentley trophy cabinet so we understood who he belonged to. *Spiteful but true. Why did Dad have so little pride?* Then there was Christmas. Natalie invited Dad to come to them. Dad refused, said he needed to stay around while Gronya went to her family. When they got drunk and made snide remarks Gronya wanted him home so she could retreat and him be there to comfort her. *It was like we didn't count.* Daniel's instinctive repulsion over the photo thing nagged at him. If everything Dad said about Mum was true it didn't excuse what Dad and Sabina did. Daniel's bewilderment since opening that email was relentless. It went against every ethical bone in his body, worse than Dad's adulterous relations with a millionaire ex-patient. *Why won't these thoughts stop whirling? Just need to sleep.*

The next morning they packed to go home.

"Well that was some goodbye," said Natalie.

"Don't start."

"So explain why your dad left us to get breakfast and entertain ourselves, then wave us off from an upstairs window instead of coming down."

"Don't know. Don't want to."

"So… Are you going to tackle him and Sabina over the photos?"

"I need to concentrate on driving. Let me be."

Ↄ Ↄ Ↄ

SOME DAYS LATER DANIEL spoke to Sabina who offered short shrift. Sabina contended she did nothing wrong, Mum forced them to do it. All their lives Daniel hated to challenge his sister – Miss Bossy Boots he called her. He disliked the way she would glare and go silent if she didn't like what you said, then ignore you. But this was impossible to overlook. Daniel asked why it wasn't left to the solicitors, but Sabina insisted Mum was aggressive, devious and uncooperative, demanding more than she should. Daniel didn't know what to believe. Dad lived with a wealthy woman in a mansion while Mum occupied a two-bedroomed flat with little from their married life. What was Dad on about?

Daniel phoned Dad.

"I need to ask. Were you aware of what Sabina had planned? Did you approve?"

"Can I refuse to answer?"

"It would help me understand."

"What's done is done. Can't be undone."

"But I need answers."

"How will it help? Sabina told you everything."

"So you know we spoke."

"She told me she explained what needed to be explained."

"Why will neither of you tell me whose idea it was?"

"Because it's irrelevant."

"To you maybe. Would you have forbidden Sabina if you did discuss it?"

"Sorry, son. Can't help."

Daniel hung up. *Can't or won't?*

ଓ ଓ ଓ

DANIEL TOSSED AND TURNED during another sleepless night. *Mum wanted to go to the GMC but seemed unable to decide. I should have done it, but In the middle of trying for a consultant position couldn't risk being seen as a whistle-blower. Thank goodness Natalie persuaded Mum to wait until I get my consultancy.* Daniel tried to stop thinking about Mum in her flat while Dad lived in luxury in Gronya's mansion. *As Mum pointed out, it's bigger than he could afford during their lives together. What's wrong with my parents? It was their business. Why did it spill out so badly? Now Sabina refuses to see Mum and won't let her see her grandchildren. Mum has cried to Natalie about it. I ignore it or change the subject. Don't have solutions. What can I say? No matter how bad it got between Mum and Dad, his accusations of Mum being personality disordered and abusive seem absurd. She's so gentle and loving with Alexander, and Natalie wouldn't hesitate to leave him with her. They say you only see yourself when reflected in others. If that's true what kind of person am I? See myself in Mum and Dad. Don't want to be what Dad is or what he made Mum into.*

Cß Cß Cß

JOKER APPEARED ON the screen as Daniel's tossing and turning faded. Milner's jealousy was aroused as he noticed Hera sat on Joker's lap being stroked.

"They're a couple of happy bunnies," said Joker.

"Which couple? From which episode? Anyway none of them are my responsibility."

"No…?"

"This nonsense is fraying my nerves."

"Really. How can I improve matters?"

"That sarchasm gulf is widening, Joker."

"How observant."

"As Julian said in that last miserable load of rubbish, what's done is done, it can't be undone. Can't change anything now."

"My purpose is not to change what happened, but to get you to think twice in future."

"The only thing I regret is Hera. I miss her."

"So you do regret something?"

"No comment. What I want to do badly is view the rest of these 'episodes' you've prepared. I suggest two a night and you leave me alone till they're finished. Then we'll have our 'chat' and I can get on with life."

"Interesting turn of phrase – what you want to do badly. Do you mean what you badly want to do? Although on reflection, badly is probably the best way to describe what's happened no matter where it comes in the sentence."

"Ha. Ha. Do me the honour of pushing off for now and arrange my nightly torture, will you? I'm going to bed. See you when the misery is over."

ↂ ↂ ↂ

CHAPTER 16

Lady Sibylline

Who feigns cleanliness and innocence
but wallows in a muddy waterhole
Who crawls into beehives to steal honey
and howls when stung
Who exudes chasteness
but is as empty and deceptive as froth
Who pretends to have no bristles
but disingenuously stirs settled dust
Who wants to warm an already warm bed
then slyly and contentedly lick clean their whiskers

GRONYA ROLLED OVER, raised an eyelid and stared at the clock – ten-thirty am. *Eugh! Last time I looked it said four-thirty am. Oh boy! Another endless day to struggle through. No wonder I feel knackered before I start.* She closed her eyes in an attempt to banish the tormented thoughts that rose as consciousness dawned. It didn't work. The same ideas ploughed the same furrow every morning and no matter what she did, she couldn't encourage fresh ones to germinate, or overturn the shallow, narrow trench her ruminations trudged along. The questions *'how long since I got my way'* and *'how long did happiness last once I achieved what I ached for'* niggled her. Her mind regurgitated the same response each time – *'too short in comparison to what went before'*. Contentment with achieving her goal lasted no longer than the orgasms she believed the right size equipment could deliver. Awareness of the abyss of time had turned reality into an ordeal that stretched into the future and made it difficult to contemplate.

Her intense pursuit of Julian lasted seven years – although it took the three before that to persuade Milner to offer help. At first, in the glow of pleasure at her accomplishment, Gronya smiled at how easily Julian succumbed to Milner's ruses. Now, misgivings about how Julian's marriage and family collapsed like a house of cards was dogged by regret at the haste with which her long desired new life with Julian began.

She ached to recapture the sweet satisfaction that marked the start of her adventure. If only it had lasted longer. Julian outdid himself to cater to her every whim while Gronya revelled in his attention and agreement to whatever she proposed. *Called me his Sibyl. Didn't appreciate it at first. Told him I didn't like being named after a dreadful harridan from a TV show. Made me to look it up, so I understood; felt gratified when I got his drift.* Gronya had never experienced such adoration, at least not that she recalled. Perhaps Milner worshipped her once, but for ages she loathed his attempts at affection;

the germs he breathed over her with his forced hugs. How did she bear the seven years? Or the ten before them? Seventeen years ago coincided with her plan to return to work; to be done with babies. Milner persuaded her to have another; so Hattie arrived. Lovely to start, but the cuddly baby transmogrified into an anorexic teenage monster. *Doesn't mean I don't adore her, I do, but she kept me on the back foot until Julian appeared. In therapy he taught me techniques to deal with Ollah and Hattie's crises.* Julian insisted she wasn't to blame for the girls' eating disorders; that was down to Milner's propensity to treat money like medication, one the family overdosed on. Julian helped her cope with Milner's insistence on physical contact. *It's why I fell in love with Julian, my hero, my soulmate, THE man to fulfil me.* He showed how Milner controlled her, got his way by insisting he cared and his plans were in her best interests. Milner treated her like a Madonna, not a Sybil. Enthroned her at the centre of family life to dispense goodness and caring while he supplied finance. Under his regime he asserted the right to decision-making outside the home; while she concentrated on overseeing inside. Made sense then; suited her preference to avoid work-places where she might encounter more Milners. One was enough. She shuddered as she imagined work; all those germs on legs launching themselves at her. *Eugh*! Julian, however, epitomised everything Milner could never be. From the first she loved his constant reassur-ance of her capability, insisted her family didn't value her properly.

But now every time Gronya closed her eyes in an attempt to shut it all out, she became engulfed in an imaginary whirlwind of unbridled ferociousness. Escape was impossible and she couldn't diffuse her sense of being trapped, unable to escape the whimsical nature of the vortex that enmeshed her in its restlessness and, without warning, delivered gusts that knocked her down, caught her up and swirled her around. She loathed the sensation of helplessness with no way to break free. *Never sure if I'm awake or dreaming when my mind churns.* Nothing went as planned. It seemed simple while she wanted Julian – before she got him. Goal achieved, the dream soured. *Today will be hell as usual. Hattie hasn't forgiven me over Hera. Is milking it for all it's worth. Need Julian in full support mode, but with Daniel and Natalie here last night he'll be occupied with other things.*

Her discordant thoughts were interrupted by a shrill ringing.

"Mum."

"Ollah."

"I know THAT lot are there. When will you be here? Can't neglect me because THEY are there."

"Was about to call Hattie then set my agenda."

"You thought of her first? I need you more."

"Actually, I assumed you'd be asleep. Hattie's awake. Texted me."

"I'm awake too."

"Is the coast clear?"

"Sarkie doesn't suit ya, Mum."

"You went out last night with gay friends. I don't want to meet another of them by accident, especially if they stayed over."

"Are you are inferring I slept with one of them? I got drunk, but not that drunk."

"Glad to hear it. Your father hates forking out for psychiatric consultations when you do."

"But he pays anyway, because he loves me."

"Did the cleaner do you this week?"

"It's clean enough for you and Dad, not just the pets."

"Don't get defensive. He hates your animals being distressed because you haven't found time to sort your house out."

"Will you never stop moaning about that?"

"Not while I pay the cleaning bills."

"Who pays? Ring Hattie, then text me when you're on your way here."

Gronya threw the phone onto the bed and searched frantically for her small fan. *Why do Ollah and Hattie give me grief — won't concede my right to happiness with Julian? I gave them so much of myself; can't they show the same consideration? At the beginning Julian insisted it'd settle down, but when? It's the one thing Julian and Milner agreed on. They both wanted me happy; both said it'd work out.* She fanned her cheeks, which stopped burning after a while, but the problem of perspiration-soaked sheets wouldn't be so easily solved. For years Gronya clung to the belief contentment would cure hot flushes. Her recipe for fulfilment consisted in someone to pay her attention, appreciate her at all times and confirm her wonderfulness. She closed her eyes, aware, despite all efforts, nothing had changed; it was another Saturday morning, another ten forty-five am. She'd seen a sign once that said 'Same Shit, Different Day'. *How appropriate, especially given the short honeymoon. Why haven't my physical symptoms settled? Why haven't the panic attacks stopped?*

Gronya grabbed her screeching phone. *Not again. Today I hate you, phone, you're jangling my nerves.*

"Hattie. Been trying to get you. Shall I come now? Ollah wants me there later. Anything special you need today?"

"Must I need something special to get you here?"

"No, darling. Your every whim is my command."

"Ha, ha! When will you come?"

"Soon. Was waiting for the coast to clear."

"Why agree to have Daniel and his lot? I need you. Come now."

"What's so urgent?"

"Fancied some of that soup you made, but can't face the kitchen."

"If you're serious, I'll be there. Won't bother to say 'don't move'. I'm sure you'll stay comatose till I get there."

"Sarcasm is beneath you. You aren't good at it."

"Fine. See you soon. Hope your appetite doesn't

diminish meanwhile."

"Ha, ha – again."

Gronya threw the duvet covers on the floor to air the mattress. *Will make it later with fresh sheets. Wish my night flushes would end. Hope I don't run into Julian's lot downstairs.* She hoped this would be their last visit. All those stranger germs. *Need to get the cleaner in for an extra session next week.* Thankfully, Julian was in charge of his brood. She crept down the stairs, holding her breath. She released it as she realised Daniel and family were in the dining room with the door closed. *No avoidance tactics necessary. What a relief.* The doorbell rang. Groyna noted the outline of the postman through the leaded lights. *Damn him. Why's he ringing?* She answered, signed for a parcel, took possession then inspected it. Burning sensations spread through her fingers and up her arm. She searched for a tissue to wipe her forehead. *Deep breaths, Gronya, picture the tea towel – Keep calm and keep drying.* She tried the dining room, but no Julian. She apologised for interrupting then hurried to his bedroom.

"Yours, I believe." She threw the parcel on his bed and watched him tense.

"What game's she playing?" she demanded as she went to the ensuite to splash cold water over her hands and cheeks. "Where's my fan? Where did I leave it?"

"It's probably nothing. I'll open it when the kids are gone."

"No you won't. I want to see what she sent."

"What you doing up? I thought you planned to stay out the way."

"Hattie phoned. I'm going home to sort her out then Ollah. Happy coincidence you can use to explain me away."

"Home?"

"I mean Milner's."

Julian grimaced as he undid the wrapping. Two items fell out. One was a small bible with a zip enclosing its entire edge; the other an adding machine roll, covered in xxx's stamped with an office stamp that said confidential, held together with an elastic band. Gronya saw Julian recognise them, then watched him turn to avoid her gaze.

"Come on, what is it? Must be significant. You've gone grey."

"It's from our courting days," said Julian as he gathered the items in an attempt to hide them. "It'll only mean something if we let it. I'll look later. Then I can treat it with the contempt it deserves."

"You make sure you do. We'll talk this evening."

"Off you toddle then. I'll go shopping once the kids are gone and I've tidied. They're leaving soon."

What viciousness has she managed now? Whatever's in that parcel stirred memories he'd rather forget. Saw deep hurt in his eyes as he went pasty faced – usually manages to keep the old face solid as rock, never betrays a flicker. What was her aim? To make him miserable, embarrass him? She succeeded. Means he'll be emailing me tonight wanting to make 'lurv'. Hope he doesn't sulk and want an all-nighter, there's only so much a soul can bear.

⚬ ⚬ ⚬

GRONYA WAS IMBIBING a glass of red wine in the TV room when he arrived home. She hadn't been in long. She listened to Julian cart shopping into the kitchen and fill cupboards. *Hasn't called out. Bad sign. Hope he's not sulking and practising his best sullen silence.* When he assumed his stern, hangdog look her new tactic was to ignore him. *Why attempt to draw blood from a stone? If he wants to give the impression it's not worth resolving his problem, wants to play the martyr, why fight him? Why upset myself? Let him wallow.* While he didn't verbalise, and she got her way, what did it matter? Perhaps tonight when he emailed with a request to visit her boudoir her phone/tablet would be switched off. *I'll decide when I've had enough to drink or whether I've patience to jolly him out of it with sex.* Funny how Julian once thought she was a gem that enhanced his life, insisted she fulfilled his every need. Said so in one of his honeymoon period emails. She treasured that message; pulled it up on her tablet. He'd headed up his missive 'Faith, Hope and Charity'. "You are too generous in spirit and too good for your family to always appreciate. I am certain they do love you but are too wrapped up in their own issues to understand your needs just now. You should take comfort from knowing how many other people value you and wish for your happiness. I certainly know you are a wonderful caring person and that's without bias." *Music to my ears. Shows he understood me then. Has it all gone down the plughole?*

"So there you are. What you watching?"

"The Queen video – *I Want to Break Free*."

"Dare I ask from whom or what?"

"It's been a harrowing day. Hattie won't forgive me for Hera and Ollah is set on more self-destruction."

"I thought we might discuss my parcel."

"Spent hours trying to coax Hattie to take a few mouthfuls of soup. Milner was there. He tried too, then turned on me, annoyed because he got some weird email from Adelle. Seems she's launching some emotional war on everyone. Manipulating loser. Hope you destroyed whatever she sent you."

"Wanted to talk about it."

"What for? That achieves her aim. I've enough to cope with. Hattie and Ollah aren't coming to terms with anything, giving me grief and lots of it. Any suggestions how to deal with them? When and how will you get rid – best thing for it? Wait! The email Adelle sent to Milner – did you get your forwarded copy – attempts to wheedle herself into Milner's good books. Gives me an idea. She knows we booked a holiday cottage over the long weekend that coincides with her birthday. She knows Sabina and family will be there. Said something along the lines she hoped Milner would have a good weekend and recommended some book to read. We can take her wretched parcel, invite the kids round on her birthday, light a fire in the garden and burn it."

"Is there any point me emailing later to arrange a visit after light's out?"

"Depends how drunk I get. Had enough of Milner and his attempts to hug me today."

"OK, darling. I'll start dinner."

Gronya contemplated her glass of wine. *Why do I find his apparent polite agreement annoying? Why does he agree then walk away with a sullen look? Thinks I don't notice. Why doesn't he stand and fight?* She couldn't fathom whether he went along to keep the peace, or because he agreed. Gronya found Julian's deference more irritating than Milner's insistence on having his way. Milner never offered passive resistance; he'd argue until Gronya acceded, then leave her to smoulder with resentment. Julian complied without argument; a tactic that left her confused and still smouldering.

Milner made decisions; now she was forced to make them because Julian nodded his head and succumbed. *Eugh*! She suspected if she asked him to dismantle the Eiffel Tower and reassemble it in her garden he would nod, then drive her mad discussing the many and various options to tackle the job until she insist he abandon it. Julian became difficult to deflect once he sank into a brood. Sex diverted him; but Gronya discovered that to be a temporary fix. Size hadn't proved as satisfactory as she imagined all those years.

She cottoned on to Julian's inability to make decisions after she cajoled him to move to the house she settled on as their love nest. He resisted at first. Some nonsense about being tied down work-wise and too close to Milner and the girls. They fell out. She back tracked and apologised; pretended to let it go. But she stuck at it, and overseen by Milner's persuasive tactics, Julian caved. *Julian accepted a year's tenancy. Conceded it gave breathing space to decide where to live later. Said I needed to be on hand so my lot were reassured; didn't intend to move me away from them.* Julian insisted it didn't matter if he lived a long way from Adelle and his family. He'd nurse them through the initial crises from a distance. *How wonderful to have my needs prioritised. Worked in my favour 'cause I controlled his time with them. He made a couple of visits to explain, but the trips dwindled. Phone calls is what they mostly get now.* Unspoken between them was the reality that once Julian agreed to the lease he was ensnared. Milner let it be known he was set on buying the property and if Julian refused to accept would be homeless. *Milner jiggled those pieces into place by exploiting Julian's paralysing indecision over how to ease his conscience. At least I think that's what I understood when Milner explained it to me.*

CƷ CƷ CƷ

"HAD ANOTHER EMAIL about Christmas from Natalie," said Julian.

"I thought that was settled," said Gronya.

"You know Natalie. Doesn't give up easy."

"Or perhaps you didn't make yourself understood.

You aren't going, are you? Or have you changed your mind?"

"No. I'll stay here for when you want me as requested."

"I will need you. I'm still in Hattie's bad books over Hera – why do those names sound similar – and the girls haven't recovered from their wobbles."

"Sabina wanted me to go to her. Never been so popular. Told her it was too far to drive in one day. She accepted. They don't have room for me to stay. But Natalie says they do and can't bear the idea of me being alone."

"You won't be. You can phone them and you have TV to watch."

"I plan on lobster and a glass of superb white, maybe a Pouilly Fume or a Chablis."

"Sounds better than the blow out Milner and girls have planned."

"Tantrums or food wise? Whichever there'll be the usual hangovers I guess?"

"Don't be sarkie. I need you concentrated on me, so no getting too far gone on your wine. You'll have to escort me back here when they get too much."

"Your wish is my command. I'll tell Natalie I won't be lonely and will have lots to keep me occupied. It's ambiguous enough to be true. Any point emailing for an appointment tonight?"

"Sounds like neither of your children are concerned about their mother. Where's she spending Christmas?"

"Don't know, care even less. Her relationship with them is her affair. No longer my responsibility. I'll ask again. Any point me emailing later for duvet time?"

"I'll see how I feel when you email."

They spent the evening with Julian in a sullen mood. *Is it the silence or the penetrating glares?* Gronya resented his moods whatever. They signalled his desire to have her concentrate on him, but was too cowardly to push it. Made her obliged to find the energy to wheedle his problems out. His worries held little interest for her now. She wanted him concentrated on her like at the beginning. Sex was the quickest way to entice him over his hump without long discussions, but meant germs invading her bed plus showering and a sheet change after the struggle to get him to spend the rest of the night in his own room.

Tonight she couldn't face it. She sat in her bedroom with the ring tones suppressed on her phone and tablet. Her annoyance arose from the images of Adelle that invaded her thoughts. The suggestion to Julian of the totemic burning of the items Adelle posted hadn't been as satisfying as she hoped. Julian's cold glares reminded her of Adelle's description of Julian's mother; how she kept pain and disappointment to herself, but showed it in her eyes. Julian did the same, but had honed it to martyrdom. To Gronya this signalled unhappiness and at first she wondered what she did to cause it. Now she realised the stares were due to sulking at not getting his way. *How did Adelle put up with him? He claimed Adelle insisted on everything being done her way. Maybe he never argued, just gave in the same as he does with me then laid the stare on her. Adelle must have loved him more than he her.* Gronya realised Adelle's loyalty to Julian ran deeper to him than vice versa or he wouldn't have been prised from his marriage. *How stupid was Adelle to stick by old fashioned notions that wedding vows are for life and not as long as it proves convenient. Made her complacent. Why am I obsessed with Adelle? I only paid attention to her to get closer to Julian and catch him in my web. I succeeded so why the metronome in my head, tick-tocking; why can't I ignore it?* Gronya had learned what it meant when folks said, "Be careful what you wish for". *His daughter, Sabina, does the silent glare. It's why I don't visit her. She pretends to like me, but I'm not sure. She abandoned Adelle when she failed to cope over losing Julian. Look how she spied on her mother. Milner would never use his daughters like that. Adelle boasted she taught her children to be independent and ethical. Got that one wrong.*

෧ ෧ ෧

GRONYA AND MILNER shared a coffee in his kitchen. It was Christmas Eve, and they were going through Milner's check lists to ensure everything was ready for the next day.

"Will you stay all day tomorrow?" asked Milner.

"I'll stay while I can cope. Julian and I plan to spend the evening together, so will leave in time for that. The girls must like it or lump it although I suspect you'll all be too far gone to notice."

"Hopefully things will start to settle and get easier soon. This first period was always going to be the most difficult."

"Talking of next year, Julian's been looking at his college meetings. Needs to attend to build points for his Continuing Professional Development. There's a meeting planned to mark some anniversary or other. Reckons it would be the ideal event for me to go to so we can 'come out'."

A sweat broke on Gronya's forehead as Milner blushed, burst into uncontrollable giggles then choked on his mouthful of mince pie. Gronya had never seen Milner react to anything that way. Prided himself on control of his public demeanour; told her so many times.

"So that's what you think is it?" Gronya splashed cold water on her cheeks and hands then grabbed kitchen paper to dry them. "How dare you mock me? I'm off. See you tomorrow."

Milner spluttered and cleared his throat.

"Gronya. Gronya. Don't leave in a temper. I apologise."

"Sorry; won't cut it. You never respected me. Now I've proof. Just couldn't control yourself."

"I behaved badly. I lost it because I'm shocked at the realisation you're achieving your dream and plan to do things with Julian as a couple. I'm nervous for you and hope you'll be ready to face a conference full of psychiatrists. The scrutiny will be hard, particularly with your anxiety symptoms which stopped you coming to my business meetings. If you're sure you can deal with such situations – good – go for it."

"If that's the only reason, I accept your apology."

"It is."

CZ CZ CZ

GRONYA ARRIVED TO BE greeted by the girls in high spirits. Milner was busy in the kitchen with meal preparation while Hattie and Ollah were occupied with uncorking a second bottle of champagne. A hot flush swept over her. *Won't be any different, will it? How to get through till after lunch?* She hung her coat in the downstairs closet, anxious to discard as many garments as possible. She wrapped up for the walk, but as usual, had too much on in anticipation of the cold.

Last night at home proved difficult and Gronya felt drained and unready to face the routine nightmare of Christmas day with her family. She dreaded 'duvet time'. She and Julian had different ideas about what it meant and Julian's did not coincide with hers. She hated that Julian wanted to stay under her duvet longer than she could tolerate and kept her awake. If she kicked him out, he rewarded her with sulks. He wanted all-nighters, but she loathed his snoring. She banished Milner from their bed for the same problem, why put up with Julian's? *Why am I attracted to men who snore? Am I fitted with some invisible honing device or a tattoo that says 'snoring causes this woman maximum frustration'? Don't remember*

Adelle complaining about it although Julian moaned about hers. For years Gronya despised Milner's demands for physical closeness, so it was wonderful when a valid excuse presented itself and enabled her to lever him from under her covers. Now Julian expressed the weird idea that sharing a mattress all night brought you closer. *Doesn't do it for me. Eugh! All those noises and unpleasant odours.* Gronya had a particular dislike of Julian breathing in her face, worried about the germs he exhaled. He left last night, eventually, but only after she'd been up and down twice to the shower and changed sheets several times. She thought he'd never get the message. The result was less than four hours sleep. *Pull yourself together, Gronya, you've a long day ahead.*

"Ah… Bird about to perch after flight from love nest," hollered Ollah.

"Am I sorry the Cat Murderer is deserted, alone and/or lonely?" chimed in Hattie.

Milner appeared at the door.

"Now, girls. We discussed this. No mum-baiting today. We need to practice sweetness and light towards each other."

"OK, Dad. Can we open presents?"

After frenzied present opening, the girls and Milner drifted to the kitchen; Ollah in search of wine, Hattie water. Gronya gathered up the discarded wrappings and labels. Milner spent his usual fortune getting everything on their Christmas lists. Their complaints he hadn't got the right brand or size or model followed by promises from him to change them for what they specified left her exhausted. *Why is it always the same? Why do this? What's the point? They insist on me being here to prove I put them first, then behave in ways I loathe. They abuse me with constant entreaties for attention.* She wondered if the exchange was fair – the privileges Milner granted in return for her being on call; the house, the use of the Bentley, the London flat. She'd been adamant she'd not give them up for Julian, determined he would live around the edges of her family, there to help when they became overwhelming. *Must get out of here, now. Except I can't – need to see lunch through – agreed that with Milner. Will phone Julian and tell him to come mid-afternoon.*

CB CB CB

"SO – WAS IT as awful as anticipated?" enquired Julian when they got home.

"It was bearable."

"So why the panic to leave? I missed the Queen's speech."

"Don't know. Thought you never listened to the speech. I find my lot all together overwhelming, but can't stay away. Thought I'd achieved some control since I left, but today made me doubt it."

"Are you interested in whether I enjoyed my dinner?"

"Hattie won't forgive me over Hera. Her untimely demise disrupted progress and undermined Milner's attempts to get the girls to accept things. Their hostility to you seems worse. Ollah's cat, who is staying with

Milner, is peeing up the curtains at home, despite my efforts to cure the problem, and he has backed off moaning to her about it as he's on the back foot over Hera who he misses. Milner is all mouth and no corduroy over his daughters. Ollah refuses to have the animal rehoused or put down. Milner tried to persuade her to remove it to her house, but when he visited the state of her place made him sorry for the cat; said he wouldn't condemn anything to live there, then spent a fortune getting cleaners in to sanitise Ollah's house."

"I thought you said it was bearable. You referred to that place as home again. I've told you not to give in to your girls' tantrums. I watched some recorded rugby this morning by the way."

"Look at us. Bare walls. Every room the same. Milner won't let me have permanent use of any of the paintings we collected over the years. Says he paid for them. Adelle shouldn't have denied you some of your collection."

"She said the same as Milner. She chose and bought most of them so reckoned she should keep them. This is miles from misery over a difficult Christmas dinner. What bought this on?"

"Don't know."

"I have a cure, if you're interested."

"Not now. Need a glass of wine and to relax quietly – alone."

Gronya carried her wine to her bedroom and showered. When dressed she stood and looked around. Bare walls annoyed her. *Why? I want colour to brighten this place up – in contrast to Julian's sullen face. Wish Milner would go away more so I could borrow pictures from his house. He lets me when we have visitors, but isn't aware I do it when he's not there. What he doesn't know doesn't hurt.*

Gronya rehearsed her list of regrets, a new pastime she'd discovered. *Do I regret Milner lied to Adelle about our divorce? Not at first.* It proved another means to ensnare Julian in Milner's finely spun web. What they didn't foresee was Adelle suing for divorce. Gronya heard somewhere that Adelle said Julian forced her into it because she saw everyone being manipulated and wouldn't be part of it. The filing came soon after the birthday trip. Gronya realised they must be connected. It was Adelle's attempt to punish and force him to face the issue. *She never knew when to leave things alone. It was how I won him, promised not to do the same. Now I do. Perhaps it's why he sulks?*

Do I regret Adelle doesn't see her grandchildren or daughter? No. That's Julian's problem. Gronya felt smug Milner kept his family together. She had sympathy with Adelle's hurt and anger over Sabina and Julian after the photo incident. She'd be the same; but Adelle's other angry outbursts had no justification and frightened her. *Like when she phoned Julian at two am once and complained loudly about texts I sent her by mistake. Said she shouldn't have to endure texts from me in the early hours and to get me in order.* He tried to reason, pointed out they were mistakes, but she insisted they were callous and upsetting given he'd abandoned her for me. Once was fine, but it happened several times, woke her up. Gronya explained to Julian her fingers made silly errors with her phone at night. *Julian understood; Adelle also lost it badly over me texting whenever he went to visit her. I wanted to be sure he was OK, wasn't going to surrender his autonomy again. Why was my concern unreasonable? He'd left her to be mine. Why did she reckon she deserved his full attention when with her? She forfeited that when her behaviour forced him to leave her. Excused herself by blaming grief. Grief my foot. Julian saw through that and put her right; told her to stop dwelling on it and wouldn't give her reasons. I agree he owed her no explanation.*

Do I regret how devastated Adelle was, so she didn't do what Milner and I hoped? Milner swore he thought she adored Julian so much she'd do the cooperation thing; accept Julian staying with her sometimes to see she was all right. Gronya decided it was Adelle's fault she lost Julian, her behaviour entitled Gronya to prise Julian from her if she couldn't make him happy. Everyone deserved to feel autonomous and loved. Adelle dragged him down with her insistence she was always right, that his indecisiveness and inability to take decisions forced her to behave that way. Milner threw the same accusations at me, but pointed out in Adelle's case her argument that Julian and Gronya could never be content were expressions of despair. *If Julian reconciled his professional ethics Adelle should've accepted it. Wasn't for Adelle to judge or describe our relationship as inappropriate.*

Gronya jumped as her tablet tinkled out the sound that indicated an email had dropped into her Inbox. *OMG – suppose I'll have to play ball tonight.*

⚃ ⚃ ⚃

THREE MONTHS HAD passed since Christmas. Hattie returned to studies after the New Year break. It all went well – for a while. But today Gronya was on her way to Milner's in response to a summons from Hattie.

"Dad tells me he spoke to your tutors at uni."

"He's got 'em in control same as before."

"So what's happening? Will they allow you to repeat the year?"

"Apparently. Say they recognise my family circumstances are the reason I can't cope and have relapsed."

"I'm surprised they're so tolerant."

"They say I'm bright and clever and will pass my exams when strong enough to take them."

"But to agree this twice seems a bit of a luxury."

"If Dad's willing to pay for another year of study, why are you bothered? It's not as if the money comes from your pocket. He makes certain you and the Cat Murderer are in clover."

"Wish you'd stop calling him that. It was an accident."

"Won't ever forgive him. Want to scratch his eyes out."

"I'll overlook your remarks. You're obviously not well. I'll stay for a bit and make you comfortable. Go shower and jump in bed. Sleep is the cure for your problems."

"OK, Mum, but promise you'll come if I call."

"My phone won't be switched off."

Later than evening she faced a difficult conversation with Julian. He insisted she and Milner were pandering to Hattie, whose self-image came from distorted views of herself; that they should correct it by denying her exaggerated claims to be fat. He was fed up because he thought he'd escaped this nightmare in leaving Adelle whose warped ideas about herself and her abilities had frustrated him. The only difference was Adelle never used food to manipulate, just proclaimed her unworthiness and catastrophized everything. Why couldn't Gronya devote more time to him? Gronya was disturbed by Julian's rant as he usually stayed tight-lipped about her family these days. She went to bed determined not to respond to his email. He'd set off her memories about Adelle again – she found this unforgivable. *Why am I obsessed with Adelle? The man I live with is not the one I imagined all those years I plotted and schemed to lure him into my web. He's not the Mr Perfect I believed in. Why does reality do that? Rob you of dreams? Why is he so damned deferential? If the girls got any hint I'd abandoned the fantasy of happiness with Julian, given how it's working out, they'd roll about laughing at the irony.*

CB CB CB

CHAPTER 17

Tragedie

Once entwined with honour –
now entwined with dishonour
Once delivering healing and compassion –
now attracting anger and hate
its poison diverted
not to search for Wholeness
but to Maim, Destroy and Incapacitate.
His totem should have remained sheathed
in its scale headed helter-skelter
Impotent to cause harm
imbued instead with power
to disperse peace, healing and understanding

J ULIAN BLINKED AS a shiver convulsed him. The warmth under the duvet didn't resonate with his mood and the stark, cold atmosphere that enveloped his bedroom. He yawned. *Why do I feel as if I'm in a half drained ditch, no boots on, my feet mired in the gooey muddy mess at the bottom.* The volume of unoccupied space he stared into swamped the single bed, white side table, small desk and bookshelf. The cream-coloured iron bedstead originally made a pair, chosen for a guest suite in the French gîte which Adelle's attention to detail developed into an inviting, comfortable holiday home for visitors. Now it stood alone in a functional, neglected rear room in a London house. Apart from the bedside table the other bits of furniture were cheap, self-assembly jobs – bought to make do. Not like the beautiful oak bookshelves he installed in the library/study in France. In his mind Julian pictured them and the books that lined them sorted and ordered with care by Adelle. His mind swept past the volumes to remember the view from the window which overlooked the courtyard, where a stately and aged Judas tree dominated. France had fulfilled a lifelong dream. It gave him hours of pleasure construct-ing those shelves. He'd quality material to work with; rich, grained wood that reflected the calm and beauty of the valley and countryside the house occupied. *How quickly it turned sour. The fantasy of forty years defaced in the span of two summers and one miserable winter.*

Daniel and crew had come for their first visit since the photo incident wreaked havoc over everything. Gronya was leaving him to it as usual – staying out of the way. Julian dragged himself from under the duvet. He heaved opened a wardrobe door to search for something to make himself decent for a trip to the bathroom, but then stared at the shelves paralysed with indecision. *Can't face it. I'll get back under the covers. Maybe it'll all go away.* He loathed shopping; kept his garb to a minimum.

Adelle gave up on his attitude to clothes early in their marriage – shrugged her shoulders and left him to it. Gronya struggled to do the same. Used to Milner's extravagant tastes, she nagged him to spend unconscionable amounts on things he would never dream of buying. *Thankfully Gronya also abandoned the battle in the end. Adelle blamed my parsimonious Scottishness. Gronya declined to offer a reason – just went silent.* The evidence was there in the half-empty cupboard. Perhaps he should waste money; fill hanging spaces, drawers and shelves. It might lessen his inclination to describe himself as a drifter with squatter's rights.

He slept alone on this far side of the house; the room allocated on the basis it was furthest from Gronya's bedroom. The 'duvet time' she longed for and promised before they got together had failed to materialise. It hadn't taken long to banish him from her bed on the pretext his snoring stole her rest. There was a precedent; she employed the same excuse when Milner was banished from their bed years earlier. Ironically, Julian suggested that solution during a therapy session in response to constant complaints about Milner's snoring and her sleep deprivation. Julian tried to solve his difficulty – sourced and purchased nose clips – to no effect. The only thing achieved was to give Gronya a laugh at his expense while the problem remained. At first she joked about how she preferred to enjoy his heavy breathing while awake. The line was repeated so often his reply descended into a muted 'ha, ha' as the wisecrack wore thin. His lifelong routine had been to retire and be asleep between ten and eleven pm, but Gronya proved a late bird; never retired before one am. So they established a pattern where, if he wanted sex, he emailed in the middle of the night and asked to visit her room. Most nights now she refused. *Seems my tackle is not as desirable as she insisted it would be.*

Those first heady days with Gronya were recent enough for him to miss with deep longing and regret. The honeymoon didn't last – if it might be called that. The satisfaction he got from sex was like a halo fashioned from a sense of security that confirmed he did right no matter the difficulties and upset. He and Gronya had properly prioritised their happiness. In post-coital whisperings, Gronya told him how he satisfied her. *Music to my ears it was. Proved Adelle never understood my needs and was wrong to deny me. Not denied, rationed, with the ration inadequate.* Milner had long been refused sex by Gronya – the issue loomed large in his therapeutic alliance with her. Early in their patient/doctor relationship he tried to help her overcome her repugnance of Milner, but over the years realised he was the man to provide Gronya's sexual and emotional wellbeing. *Shame it turned out such a short month of honey.*

He remembered Adelle's response when told Gronya would be his life from then on – 'Stop talking nonsense and let's sort our problems.' Julian told her that would never happen; he owed no explanation and would never give one. He stuck to this line despite Adelle's protestations that their forty-five-year history meant she deserved one. Adelle accused him of cowardice, which he denied; he argued he was right to protect Adelle from the suffering that would ensue if he prised open Pandora's Box. To make her face her responsibility for their failed marriage would be odious, like examining stomach contents post mortem. Best everyone walk away with limited or no exposure to the fault lines. They should move forward, not back.

He gazed at the ceiling. *I was right to follow that line especially as Adelle's behaviour got more bizarre.* He wanted to wipe the memory of that conversation with her when he went to France to pack up the stuff they agreed she could take to her flat. Books, shelves, sun's rays, furniture vans, bees humming, cardboard boxes in supermarkets – all made him involuntarily relive the scene. He could find no tactic to erase the vision of the room, the window and the courtyard beyond dominated by the Judas tree, when he stood in a shaft of sunlight gazing at the tree, talking on the phone with tears streaming down his face.

"I phoned 'cause I don't remember which pictures you wanted."

"You've got a list. We did it together when I came with you a few months ago to sort out what I could take."

"Can't read my handwriting."

"You didn't write it, I did. So why call me?"

"You forbade Gronya the house, so she's in the village with Madame Rousselly. I'm here alone with difficult memories."

"And that's my problem?"

"I'm struggling."

"I haven't forbidden your tart the courtyard. Phone her. Get her to drive up, sit under the Judas tree and wait on you. She can futter and you go out and console yourself when 'overcome'? Most appropriate place for her in more ways than one."

"Don't call her names."

"Why not? It's what she is."

"Don't call her names."

"Why not? Why turn to me for sympathy? It's not my problem if you're overwhelmed with emotion at destroying our life. Want me to say 'there, there, poor baby, sorry you're upset'. You chose your tart for that. Go get comfort there. Tain't my responsibility any-more."

"But we loved each other."

"Loved? I loved. You needed. You took advantage of me for years and even now turn to me for consola-tion 'cause your tart's not up to it. Phoned to see if I'm soft enough to do her job. Shame on you."

"Stop calling her that name."

"What should I call her? She pretended to be my friend. You both betrayed me and now you want sympathy because it's hard to pack up forty-five years of shared memories and she's inadequate. You offered to do it, not me."

"Please."

"Go to hell. I begged you to explain your betrayal, but you told me I'm owed no explanation and you'll give none. That's why I call her a tart and couldn't care less how much misery you're in. Go seek comfort from your Madam in the village."

Julian tried to close down the memory and concentrate on the cupboard and its contents. He retrieved a pair of shorts. *Stop feeling guilty. It doesn't help. Anyway, it's Adelle's fault she faces those twin-headed hydra she dreaded, poverty and loneliness. If she hadn't been unreasonable I'd have looked after her, made sure she never wanted. Stayed with her between times with Gronya. Why wouldn't she cooperate in her best interests? Always was stubborn.* He was proud he'd not descended to Adelle's level. Gronya saw to that. Encouraged him to be forgiving and magnanimous and allow Adelle to live in their jointly owned flat rent free while the divorce proceeded. It shook him when someone suggested it was no big concession, that the court probably considered it fair, not generous. The length of their marriage, and Adelle's contribution to joint earnings, meant a judge saw her as entitled, given Julian was adequately housed by his mistress.

He pulled on the shorts and a robe and surveyed the room. This house was not his choice. After the hassle of re-joining the medical register, job hunting proved difficult. He resigned from his substantive NHS post ten years prior to retirement to concentrate on private practice, so wouldn't be successful if he applied for a permanent position now. Besides, there were few jobs in the London area, and those advertised would go to younger men with more academic CVs. Adelle managed his practice and without her it was impossible to rebuild. He'd not appreciated how crucial she'd been, or how much was involved until Gronya urged him to consider it as a way to finance his life with her. Convinced it was feasible, they spent long hours planning their future on the strength of Gronya's belief in his ability to do it. It annoyed him to acknowledge Adelle was right about one thing: you never appreciate how well an enterprise performs until it begins to run badly or not all because key people are gone.

He'd given way on the house because Gronya convinced him it would make her happy. She became set on it after her initial visit; insisted it was the perfect place to imprint their personalities and fashion their first home. A bonus was that it put her close to her old marital abode where she nursed Hattie and Ollah during illness episodes. According to Gronya this meant Julian would be caused 'minimum inconvenience' when her girls needed her. Milner told Gronya if Julian agreed to live there, they might borrow his Bentley. Milner liked this idea as it kept it running when he took holidays or business trips. These days, the most frequent visitors to the love nest were builders doing renovations to Gronya's specifications. Supervising tradesmen interspersed with attendance on Hattie and Ollah's whims meant Gronya's life changed little from when she lived with Milner in the mansion up the road. The title deeds registered Milner and Gronya as joint owners. Julian was a kept man. *How did I end up here? If Gronya dies, I'll be homeless. How will I cope? Gave away too much capital in the divorce.*

He heard his phone ring as he trailed back from the bathroom.

"Dad."

"Sabina."

"Won't keep you with Daniel and Natalie there. Need a chat but you mustn't repeat what I'm about to say."

"Why?"

"Promise not to tell. Don't put anything in emails. Specially don't want Mum to know."

"Don't worry. Ensured no more emails go to wrong places. How would she find out? There's been no communication for ages."

"Adam and I are splitting up."

"Oh. Sabina."

"Can we talk later?"

"Sure. I'll make time this afternoon when Gronya is out. Hattie is having another relapse and refusing to take final exams."

"So Gronya will be there a lot."

"Yeah."

"Sorry to hear that. You need support now you and Daniel are trying to patch it up after the photo incident. Hope it went well last night."

"We made progress, although Natalie seems hostile. Sure we'll win her round though."

"I'm still smarting from his telling off, but if you sort things with him, then I'll try. We three must unite now Mum is banished from my life."

"Fine – talk later."

Sabina's call forced him to join Daniel and family for breakfast. After his efforts to seek rapprochement with Daniel, it was unwise to leave them on their own like last time. He searched the bottom of his wardrobe for slippers, but stumbled over the hidden paper package. He'd lied to Gronya about burning it; had put a replica on the bonfire, unable to bring himself to destroy the original. He pulled it out, opened the till roll and perused the love letter he wrote all those years ago. His head dropped, and he sighed as the roll fell from his hand onto the bed. He covered his face with his hands. After rubbing away tears he read the note from Adelle. 'You created this, you destroy it, together with the poems I kept in your Bible, especially the one you composed for our wedding day.'

Julian undid the Bible zip. Several verses in his handwriting fell out. He examined the one based on Corinthians chapter 13, read at their ceremony. The passage ended 'And now abideth Faith hope and love, and the greatest of these is love'. He remembered some versions translated St Paul's words as 'Faith hope and Charity', but he and Adelle insisted 'Faith, Hope and Love' be used. Déjà vu hit him and he picked up his tablet to search old emails. He located the one that troubled him. When he wrote it he'd been particularly proud as Gronya was having bad time with Hattie and Ollah. He read it over—

My darling Gronya. We are so in need of Faith, Hope and Charity to sustain our love. I feel for you so much just now and know how you must be hurting with all that is going on and, perhaps still to come. I wish I could hold you and never let you go.

You are too generous in spirit and too good for your family to always appreciate. I am certain they do love you but are too wrapped up in their own issues to understand your needs just now. You should take comfort from knowing how many other people value you and wish for your happiness. I certainly know you are a wonderful caring person and that's without bias.

Be sure to rest and eat and avoid too much other stress as you always tell me. It will take time, my love, but I know we will get there and enjoy our wonderful love together. Others will have to habituate to this and may not always like it but 'there you go'. I am sure we will have many more laughs together.

All my love, Julian

Did I really feel that way when I wrote that roll and poems to Adelle then expressed identical ideas to Gronya all this time later? So much has happened.

CB CB CB

HE FOUND DANIEL in the kitchen making coffee.

"Morning, Dad. Natalie and Ben will be down shortly."

"Better get breakfast ready."

"You look pale. Bad sleep?"

"Never rest well these days."

"Nothing you can't fix, right?"

"Oh hell! Your mother makes life so difficult."

"Always was stubborn. We discussed it lots of times. What memories are you struggling with?"

"The parcel of sentimental items she sent that I'd forgotten about. She did it to hurt me."

"Your face says she succeeded – then and now. Anyway, we did a ritual burning."

"True."

"So what's the problem?"

"Sabina rang earlier. Started me off again. It's Mum's personality disorder. That incident was proof of what Sabina and I said all along. She is dangerous and you should make sure you keep her away from Ben like I advised Sabina with her kids."

"That's difficult, Dad."

"I know, son, but think about it."

Natalie and Ben appeared at the kitchen door.

"Think about what?" asked Natalie.

"Nothing," said Julian. "Let's eat."

After breakfast Julian helped them pack up. As Natalie and Ben sat in the car with the engine running, Daniel had a quick word with his dad.

"By the way, what did Sabina want?"

"Said she was hoping we might get together, plan for the cousins to meet and put to rest the nastiness after the photo stuff. Asked if you would be amenable? Said I'd ask. Can I tell her we'll progress the idea? Can Natalie be talked round?"

"Sure. She'll do what I say if I put it to her the right way. We'll make plans soon."

CB CB CB

WITH THE KIDS' DEPARTURE, Julian tidied up, finished the shopping list and went to do the necessary. He dreaded the talk with Sabina. Been a fool not to be more careful with emails and regretted getting Sabina into trouble over his carelessness. Good had come from bad though because it brought him and Sabina closer by twisting Adelle's fury over the incident to his advantage. Now Daniel was coming round. Natalie was the problem, but he was sure she could be persuaded Sabina had done what was right because Adelle was unreasonable. Everything would get back on track. *Need to find more time for Alexander. Show Natalie I'm good with him too. Prove Adelle is a fantasist who dreams up ruses to manipulate. Perhaps I should tell Daniel and Natalie how she lied over Milner saying he intended to divorce Gronya. Adelle was deluded of course, Milner assured Gronya he never told her such a thing. Generously said Adelle misunderstood him. If I say it was due to her grief, it will suggest we are not unsympathetic to her delusions.* Gronya had reassured him he was right not to explain himself to someone so irrational. Natalie would understand.

CB CB CB

"HI, SABINA – SORRY IT took so long to phone. Lots to do."

"Don't worry, Dad. Just spoke with Natalie. Astonished she phoned as soon as they got home. She asked if everything was OK. I nearly spilled. Wondered if you betrayed me."

"I promised I wouldn't, and I didn't."

"Know that now. She wanted to gossip about you two. Says she caught Gronya in the kitchen last night crying. Asked her why and Gronya said she was fed up with the McPherson sullen silences. Said when you do talk you moan about her continual pampering of her girls, but then heard footsteps and fled before Natalie could interrogate further. So are you OK?"

"Of course. Gronya gets down when the girls play up. I have it in control."

"Wondered if Gronya was relapsing and whether Mum was stoking it somehow."

"No. Cured Gronya's problems when she was a patient. Relapses rare. Difficulties now easily dealt with. I correct dysfunctional thinking immediately. No more six-day waits between therapy sessions so no time to brood. Hardly happens nowadays. Got it all in hand."

"So why the complaint about 'sullen silences'?"

"No idea. I phoned to discuss your problems."

"Adam and I had another row where he ranted and I listened. Made up my mind it was enough. He's too unreasonable. Complained about my sullen silences, which is why I wondered if Mum was stoking behind the scenes. Wonder if Adam's been talking to Mum or Natalie?"

"How? Why would he? You told me he refused to answer her email about why you took the pictures. Your mother spent most of last year travelling according to Daniel. Saw her mother in Australia. How can she know the lie of the land?"

"Communications are international now, Dad. I got an email from Mum's mum asking for photos of Ben."

"Did you send any?"

"Just one. A picture of Ben with his tongue stuck out and his thumbs in his ears waggling his fingers at the camera."

"Was that wise?"

"Ben will never see his great-grandmother if I can help it. Not sure why she wants pictures. Anyway, back to my problems. Said I would move out so Adam demanded to know about his mum and that flat she lives in. Told him she wouldn't get kicked out by me. That agreement we signed with Mum made certain of it. Says he doesn't trust me 'cause I seem demented."

"On what evidence?"

"I suspect Mum. She ruled by dictatorship – hated committees – quoted Milner as her authority on the grounds he would agree based on his experience as a board chairman in big companies. She offered negotiations over the photo incident – I refused – it was her way of manipulating us to accept she was persecuted when it was us she wronged. You were wise to suggest I stop her seeing the kids. She doesn't deserve them in her life. I'm more convinced than ever, especially if she is meddling. We need to persuade Natalie. She's the weak link."

"Why do we spend time talking about your mother? She's out of our lives. Made sure she won't be back. What arrangements have you arrived at with Adam over my grandchildren?"

"I've agreed shared custody fifty-fifty as long as he behaves."

"And your house?"

"We'll sell and split proceeds. He'll go his way and I'll go mine. No divorce or stuff to argue over."

"Sounds simple. Hope it works out."

CB CB CB

JULIAN SAT IN the TV room with a half empty bottle of red. *Look at our bare walls. Only a TV screen to stare at. All Adelle's fault. Everything that's gone wrong. If only she'd conceded my right to be happy – accepted Gronya in my life and what she and Milner were prepared to offer. Could have stayed like before – art gallery visits, theatre nights and stuff like that. All the things she liked doing. Could have been perfect.* He heard a car in the drive, necked a glass of wine while he listened to the engine die, then waited for the key to turn in the lock.

"Been at it a while," said Gronya nodding her head at the bottle Julian waved in his hand.

"So what?"

"Not complaining. Means you might talk instead of giving me the silent treatment."

"Don't you mean 'sullen' silent treatment?"

"Who suggested that?" said Gronya, rummaging impatiently in her bag to locate a fan to cool her burning cheeks.

"A little bird."

"What are you saying? I've complained to you about your silences and refusal to talk. Seems it's a common complaint in your family. Seen Sabina do it. I thought you did it with Adelle because you grew apart. That was the reason you gave. Said she didn't listen, so you stopped talking."

"You never referred to my silences as 'sullen' before."

"Yes I have."

"No you haven't. Someone put the idea in your head. Who was it?"

"No one. More pertinent is which little bird put ideas in yours?"

"How is Hattie by the way?"

"Coward – changing the subject?"

"Bin thinking I need to spend more quality time with Alexander, Ben and Katy."

"You do that. As long as it doesn't mean I'll get less support with my girls as promised."

"Hattie and Ollah are adults. My grandchildren are just that – small children. I've been here for you over the girls for ages. Should devote myself to my family for a change."

"Is this another way of saying you reckon I spend too much time with mine?"

"No. It's come to my attention that despite trips away, Adelle sees Alexander more than me. You know why that's not healthy."

"Why are you obsessed with Adelle? You made sure she doesn't see Ben and Katy, isn't that enough?"

"No."

"For someone you suggest is a nonentity, why do you allow her to dominate proceedings."

"You're a fine one to talk."

"I never denied my girls dominate my life or that they frighten me with the unpredictable nature of their illnesses. But for all their foibles and demands, Milner has somehow held our relationships together and we support each other."

"What are you suggesting?"

"That if you'd seen the consequences of the photo thing, you might have reconsidered. For all her faults, she is the children's mother and grandmother and deserved respect. Milner would have found another way round her stubbornness. Or did Sabina plan it and give you no option? Was it your habitual hesitation and inability to say no immediately that gave her the signal to go ahead then you didn't know how to stop it?"

"Quite a speech. Someone must have been putting ideas in your head."

"Don't get paranoid with me."

"Your diatribe suggests you feel guilty about the misery we spread around with our decision to get together. I told you at the beginning. No hesitations, no regrets and no explanations."

"Is that why you give me silent stares and no explanations unless you get inebriated? Can't shed the habit of a lifetime. Thought we'd be different like you said we would. We were when we started. What's changed? What made you shrink back to your old self, the one I believed I was freeing you from?"

"Had enough of this. Off to bed. Any chance of a visit to your boudoir tonight? Or will my email request be met with silence?"

03 03 03

JULIAN CLIMBED THE STAIRS, lightheaded and weary. He lay down and stared at his wardrobe in the gloom. He and Gronya had inflicted pain on everyone. They acknowledged it at the time, but convinced each other they could overcome it and everybody would end up happy, or at least accept it. Julian recognised much had disappeared from his life and envied Milner's ability to keep his family together through it all, with Gronya continuing to lavish most of her attention on them and not him. His own family had collapsed, his grandchildren had no grandmother, and he saw little of them himself. He was right to blame Adelle. He had no other solution. It'd gone too far. *I'm sick of Gronya's moans about my brooding silences. Why can't I find relief; empty my mind of the ideas that rattle round it? Hope I don't have that dream again about the hellish place with the frame-like structures spun from webs by large spiders, where goblin prisoners are led out of a side building by a troop of guards. One resembles me and I get stripped naked and strung on a web. Then the Komodo dragons appear to strip flesh off my limbs while I howl until a replacement piece grows. It's like Groundhog Day. The dragons feed for hours. The bits of flesh that regenerate are not as tasty, so the dragons avoid them until they've had a go at the fresh stuff, then return to the first bit to degrade that more. The hell is the closed drawbridge; no way back or escape. I plead my case; say I never meant to betray my wife and family, but nobody listens. I insist it was Gronya got hold of my balls and made me want to relive my youth; gratify my sexual whims. Gronya appeals to my passionate side. Trouble is she can't satisfy the spiritual, the part that displayed dignity. Now I'm tortured and trapped in a miserable existence.*

Enough. No explanations. No regrets. No looking back. Let's email Madam and see if she'll accommodate me. If not I'd better find a boring, mundane book.

ᎈ ᎈ ᎈ

CHAPTER 18

Madame Wanhope

Who sports a synthetic blindfold
enhanced by a spirit level
while claiming impartiality
Who sleeps with danger
unbalancing the scales
then indulges in feigned wanhope
imperiously declaring innocence, fear and regret

O LLAH LIFTED HER EYELIDS – then shut them. Light caused pain, metaphorical and physical. *Perhaps if I lie absolutely still whatever is banging and rattling inside my skull will give up and stop worriting me.* It didn't work. The cacophony in her head increased in proportion to movement. *Why did I do it? Another Friday night, another bender.* Saturday morning regret punched her consciousness. *Why can't I avoid this bit?* She needed pills and water. Take the edge off. Being inebriated numbed the misery, but offered no solution. *Wish I'd some other recourse, but I don't.* At least today she awoke in her own bed and not some gay guy's. Someone shoved her in a taxi last night, but it was a blur.

Seemed ages since 'that man' seduced Mum and betrayed Dad, her and Hattie? Her family were happy in their own miserable way until he landed in it. For the best part of ten years Mum forced them to tolerate his interference. Then he inveigled Mum into the unspeaka-ble. *Why did Dad put up with it? Even paid the idiot for the privilege of preaching at us. What possessed Dad? Then after 'that man' supposedly retired and Dad accepted him and his unbearable wife as friends, we'd to stomach Adelle telling Mum how wonderful she was and how she shouldn't allow us rule her life. It was awful.* Then after they did what they did, Dad provided them a house. Watching them play lovey-dovey proved nauseating, not that Ollah cooperated in indulging their fantasy.

Ollah knew why she disliked 'that man'. After whee-dling himself into Mum's life under the guise of psychiatrist and therapist, Mum started to behave in ways Ollah didn't appreciate. Mum discovered assertive-ness, argued with Dad, kicked him out of their bed on the pretence of his snoring, and although around when needed, showed less tolerance and spoke up for herself. *We experienced our ups and downs, Hattie her anorexic crises, me my bulimic ones, but Mum nursed us through them. Now she lives down the road and comes to fuss over us at Dad's when we get sick or on our birthdays or at Christmas.* But was it Dad's house? Mum spent so much time there it seemed nothing changed. *Dad said we'd to accept it, but I hate how she insists on going 'home' to 'that* man'. *It's not right. She's our Mum.* Ollah loathed it when Mum went away with him to Exeter near Mum's brother. Before that our uncle would come to Dad's where Mum nursed him through his bad patches. After 'he' seduced her, Mum insisted she visit Exeter to help her brother and left Dad in charge in London. *It's what she does, puts us to bed to sleep and rest while she takes care of everything else. Pity she allows her attention to be diverted by 'him'.*

Ollah dragged her limbs from under the duvet, donned a dressing gown and shuffled downstairs. Clothes lay around the bedroom and on the stairs. She picked up a jacket and threw it aside. It stank of vomit. *Eugh!* Was it hers or a friend's? She'd no idea. Whatever, she'd deal with it later. At least the house was clean and tidy. Ollah slouched into the kitchen, filled the kettle and hunted the cupboards for a mug and stuff to make coffee and swallow painkillers. Ollah leaned on her table and stared at the olive leaf pattern on the tablecloth. The images made her long to taste olive oil sitting on a beach, drinking and eating with friends somewhere far away. It helped summon up visions to displace 'that awful man' from her thoughts. A cat sidled up and rubbed her leg. Ollah bent over to pick her up. The dog and other animals had been removed to Dad's where Mum looked after them during the week. *How has this one been missed?* Hattie being nursed at Dad's meant Mum took Ollah's pets along for the ride.

The kettle boiled. Ollah poured water into her mug.

She fished in the fridge for milk then struggled to open the carton. Mum and Dad must've been round. Ollah couldn't decide whether to be grateful or annoyed. Ollah didn't 'do' housework; it was good to get the place cleaned, but it cost her. Mum and Dad ranted about how she lived in a pigsty and didn't want her pets should suffer. It's why they employed a cleaner to spring clean every few weeks and adopted her cats as well as Hattie's Hera. Her cat peed up Dad's curtains. *They said living with me traumatised it, and Mum wanted to help the thing by giving it a sense of security, so maybe the problem would resolve.* It never did. When she went off with 'that man' Mum dumped Ollah's cat on Dad and took Hera. Ollah suspected Mum loved Hattie more than her, and Hera proved it. That reminded Ollah the cat she'd been petting needed food. She phoned her mum but got no answer so rushed off a txt – *'Mum, cat needs feeding, when can you come down to see to it, or shall I bring it to you?'*

Ollah laced her coffee with milk, spilling some. She looked for a cloth, but decided it was too much effort and left it. She carried the mug into her sitting room, her unsteady hand slopping liquid along the way. *Good job I put my slippers on so I can stand on the blobs and soak up the wet. Can't be bothered to find kitchen paper.* Ollah scrutinised the clean, organised space, wanted to mess it up, but didn't have the energy. It was a paradox in her condition her therapist spouted on about. *According to the theory, my bulimic symptoms don't fit the usual mould. I'm not perfectionist in everything, eager to please or* sensitive to criticism. I just see others as interfering. Don't do self-doubt, I'm too clever, except when in a crisis. Ollah was proud she had the therapists confused, unable to wedge her into any single illness mode that fitted their DSM manual. It proved useful having Hattie at med school. She told Ollah about the DSM book psychiatrists and psychologists used to diagnose what disorders their patients suffered from. Made interesting reading.

Ollah's mobile beeped. 'Will come to feed cat just now. Mum X'. Ollah located the TV remote behind a cushion. She flicked through the channels but saw nothing worth watching. She decided to crawl back to bed to sleep for a bit, but her attention was caught by one of those stupid programmes that offer endless prizes. Wonder what I could win in life that would make me permanently happy? Get a rich man like Dad to love me, acquire the perfect figure, get Mum and Dad back together? Reckon it would be great to have a baby. It'd keep me busy and fulfilled, and these days you don't need a man to achieve that, they're incidental to the process. Trouble is I'm nearly past it. Maybe Dad would give me the money to get my eggs frozen, then when I'm ready go for artificial insemination? There's an idea. Must research later when the pills kick in.

She turned off the TV and crawled upstairs. She flopped into her pit, pulled the duvet over her head and drifted off to sleep. She awoke startled when her mother let herself in and shouted down she was in bed. Ollah tried to compose herself but when Mum appeared in her bedroom doorway a few minutes later, Ollah could not contain herself.

"You look paler than usual, Ollah."

"So would you after the dream I just had."

"What was it about?"

"Werpils."

"Were they ghastly creatures, blind, half snake and half worm, immersed in a foul bog?"

"How'd you know?"

"Hattie described a similar dream. Did one of the Werpils resemble you?"

"Yeah."

"Same as Hattie. One in hers looked like her."

"Did Hattie's Werpils wave their back claws in the air, and stuff their mouths with prescription pills, bags of illegal drugs, syringes and money?"

"Sounds identical."

"Eugh. The foul stench they gave off is stuck in my nostrils."

"Poor dear. Where can I find cat food? Poor unfortunate animal needs feeding before it chews its paws off from hunger."

"Before you do I've an idea."

"What's that?"

"I want a baby."

"Right…?"

"Did you hear? Fancy having a kid. Before it's too late. If I leave it much longer, I'll be too old, biologically."

"Don't you need a husband or partner, even if only

for the procreation bit?"

"There will be hurdles. I must research. But reckon it would be good for me."

"You do that, dear. Research, I mean. In the meantime, rest while I feed the cat. When are you due to see your therapist? Perhaps you should discuss the idea with her?"

℘ ℘ ℘

OLLAH WAS ON her way to her therapy session armed with research into having babies. Her parents would be hard to convince. Before she tackled them on funding her proposals she'd to prove she'd considered it in detail. Her therapist's opinion would carry weight with Mum and Dad. So, if Ollah won her support, they might be persuaded.

"Good to see you, Ollah. Where were we when we left off?"

"I want to discuss happiness."

"Any particular aspect?"

"I believe my family have a right to be happy. All of us."

"I wouldn't argue against such a proposition."

"I understand happiness is never a permanent state of affairs. Otherwise how can anybody discern the difference between that and melancholy?"

"Your point being?"

"We've discussed 'that man' and how he destroyed my family's happiness. Tried to take Mum away. Hasn't entirely succeeded, but it's not fair he takes any of her time."

"Are we back to Bentham's Happiness Principle? We've aired it many times; how he based it on the notion that the happiness of the majority should prevail. But your mother's object was to increase her individual happiness quotient, which is just as important. I thought you reconciled yourself to the idea that if your mother is happier with her lover, she'll bring more happiness to your family because she's fulfilled and content, whereas inside the family things were strained by her unhappy relationship with your father. You seem unable to overcome resentment at her finding personal happiness outside your family."

"We did get over it. Sort of. I swallowed your logic when we last discussed it."

"So why are we covering this again?"

"Because the idea only makes sense when I'm sober."

"So if you cope when sober, why semi self-destruct by boozing? Why sabotage progress towards positive goals? If drunken inhibitions or bingeing – which are connected behaviours as you acknowledge – allow distorted thinking to emerge, why indulge, especially if it makes you unhappy?"

"I'm aware of the logic, but can't resist the booze or the food. Logic disappears when I see oblivion in the bottom of my glass or fill my stomach to bursting."

"So let's go over it again. How do booze or food blowouts help?"

"I don't know. I only know when I feel unhappy I need to get drunk and want to wipe myself out like the half-digested stinking mess I retch down the drain."

"So where do we go from here? Can you suggest strategies to stop yourself bingeing?"

"I have an idea."

"Let's discuss."

"I want to have a baby."

"That's certainly one proposal. How will it help?"

"It'll give my parents a grandchild. Bring the family together to support each other and marginalize personal needs as we all concentrate on a new life."

"How do you propose going about it?"

"Been reading up about how they harvest ovaries and store eggs. Then later on the eggs are fertilized and embryos transplanted to the womb."

"How much research have you done?"

"Trawled the internet. If my parents agree to fund egg harvesting and preservation I'll commit to getting off booze and bingeing forever."

"Huge commitments. You're nearly forty and attempted to achieve those goals your whole adult life. Do you think a child will help you achieve them – permanently?"

"Don't know. But reckon it's worth a try?"

CB CB CB

MUM WAS DUE after spending the morning with Hattie. Ollah expected her early afternoon, so went downstairs, scattered papers on baby research about the kitchen and returned to bed to nurse her hangover. *What is it Dad says? Softly, softly, catchee monkey. Mum didn't believe I was serious; could tell from her tone when she said "You do that, dear. Rest first while I feed the cat."*

Ollah heard the key in the lock. She lay still while her mother emptied shopping bags and filled the fridge; then boiled a kettle and rummage in cupboards, presumably to make coffee or tea. All went silent except for the sound of paper rustling. Then Ollah heard mumbling. *Mum must be on the phone. Wonder if she phoned Dad or 'that man'. Can't risk trying to creep downstairs to find out who she's talking to.*

A head appeared round her bedroom door.

"Are you awake, Ollah? Brought coffee."

"Good."

"Found your papers in the kitchen."

"What do you think?"

"Have you spoken with your father?"

"Not yet. Spoke to my therapist who says the idea has merit."

"Really."

"Told her how if I had a child, I'd commit to never binge-eating and boozing again. Hoped you and Dad would be pleased with the idea of a grandchild. You love cooing over babies, don't you?"

"Is that what you're banking on? Me doing the child-rearing?"

"You'd want to, wouldn't you? I'd need to work to

pay Dad back for the egg-harvesting and other treatments."

"You never reimbursed him for those two years you dropped out of legal work and went back to college."

"Couldn't afford to. Anyway, Dad paid for Hattie to do an extra two years at med school, so I reckon that about evens it all up."

"What exactly did your therapist say?"

"I'd spent my whole adult life trying to achieve the goals of stopping bingeing and boozing and said I should consider carefully whether having a baby would help me. I have and am sure it will."

"It doesn't just affect you."

"It'll bring us closer. Babies always do; bring families closer."

"You dropped out of college and went back to law because you said you didn't have the patience to face a class of demanding kids. How will baby demands be different to a schoolroom full of kids?"

"Babies have different demands. They need feeding and someone to cuddle them to sleep. That's why you like that bit so I can leave it to you while I earn."

"Babies grow into school children."

"Miles in the future."

"Not sure where this conversation takes us. You have all the answers. Not sure I do. Speak to Dad since your whole edifice is based on his willingness to pay for treatment. That could be the hurdle you can't get over."

"We'll see. He always forgives my debts in the end."

 C3 C3 C3

OLLAH WAS TO MEET Milner for lunch in the City. She'd thrown a sickie yesterday and didn't feel like bothering with work today, but Dad agreed to discuss her baby proposals over a meal before one of his board meetings. It would be bad form not to show. Ollah was prepared. Dad could always be talked round. He never denied anything she wanted. *He'll see I've changed. Will eat a good healthy meal and not touch alcohol. He's bound to be impressed.*

The morning train commute proved tedious. Solid grey skies and rain-sodden streets were barely visible through dirt-streaked steamy windows. One relief was to readjust her view and study the weed-infested gravel surrounding the tracks and impedimenta to do with sleepers, wires and signalling. The alternative was the distraction offered by the heavily graffitied bridges and walls along the track. None of it appealed. Rush hour invaded her senses with increased intensity due to the damp and humidity. The pungent odours from wet tailored wool suiting, no matter how expensive, always made her stomach churn. *Why do wives never get husbands' suits dry cleaned?* The bright spot on her horizon was the prospect of her baby plans. New life, new opportunities, new everything.

"Good to see you, Ollah."

"Dad."

"How are things in legal copyright these days?"

"Litigious as usual. It's what makes it a profitable

branch of law."

"Your mother told me of your plans."

"What do you reckon? Will you help me? Would prove how caring and supportive we are as a family."

"Why do we need to prove what we already do?"

"It would give Mum a purpose for starters."

"Are you suggesting she has no purpose to her life?"

"Her concentration is not on us the way it used to be."

"Aside from that."

"It would marginalise The Cat Murderer as Hattie calls him. It would up end that Sabina who betrayed her mother. Show some people stick to ethics and don't just talk them. What I propose would prove the opposite, how much we need Mum in our family, love and want her."

"Ollah. I came to see you because Mum said your aim was to give you a reason to end bingeing and boozing. What has that to do with your mother and her lover?"

"Their relationship is why I can't recover. He ruined our lives, destroyed our happiness and took away any chance I had of getting over my problems. Look how Hattie relapsed. All down to him."

"You are incorrigible, Ollah."

"I know, Dad. It's why you love me. You see yourself in me."

"I've seen no costings. Send them so I can consider before we talk further."

"Sure, Dad. I'll email what I've collected. I'll give you a week then call to fix another chat. Don't want you thinking I'm not serious or will lose interest if you don't get back to me. No delaying tactics please."

"Would I?"

"We've played this game for years. Learnt the rules from you."

"Trained you well, didn't I?"

"Sure did."

"I promise to give your idea careful consideration. But no badgering. This is heavy duty, not to be treated with frivolity. A baby requires a big commitment."

"I know. I've thought about it lots. I do have some principles."

CR CR CR

CHAPTER 19

A Long Night's Journey into Day

Who saw only good in those they believed friends
and expected no harm from those they trusted
Who naively judged others
to have honesty and integrity
Who believed hot water never came from cold taps
and learned 'I mean you no harm' and 'I want only the
    best for you'
were misleading duplicitous lies

ADELLE BRUSHED AWAY the tears aroused by the vivid nightmare burnt on her memory. She never used to remember dreams. Now she did. Confused, she wondered if she was awake or dreaming. Acute pain accompanied both states. No – at this moment she was fully conscious – the framed print triptych of Bosch's *Garden of Earthly Delights* on the wall opposite her bed accentuated the irony; a painful reminder of past and present. She lay and contemplated the idea of reality vs nightmare a la Bosch. Were they different beasts? How long was it since Julian abandoned her? Seemed like yesterday. Perhaps the forty-five-year marriage was the dream she woke from this morning. The misery clawed at her insides to disabuse her. Words by Sir Thomas Browne meandered through her thoughts. 'But who knows the fate of his bones, or how often he is to be buried.' Browne wrote about human remains found at archaeological sites, pleading with those uncovering them to '…mercifully preserve their bones and piss not upon their ashes…'. Julian did that, metaphorically speaking – pissed on the ashes of the bonfire on which he tossed the bones of her life, hopes, dreams and all she spent decades building.

She rolled over to pick up the tablet that filled the space Julian had occupied for so long. She swiped the screen to access her poetry folder. It was her morning ritual after asking – *will this pain ever go away*? The wraiths of memory would not release her. Attempts to put her agony into words helped, but the fix was temporary. She edited the verbiage poured into verse yesterday.

Asclepius

What hubris caused you to believe the lies
to abandon Asclepius and his healing rod –
there was no ambiguity in the venom you espoused –
just poisonous decay
that sped through the bloodstream of our love
like a canker – debasing, corrupting

and destroying trust

Your obdurate bafflement at my grief and anger
were necessary to alleviate your guilt
but why was it necessary to destroy my life
deprive me of my child's trust
and the hope vested in my grandchildren

To assuage your lust and loss of dignity –
you poisoned my wells
made me a whipping post and scapegoat for
    your failure
turned me into Aunt Sally
cast evil into me like the Gadarene swine
What for? –
there is no panacea for you
in the nebulous promises
of a misguided fantasy
that tainted everything it brushed against
adolescent at its very core
and incapable of endurance

Satisfied for the moment, she closed her Dropbox
and forced herself out of bed. She'd delayed enough. She
must face it. The daily routine assaulted her senses as
memories escaped the fortress where she attempted to
incarcerate them. Most provocative were music and
smells. Disembodied radio voices blathered away –
allowed her to embrace the illusion she was not alone –

when a tune from their early life drifted into consciousness. As the words and melody penetrated her memory,
her stomach churned, an indigestion-like spasm seared
up towards her throat and tears coursed down her
cheeks. *Why can't I control these feelings? Why can't I fall
sleep and not wake up?* She didn't want to die, just arrive
at permanent oblivion so the dreams might end. One of
her maxims was heaven or hell was created on earth; no
need to wait for death to transport you to imagined
nether regions. She had evidence. She lived in a hell
created for her by the man she adored since sixteen, the
year they saw *Countess Billy* at a local theatre. The
programme from the performance was in her collection,
although now lost to her, locked in an attic of a house
barred to her.

His sock and winter vest drawers were saturated with
his odour. Scented liners couldn't banish him. His smell
would spill out and dance in her nostrils whenever she
opened them. Caught unawares – hoping the perfumed
scraps of paper she lined them with had done their job –
she found it ended the same way every time, with a
visceral reaction identical to the one that erupted to
musical prompts. Blowing a snotty nose didn't wash it
out. The whole thing squatted in her head, like an old
vinyl record with a stylus stuck in a groove that summoned words, notes and memories scrambled together in
a never-ending memorial dirge. She banished his essence
from the bed with a new mattress, pillow and linen, but
he was ingrained in the drawer joints and seams from

where he refused to be dislodged.

Everyday tasks dragged out mixed emotions. Smiles were conjured up by memory flashes of happy days when they revelled in a loving, caring family, held together by an emotional superglue unique to themselves. Asked then if she played the lottery, she insisted she'd no need; she won it when she found Julian. They escaped adolescence as one, supported each other through whatever life threw at them. Now he was gone, forty-five years of love and devotion discarded. *On what? Would have died for them all. Wouldn't have questioned why. How did this betrayal happen? None of it makes sense. Did I live under an illusion?* It didn't help when counsellors and friends said she'd done nothing wrong; legally he committed adultery and deserted her. She realised she had, over time, mistakenly constructed his identity out of desire with no solid foundation. She longed for her memory bank to transmogrify into a sieve, to grind her recollections to a fine dust to be washed away through the mesh.

Even this she was ambivalent about. The ideal would be to discard selected memories. She wanted to treasure good times but feared they might be diluted or swept away by heart-breaking ones. How to forgive the tsunami of misery he drowned her in, that overwhelmed and wiped out what they created with love? *Why cruelly and deliberately abandon what we built? I believed our hearts and bones had been fused never to be separated.* It resembled an amputation. The limb was gone but the phantom remained, registering pain. Why separate himself the way he did? Turn off love and affection like a tap. Had he loved or merely needed her? *How deluded was I?* She put away pictures of him from around the house, unable to bear his face staring out from cold, stiff picture frames. The wedding album was worst. She hid it at the bottom of a cupboard. Her urge was to slash every picture to shreds as he had her life and all she nurtured. One day she would; if she ever arrived at calm acceptance he was gone and she was better for it. How she longed for that dawn. Sometimes she caught glimpses of how it might be, but most days were vast emptinesses of excruciating longing.

Her memory conjured up unwanted thoughts of the last time she saw him, when she noticed his wedding band. He prattled on about how she'd no need to worry, she'd never be alone or lonely, would always be loved and looked after. The ring focused her anger; she demanded to know if he understood the disrespect he showed her and his whore of a lover by wearing it. Julian said he hadn't considered it, assumed Adelle was still his wife and would do what he wanted. Adelle should accept Gronya as part of their lives and not indulge in name calling. *What distorted egregious thinking.*

Adelle dressed mechanically. She was to meet a friend for coffee, but getting past the front door was a chore. *Can I ever face the world? Be excited about life again?* Eventually, she dragged herself to the café, ordered a drink and sat. *I mustn't go on about him and my unhappiness if I hear trigger words. Why can't I stop myself? I know it's stupid the moment their eyes glaze over.* She read somewhere loss brought more loss in a pile up of calamity it was difficult to crawl out from under. When she asked Julian why he slept with his patient he responded he owed no explanation and intended to give none, then suggested they live in a kind of ménage à trois. His answer, though revelatory, stung because she had to accept he hadn't grown up, just got old. *What an incredible response, him being a psychiatrist an all. It was true – cobblers' children wore the worst shoes.*

Her friend arrived and ordered coffee for herself and another for Adelle. While she waited Adelle stared at her empty cup, the frothy remnants from the whipped milk stuck round the rim. *Why does everything have to remind me? I must be strong. Talk about anything except 'him'.* She looked up and smiled as her friend put a tray down. As this happened Adelle glanced past; immediately her smile froze and tears welled. She fished for a hanky, but her coat was hung inside out over the back of the chair; she twisted to pull at it, expose the pocket and find one. No luck. She lugged her handbag up between her knees and searched frantically in its depths.

"What's the matter?" asked her friend in a tone that said she knew what to expect.

Adelle nodded towards the entrance where a mother struggled down the stairs with a buggy in one hand and a curly blonde eighteen-month-old held tightly with the other. The child stood on the top step, sucked a finger and shook her head.

"Come on, you wanted to, you can manage," pleaded the mother.

The proprietor rushed to help with the buggy while the mother concentrated on the child, who consented to take one step at a time. At the bottom she smiled and reached to be picked up.

"Still no contact then?" said her friend as Adelle wiped her face and blew her nose.

"No. Don't suppose there ever will. It's been three years. I miss them so much."

"Do you want to go?"

"Give me a minute. Just can't stop the sad feelings hitting me like a tornado when I see a child resembling Katy. She was small enough to cuddle, feed a night time bottle last time I saw her. Guess she's too big now; wouldn't remember me. Don't know what she looks like. Not allowed photos. Wrote a poem about it. Not sure it helped. Sometimes it does, but if I stayed home so I don't see babies, I'd never come out. Perhaps that would please Sabina. Don't know. Hasn't spoken to me in three years."

"Have you a copy of the poem?"

"It's in my Dropbox if you want to read it."

"OK."

Adelle located it and handed her phone over.

Hurt

(to a lost daughter)

No one can hurt you like a child –
lured into a mire of guilt
entrapped in a bog of discarded ethics
presided over by a callous manipulator
whose shallow simpering
hid a stagnant reservoir of calculated selfishness

Why is a child so quick to destroy –
the fragile web of love so carefully woven
in favour of self-serving falsehoods
that deny dignity and respect to a mother
through scathing language and abuse of long
    held trust

Why is a child so quick to discard a mother –
whose struggle and sacrifice was willingly made
who took pride in her child's achievements
whose loyalty was unquestioning
who cannot understand why her child would want to
sever the bond that should never be undermined,
    fade or die

Why is a child so quick to forget –
the happy times
the preciousness of belonging
the safety and comfort of being accepted for what
    they are
and belief in their potential

No one can hurt you like a child –
who chooses not to understand the pain and grief
of a shattered togetherness
that should have stood like a fortress on
    strong ground
but was instead
built on foundations of sand whipped by
    carnal winds

While her friend perused the poem Adelle's mind wandered through the torment that caused the rift with Sabina – Ben's birthday party. Daniel and Natalie arrived that day with Alexander, followed shortly by the cousins, who burst in with childish abandon at being released from car seats. Adelle remembered the fervour exuded by their excitement. Shopping for the party had taken energy. It was Ben's second that year; the first held the previous day in Julian and Gronya's honour. In the end granddad turned up to that party – late and alone. Gronya's cat, Hera, had been killed outside the love nest, run over by a car. Adelle heard Daniel and Sabina whisper about it as she made tea in the kitchen. Gronya was too distraught to attend and pleaded with Julian not to go, she needed his comfort. Gronya and Milner had faced Hattie; the row had been terrible. Hattie accused Gronya and Julian of negligence and selfishness, said if they'd not wrecked her family, Hera would be alive and they had killed her. *Such fuss over a cat? Shouldn't Julian's priority be Ben? Of course not, stupid, in new relationships lovers take precedence over grandchildren, don't they? Anyway, if Ben had a good time at my party, he may have remembered and preferred mine in future. Ungracious and spiteful maybe, but all's fair in love and war, don't they say?*

Adelle wondered if what happened next was karma, then dismissed the idea. Divorce proceedings were commenced and Julian, who couldn't remember what furniture he agreed to let Adelle have, demanded a list, which Adelle readied to send to her solicitor. It was a game. Julian had a full manifest of the items. Indeed, went to France with Gronya for a week to pack and load them onto the moving van. He'd phoned from France crying copiously, saying he couldn't face it. Adelle told him it wasn't her problem, if he wanted comfort his woman was down in the village. She got some response that Gronya wasn't coping. Julian didn't appreciate the irony; gave the impression he expected Adelle to support him the way she always had.

The day after the party the photos surfaced. Emails went to unintended recipients. Sabina had taken photos of her flat for Julian. In the email to her father, Sabina wrote 'Let me know when you have what you want and I'll delete the evidence.' *Why didn't Sabina and Julian simply hold me down and tear out my heart with no anaesthetic? Would have been less painful. At least I'd be dead.* Since then Adelle dreaded the nightmares where she relived the pain of the stunned sense of betrayal that engulfed her. Misery piled on misery. When asked why, Sabina said she did nothing wrong, wouldn't apologise;

Adelle had been abusive; could no longer see Ben and Katy – not until the divorce was finalised. That took twelve months. Adelle woke every morning in agony, tempted to swallow all and every pill she could lay her hands on. She was undecided on whether to be grateful she had none to hand.

"You told me before, but remind me again. Why did Sabina hint at abuse of some kind?"

"She knew how it would hurt me. The best form of defence is attack. It's how bullies behave, they justify themselves at others' expense."

"How do you mean?"

"You avoid shame and guilt by insisting others forced you to do what you did."

"Guess such logic explains Julian's behaviour."

"For sure. Enough. Let's change the subject."

Coffee lifted Adelle's spirits. Her tummy fluttered as her friend talked about a planned outing later in the week. Adelle thought about the old house where she worked at weekends; how she loved the place, its history and the marvellous sense of belonging it brought. But her elation didn't last long. It hit her as she walked home; the painful decision never to see her grandchildren again. Sabina's vindictive, unfounded accusations and willingness to use her children to punish her meant Adelle daren't risk Ben and Katy being used that way in the future. She must protect them and herself from Sabina's whims. She missed them every day, her grief like suppurated wounds, her heart a hollow, rattling tin box.

Some expert, in an attempt to assuage her misery suggested, with time, anguish would turn to nostalgia. She would cry over them, but not with today's raw pain. *Will that day ever come? Will Ben and Katy come to despise me because Sabina is unable to appraise the consequences of her actions?* What irony Sabina supervised clinical psychology PhD students. *Strange how mental health practitioners apply the maxim 'Don't do as I do, do as I say.' Wasn't it Sartre who wrote, "Hell is other people"?*

Adelle peered at shoppers loaded with bags of stuff; food, clothes, cosmetics. *Are they real? Is what they carry substantial? Look at them. Do I hate them or am I jealous? How do they go on as normal? How do they laugh, shop, drive, take holidays while my world has collapsed down a sinkhole? Maybe theirs has too and they shop as a form of therapy. Never worked for me. Maybe they are just skeletons adorned with skin, titanium implants, jewellery and empty plastic bags covered in advertising, there to taunt me?* In dreams she visualised the bottom of an abyss, where fiery flakes rained from the sky, landing on a surface of quicksand, pockmarked with craters of boiling blood and fire. In this vision she huddled with her grandchildren on a small island under a makeshift shelter that offered limited protection from the deluge. Walking past her on a wobbly bridge was Milner protected from the molten torrent by a Kevlar umbrella.

Adelle entered a shop. On impulse she sought comfort in a bouquet of flowers to take home. *Am I a hypocrite or what? Criticise bags of bones who shop as a form of therapy, then I do likewise.* She longed to stare at King Proteas, to wallow in memories of Africa where she and Julian had met and married, where they viewed the Victoria Falls, or as the locals called them Mosi-oa-Tunya, the Smoke that Thunders. She closed her eyes; allowed her mind to transport her to stand in front of that solid wall of water cascading over the rocks; the sound echoing in her ears. The lush rain forest nurtured by the gentle mist thrown up from the valley below had, for her, been a symbol of their life. Now she pictured the Falls as a place where hope was dashed down a chasm, battered on rocks, pounded into foam and froth, then washed downstream to disappear in shallows.

Once home, she arranged the Proteas in a vase, set them on a table, sat down and stared at them while she chewed on food that tasted of sawdust. Nothing had flavour. An idea came to her. There was something she'd to do. There was no point keeping 'it' any longer. She'd send it back. He created it; he must destroy it, just as he destroyed everything else. She retrieved the tin from her bedside cabinet, the one that held Julian's love letters from their dating days. In an idle moment at work he used an adding machine roll to scribble thirty-nine inches of nonsense spilling out his adoration – then fashioned and fitted neat handles at either end, rolled it up, stamped it with the office 'confidential' stamp and covered it with XXXXXX's. She remembered her delight when he presented it to her on a cushion, his face serious as he watched her read, anxious for her to understand how much he wanted to marry her. Would she ever feel that way again; safe, secure, loved and treasured? The other items to return were the bible he gave her as a present. Slipped into its pages were his love poems. His handwriting was tidy and precise and they joked how he might fail his medical exams because it was legible. Returning these items would signal acceptance that all affection and devotion had gone, trampled to dust with his ethics.

She sought to delay the inevitable and disperse miserable memories by grabbing pen and paper. The words spilled onto the page and distracted her for an hour or two as she fashioned thoughts into ideas. She dawdled a bit more searching for an envelope strong enough to protect the items in the post, before ritually sealing her life inside a bubble-wrap tomb to be carried in a mailbag to their creator. It seemed simple. *Why then was it so difficult? Why the need to finish my poem before despatching the parcel?*

The Indefinable Thing

What is that indefinable thing
that veneer that professionals
wear like a cloak
to define 'honourableness'

They strut like peacocks in their self-styled cloak
woven from noble verbiage like –
    decency

        decorum
and concepts like
        fitness to practise
            rules of conduct

How easily the cloak is thrown off
How easily the weave tears and separates
How quickly the pattern distorts and disintegrates
when honourable conduct
clashes with carnal desire
in a web of compromise
where self-interest garrottes compassion

Four-plus decades of patiently weaving a love with
        loyalty, trust and devotion
its delicate pattern carefully counted and
        intricately stitched
then –
one pull of a loose thread
by an egocentric with superficial charm
and I am left holding the torn pieces
wondering where 'honourableness' has got me
and why it failed to hold together the fabric so tightly
        and carefully woven

She stared at the ideas she elucidated. It was Julian's
rejection of professional ethics she struggled with. They
were the reason she admired and loved him. He stuck to

principles. Those collapsed like a house of cards when that woman appeared. *Ugly witch. Mean and meaty, big and beefy. Why can't I stop terrible ideas about her possessing me? Will I ever overcome my disgust for that spiteful woman, who pretended to be my friend to steal Julian and my life?* Logic suggested a woman so desperate, with a millionaire husband and every whim catered for, but who needed a bit of 'rough', must be inadequate, would never be fulfilled, and Julian was a fool to believe happiness depended on sex with her.

The trouble was the evidence of Milner and Gronya's calculated plan and Julian's gullibility proved over-whelming. Adelle remembered when Julian misdirected emails between him, Gronya and Milner. It started when Adelle wrote to Milner who told her he wanted to be her friend. *How naive was I to believe that?* Adelle knew Sabina and family, Julian and Gronya were in Exeter over a holiday weekend. So she emailed Milner to say she hoped he'd have a good weekend. It was an attempt to reach out, let Milner know she had empathy for his aloneness – as friends do. Milner forwarded Adelle's email to Gronya and Julian, mocked her and asked them what Adelle was up to. *Milner, ever the schemer, saw ulterior motives. Should have consulted those psychiatrists and psychologists he'd spent a fortune on down the years. They'd have told him he was projecting his motives onto the innocent.* What more proof did Adelle need of Milner and Gronya's appalling actions and Julian's naivety? Julian listened to Gronya's moaning about Milner's failures and her children's selfish attention-grabbing behaviour during ten years of therapy. His solution during therapy had been to deliver her a master class in how to manipulate and control them. Now he'd allowed her to do the same to him. What a monster. Gronya's pain was the only pain that counted and she never hesitated to exploit the entitlement she believed went along with it.

Adelle once discussed Jeremy Bentham with Milner. It gave her another idea for a poem.

The Happiness Principle

Oh Jeremy – you auto-icon you –
sitting in your box –
all wax head and hay stuffing

Unlike you –
my dissection took place while I lived –
leaving me alive and in agony –
as every facet of my happiness
was disembowelled –
strewn like carrion
for vultures to feed on

Do I qualify as an example
of your 'Happiness Principle' –
accepting others right to happiness
at the cost of my own?

Perhaps my brain –
made waxy with pain and betrayal –
staring into the void
that has swallowed all I loved –
is wrong to fantasise
that those who destroyed my piece of mind
are unhappy –
that in some way –
they too feel the grief and endless emptiness
caused by their selfish pursuit
of the 'Happiness Principle'

Bentham got it wrong. Should have called it The Pain Principle, based his philosophy on the idea that it is an individual's duty to ensure what they do causes the least pain to the least number of people. *I spent my life trying to make my loved ones happy and they turned on me. Now we are all in pain – caused by two selfish individuals who believe they have the right to seek personal happiness above everyone else.*

Adelle thought she understood Julian. All those years together she believed his identity had grown from an accretion of layers of influence from his parents, built on by medical ethics. She thought he was strong and unshakeable, but Gronya gnawed away at him and robbed him of honour. As a result he dragged his family into an ugly morass where no one was happy and everyone cheated and lied.

Adelle held Julian's identity in trust all those years and never betrayed or tried to change it; she loved him unconditionally. She believed they reflected each other, steadfast, true, loyal and loving. Now his silence clamoured in her ears, she felt him there in her pores and her thoughts, as she had all their adult lives. He ticked away inside her like a clock, tick-tock, tick-tock. How to rid herself of him? There must be some way.

CB CB CB

CHAPTER 20

The Cat Whisperer

Who publicly affects to digest the past
but forgets he is not omnipotent
or able to dispel remnants of discontent
Who publicly affects to face problems with courage
but capriciously exploits weakness
making cat's paws of victims
Who publicly affects to sooth worries
but relies on selfishly acquired gains
without understanding the inadequate,
    ineffectual nature of his tools

CAR WHEELS SCRUNCHING GRAVEL coincided with Milner surfacing from a troublesome dream. He recognised the distinctive engine growl that signalled the visitor as Gronya. He bought her the vehicle shortly before his plans came to fruition. They shared an interest in cars and engines, and she drove well, provided she had a navigator. Now she had a new one – navigator that was – although Milner guessed Julian's habit of studied slow responses would be frustrating in tense traffic situations. *Don't waste thoughts on him, he's her problem. I got her what she wanted.*

In the aftermath of his return from France he struggled to decide if Belldeep was ghostly or ghastly. Had he dreamt it, had an out of body experience or physically visited an alternative reality? His struggle to budge Jester's interrogations from consciousness didn't clarify or provide answers. With the lapse of time and distance he believed he'd successfully hewn the annoying experience into perspective and decided he dreamed the whole episode. He had it under control. If only Jester hadn't reappeared on computer screens lately with taunts that forced him to reconsider earlier challenges. *What happened to my well-honed ability to rationalise situations; get the proper slant on things?*

He'd begun to suffer frightening episodes of sleep paralysis when he woke immobilized, unable to move his body or turn his head. He'd call out, but his mouth wouldn't open and emit the words his brain screamed. These were accompanied by a sense of pressure on his chest that weighed him down – made him short of breath. A deep sense of dread or danger petrified him when he intuited Hera was there, lying on him and he was unable to move to shake her off. Limb movement returned after he sensed her jump off. *Hera would never turn against me, I loved her, she was my guide and helper at Belldeep. Surely she would never torment or desert me?*

His frustration arose because he'd watched with satisfaction as the new situations and relationships settled into acceptance and routine. What right did Jester have to come back and challenge that? The one disappointment was never to return to France; couldn't face it despite his fondness for the village and the people. He and Gronya kept contact with Madame who they promised to visit, but that was to maintain strategic lines of communication. They'd need her if Julian sold that wretched house of his in the village. Milner envisaged lots of hand-holding, if only to keep Gronya in order while everyone got worked up over the legals. *Unwise investment if ever there was one. Caused endless difficulty. Still, shouldn't be too critical, Julian and Adelle's legal difficulties with that landscaper facilitated my aim to pervert Julian's ethics. Sure didn't get anywhere fast trying to undermine them any other way.*

Milner had retired the night before because he almost missed the last train home. Poor sleep left him tense and irritated. He wanted to drift back to unconsciousness, but the engine cut-off switched his senses to full alert. He anticipated the sound of the key in the front door, which overrode his wish to avoid the necessary effort to get up. Gronya came to see to Hattie. It might be Saturday, but she kept her priorities ordered. *Suppose I should be grateful Julian isn't one of them, or doesn't appear to be.* Hattie and Ollah took precedence as planned. As much as Milner disliked her betrayal of their marriage, he adjusted, gave in to the inevitable, and helped her achieve her desire to have Julian. In doing so, he aimed to keep intact Gronya's subservience to her daughters' whims. He refused to cope with them; needed her to bear the brunt. He supplied the dosh while she ensured his input was minimal during illness episodes. Despite their difficult personalities he loved Ollah and Hattie and considered their mother best for them, her patience with them far outlasting his.

Yesterday's visit to the City had wearied him, something unusual for him. He was more accustomed to feelings of elation after city escapades. He enjoyed board meetings followed by chit-chat, a chew over decisions taken, achievements achieved; then dinner with colleagues to sound out future schemes and investments; economic indicators to watch for; market movements to be aware of; paths to take in different scenarios. Gronya's arrival forced him to subsume these ideas into general concerns to be dealt with later. He decided his immediate priority should be to get up and offer help. If he didn't, she'd knock on his door – an undesirable outcome. He guessed he'd need to shop to stock up items for the house. Gronya would have a list and he would sort it – pursued the same routine for years. She hated the idea of bugs on supermarket trolley handles. If forced to use one she took bacterial wipes to decontaminate them. She treated him the same for yonks, the nadir coming when she kicked him out of their marital bed on the pretext of his unbearable snoring. He knew it was because he physically repulsed her. Her shudders and squirms when he hugged her confirmed it. He accepted it, but it still shocked when it finally dawned why she behaved as she did.

How long since it all kicked off? Little changed after her move to the house he bought her to create a love nest for Julian. She'd been full of it; happy and excited. Although unable to predict how long it might last, he calculated the peace and quiet payoff was a bargain. He hoped for a lengthy reprieve before she discovered it wasn't what she expected or desired. When that day arrived Milner had plan B to manage the fall out, which he determined she'd live with. She must grow up, shut up and put up; learn to accept consequences. He began to experience mixed feelings about the high financial cost when, all too soon, the short-lived reprieve of the calm haven he longed to spend time gloating over was blighted. At close quarters she discovered Julian's difficult personality. *She tried to moan to me about it, but I cut her off. Not my business; that was the deal. I got her what she wanted – that ended any obligation on me to listen to her whine.*

At the start, Gronya turned up at his house all sweetness and light in an effort to solicit Milner's cooperation, then go back to Julian where he supposed she bitched about him and the girls' unreasonable demands. Did Milner feel sorry for Julian? Not at all. Julian knew the score; he entertained her gripes in therapy for years. Milner heard gossip about how the sympathy Julian showed in therapy sessions and during their honeymoon period changed to cold unresponsive stares. She moaned Julian no longer responded to her; but sat in silence while she rattled on. She complained he used to cuddle her and show understanding, but now, if the gossip was true, the physical stuff had evaporated. *Ironic. I paid him an hourly fee to listen to her for years. Liquidating shares to buy the house for her cost more than therapy short term; but now Julian is at her whim – day or night. Maybe it is still a bargain.* In terms of shedding stress, Milner had arrived at a win-win. He wouldn't lose money on the property long term as the purchase ended up in a family trust. Julian would be homeless if Gronya predeceased him, but Milner calculated the world wouldn't blame him because he was the cuckolded one. Reasoned he'd be seen as tolerant and benign, a long-suffering man who did everything to ensure the lovers realised their dreams. It wouldn't be Milner's fault if it didn't turn out the perfect romance Gronya fantasised and obsessed about.

There'd been the odd occasion he wanted to provoke her; ask if the dick proved as fulfilling as she imagined. Milner had no need; he was sure it wasn't because he knew she was incapable of change. Julian would discover for himself she was impossible to satisfy. Milner never found the secret. In the end he settled for buying periods of peace and calm. Sometimes he doubted the effort and expenditure were worth the price he and his girls paid. The initial period of adjustment was painful. It was hard to swallow Gronya's and the girls' antagonism as well as her guilt and misery, but he endured it to ensure she nursed Hattie and Ollah when they needed her. On the positive side, Gronya owed him and had to deliver without reference to Milner's shortcomings. Her new target was Julian's inadequacy.

Why can't I stop the memory dance? Why do I relive scenes between us? It's like a jack-in-the-box; I shut the lid, someone turns a handle, plays a tune, the lid flies open and the clown springs out to mock me. Milner was contemptuous of Gronya's insistence she could meet Julian's needs. His own experience informed him she would fail. Like the day she told him she planned to accompany Julian to France to support him while he packed up the furniture he agreed Adelle could have for her flat. Milner struggled to hide smirks or control the laughter that welled up. He predicted disaster, and by all accounts was correct. Madame later spilled the story about how Julian slept alone at the old marital home the whole visit, while Gronya sat in Madame's kitchen in the village sobbing. Julian didn't eat with them in the evenings, skulking alone and miserable up at his house. *Can picture Julian assuming the task like a hair shirt in an effort to ease his guilt. Wonder if he crawled around at night on his knees flaying himself? Certainly acted the martyr by all accounts.* This tied in with Gronya's tight-lipped refusal to discuss the trip when she returned home. He was sure the greater part of the failure was Gronya's given his knowledge of her ways.

Long ago Milner concluded WB Yeats was right when he said 'Was there ever a dog who praised his fleas?' The more he learned of Julian, the more he struggled to figure out what Gronya saw; or Adelle for that matter. *Why were they besotted by him? Pompous stick-in-the-mud, dog-in-the-manger sort.* He remained civil to Julian in public. In private Milner used the tactics he taught himself to hone in on in opponents' pain, guilt, unhappiness and arrogance so he could ignore these annoying traits or alternatively use them as weapons to undermine. It was one way to ensure he avoided the misery of Gronya bestowing love and affection on Julian while rejecting him. Julian wasn't big enough to do the same for his lot. That was Milner's horrible misjudgement; how shallow, incapable and petty an individual Julian turned out when dealing with personalities and keeping everyone corralled. No psychiatric skills or understanding of personality. *Don't they say cobblers' children get the worst shoes?* Milner didn't regret the price paid by Julian's family. That was Julian's responsibility. He made sure his family didn't pay. Julian's lot became fodder because he allowed them to. The only absolute Milner accepted was there are no absolutes.

Milner dressed and trolled down to the kitchen in search of decaffeinated coffee and breakfast. He cut out caffeine ages ago and sensed he was better for it. He acknowledged Gronya fussing as she prepared a tray for Hattie. He carried his drink to the study. He'd finish it before he talked to Gronya and tackled the shopping. Despite their years together, he continued to be amazed at how Gronya approached the world with the air of a satisfied connoisseur of Limoges china who didn't care if she dropped and smashed pieces of it; there was always more available, and she was entitled. He thought of her as the north face of the Eiger that he never conquered no matter how many times he resolved to do so.

Tired and distracted, Milner powered up his computer. As he waited for the screen to resolve he sensed something land on his lap. He looked down to see Hera's eyes concentrated on his face.

"Hi, young lady. Been expecting you, although now might be a tad inconvenient."

"It's the end of the process and Jester needs a chat."

"Can't it wait 'til later this evening?"

"It won't take long."

"How tedious," muttered Milner. The screen revealed Jester staring at him. "Let's get it over. At least it signifies the end of the process so I won't have to view more miserable scenes when I'm tired and want to wind down with a whisky or whatever at the end of the day."

"Welcome, Master Milner. Pleased this app thingy works. Good to see you. Trust you're well?"

"All the better for seeing you," said Milner, irritated with Jester's upbeat response.

"Now, now. Let's tone down the sarchasm; 'specially since I came to inform you there'll be no more 'consequence' experiences. No more forced screenings of unhappy people. Your conscience may choose otherwise of course, but after this, I'll leave you alone and won't pursue the matter."

"How very gracious, but then I don't remember soliciting your opinion in the first place."

"Unfortunately for you, we must all face consequences. They are the result of actions. Most of the time we let conscience to do the job, but in your case, your interference resulted in such dire outcomes, it became necessary to make you face them in a more substantial form."

"Well, get you, Mr Judge and Jury."

"It won't help. I won't go away till we've chatted."

"Better get on with it then."

"Having witnessed episodes in the life of each of your victims, do any of their circumstances trouble you?"

"Only those relating to my girls."

"I see. No remorse for anyone outside your immediate circle. No potential for a crack or puncture in that carapace you surround yourself with?"

"No. At Belldeep you used images of whirlwinds to represent the grief I caused. A clever analogy suggesting everyone is supposedly blown from pillar to post at the behest of emotions. However, my responsibility lay in pulling my family from the storm. I'm satisfied my girls face occasional gusts now, which soon die down. They had issues before it started; those were never going away."

"An accurate, if selfish, piece of reasoning. So you accept no blame for the corruption of Julian's ethics and the consequences to his family."

"Absolutely not. Julian is an adult, a trained professional. If a personality weakness allowed him to abandon lifelong values at the drop of a hat it is not for me to judge. I might exploit Julian's weakness further if it all goes pear-shaped, but that's for another time. My conscience is clear. I behaved properly at all times and did the best for me and mine. I learned from craftsmen how artists' representations are just that: their own valid interpretation of reality, parts of which others see as counterfeit, even though they like the picture. There are no absolutes; everything is relative, except when I decide what is absolute for me and mine. If Julian didn't want his family to suffer, he shouldn't have indulged himself."

"No remorse then. I hoped you would've realised, despite having no pity for Julian's family, your own suffered more than necessary to achieve your aim of removing Gronya from your life into the arms of a man you trusted to care for her, although you now doubt him. You appear to have understood that in the same way he needed Adelle, he needed Gronya. No love involved."

"He has disappointed me in many respects. As for the guff about a difference between need and love – they are, always will be, one and the same. Pedantic arguments about happiness coming from being prepared to make sacrifices and you get back what you give are rubbish. There are secrets to control these things. If more people learned them the world would be happier."

"So you've no conscience about Adelle and her grandchildren?"

"None whatsoever. Julian lied to her, so why shouldn't I? The ruse over the divorce and passing on her emails to Julian and Gronya to mock were what she deserved for her refusal to cooperate in my plan. She was stronger and less controllable than I judged. She escaped from Julian through divorce. Couldn't stop him giving too much away to her. It'll be paid for, eventually, but another day, another dollar, and not by me. That daughter of hers, Sabina, is an inflexible, arrogant young madam, unforgiving and unable to understand compromise. Seems Daniel is the same. Despite frustration with my family, I will never turn my back on them the way they did on their mother, all promoted by Julian according to Gronya."

"Are you regretful about anything?"

"Hera here."

"Ah. You feel sympathy for something."

"Gronya insisted on taking Hera to her love nest because she was my favourite. I loved Hera from the moment Hattie brought her home and I took her in because Hattie couldn't cope. My trip to Belldeep was easier having Hera with me. I'll never forget the meeting between me, Hattie and Gronya after Hera died. I was concerned Hera's death would push Hattie over the edge, which it did. Her immediate anger boiled over into hysteria when she lashed out at Gronya. Not sure how I managed to contain it, but managed. Knew there'd be further repercussions, and when Hattie refused to take her final exams some months later, my forebodings came true. But I'll get it under control; it'll be resolved satisfactorily in the end."

"Are there any other issues/images that trouble you?"

"That stupid frozen lake in the final circle of hell where my and Julian's family leaned over and shouted down at me. Their arraignment of charges levelled at me was ridiculous. It was cruel to let them waft large fans of cold air to stop the ice melting while they recited their litany. I don't acknowledge the criticisms inherent in the Inferno, your allusions or allegories or metaphors. All come from religious or quasi-religious ideas based on the premise you allow dogma to dominate over reason and the proper argument of your senses. That whole system is responsible for the idea of punishment in an afterlife. Hell is here on earth, and all anyone can do is buy periods of reprieve. I've no qualms about acquiring wealth to palliate misery and make my family happy. I'll continue to provide them with what they desire. It won't be my fault if they discover it isn't what they want. They have to shoulder responsibility at some point."

"Your attitude suggests my balance sheet of your skills and faults didn't cause you to consider your actions. On current form I have to say the profile you present to the world does you an injustice, you're pettier in person than I calculated."

"Thought I came out of it well. I don't accept your judgment."

"Very well. Seems I won't find what I'm lurking for so I'll sign off. You'll never accept that to meddle in others' lives brings responsibilities towards them. Let's hope one day you meet your match. I'll make one observation though. I suggest you stick to networking in the future and don't dabble in dream-working."

Milner sensed Hera jump from his lap as he heard Gronya bang on the study door.

○ʒ ○ʒ ○ʒ

By the same Author

Norah and Emma

Based on the true story of Norah Dacre Fox (aka Elam), this fictionalised biography follows Norah on her political journey from suffragette to fascist in England during the first half of the 1900s, an era of radical politics encompassing women's struggles to get the vote, two world wars, the rise of fascism, communism, and the poverty of the 1930s.

Stubborn and forceful, Norah was ever the rebel. Was she born in an era which suited her inherent character traits, or was her difficult personality forged by the political campaigns she took on?

This is a profoundly affecting story that examines the lives of two women, one real and one fictional, whose paths cross in a maelstrom of social change. How they cope with the struggles they face and the effects on them and their families is told in a story that explores their individual responses to the conventions society used to shackle them.

The Alice Band

Carole and Alice have been friends for years, bouncing happily off each other in ways that mystify onlookers.

No one could explain how or why the friendship

worked, least of all Carole and Alice. Carole often pondered this conundrum. Alice never did.

Then 'life' happened. Circumstances conspired to force everyone out of their ruts, along the way challenging the dynamic of Carole and Alice's friendship.

How do Carole and Alice deal with the string of catastrophes that beset Alice? Can their friendship survive or will it change forever?

For more information on the author, please visit my website

www.verityshort.co.uk

VSM books

www.ingramcontent.com/pod-product-compliance
Lightning Source LLC
Chambersburg PA
CBHW061924170626
46813CB00006B/2296